W9-BAK-123

IGNORANCE

BY THE SAME AUTHOR

Novels
A Piece of the Night
The Visitation
The Wild Girl
The Book of Mrs Noah
In the Red Kitchen
Daughters of the House
Flesh and Blood
Impossible Saints
Fair Exchange
The Looking Glass
The Mistressclass
Reader, I Married Him

Plays
The Journeywoman
Child Lover

Poetry
The Mirror of the Mother
Psyche and the Hurricane
All the Selves I Was
The Heretic's Feast

Short Stories
During Mother's Absence
Playing Sardines
Mud: Stories of Sex and Love

Non-fiction
Food, Sex & God: on Inspiration and Writing
Paper Houses

Artist's Books
Poems (with Caroline Isgar)
Fifteen Beads (with Caroline Isgar)
Dark City Light City (with Carol Robertson)
The Secret Staircase (with Caroline Isgar)

IGNORANCE

A Novel

Michèle Roberts

BLOOMSBURY

NEW YORK · LONDON · NEW DELHI · SYDNEY

Clifton Park - Halfmoon Public Library
475 Moe Road
Clifton Park, New York 12065

Copyright © 2012 by Michèle Roberts

All rights reserved. No part of this book may be used or reproduced in any manner whatsoever without written permission from the publisher except in the case of brief quotations embodied in critical articles or reviews. For information address Bloomsbury USA, 175 Fifth Avenue, New York, NY 10010.

Published by Bloomsbury USA, New York

All papers used by Bloomsbury USA are natural, recyclable products made from wood grown in well-managed forests. The manufacturing processes conform to the environmental regulations of the country of origin.

LIBRARY OF CONGRESS CATALOGING–IN–PUBLICATION DATA

Roberts, Michèle.
Ignorance / Michèle Roberts. — 1st U.S. ed.
p. cm.
ISBN 978-1-60819-771-2
1. Young women—Fiction. 2. World War, 1939–1945—France—Fiction.
I. Title.
PR6068.O155I54 2012
823'.914—dc22
2011042283

First U.S. Edition 2013

1 3 5 7 9 10 8 6 4 2

Typeset by Hewer Text UK Ltd, Edinburgh
Printed in the U.S.A.

To Richard

Jeanne

The first time I tried to use paints, in his studio, I didn't know where to begin. At the edge of the paper? In the centre? He shouted: just get going! Just make a mark!

Smudges of black and white and grey. The colours of that winter afternoon when I spoke to him for the first time. The man Marie-Angèle called the Mad Hermit.

If he had glanced out from his garden at the school building, sheering up next door like a cliff, he might have noticed Marie-Angèle and me. Two children peeping out of a high window. Two white dabs of faces.

He did see us. He waited for us. He knew that sooner or later we'd come.

Late January: season of chilblains, discs of ice glazing the necks of our pitchers each morning. Thin nimbus you cracked with your fingernail. We skipped washing as often as we could get away with it. Grubby angels with shattered ice haloes. But you don't feel dirty when it's so cold.

A black and white feather began it. A magpie's perhaps. We called the novices magpies: black habits and white veils. The nuns, in plain black: holy crows. Or holy hens. The young curé, strutting plumply among us with pursed lips and folded arms,

1

was Chanticleer, from Marie-Angèle's story book. The nuns pecked and flapped for his attention. His words of wisdom. With Marie-Angèle and myself he didn't have to pretend to be cleverer than he really was. He told us about his two little sisters back home, whom he missed. He said they liked liquorice and aniseed balls. He told us jokes, too, and blushed that we found them so funny.

The feather came spiralling down out of the sky, twisting and turning on a current of air. From the dormitory window, standing on chairs so that we could see out, we watched the little plume swivel and drift above the garden wall.

Later, Mother Lucie asked me: what happened?

I hadn't the words to tell her. How could I know the words to say? They'd have been the wrong ones, fetched me a slap. She forbade us to speak of the matter to the other girls at school. She forbade them to ask us questions. Of course our classmates disobeyed. Whispering behind their hands, letting sentences tail off. Different versions of the story got out, elaborated and grotesque, coiled around the little town, darting down alleys, sidling up to back doors, hissing in dark corners of shops. My mother seemed not to know what had happened, because her friends protected her from the gossip. Marie-Angèle's mother tutted: it's best forgotten. But sooner or later, the thing came back up in my mind; it kept on surfacing, like stones erupting in a field you think you've cleared.

My mother and I had helped Marie-Angèle's parents prepare the tiny piece of land they'd rented on the edge of town. They were going to grow vegetables on it, but first of all they had to pick up all the stones. Monsieur Baudry made us heap the rocks together in a cone shape in one corner. He turned this hollowed pile, which he painted white, into a grotto dedicated to Our Lady of Lourdes. The nuns gave him one of the old statues from their attic; just her nose chipped, and the tips of her fingers missing. As though she'd been punished for trying to run away. I dreamed of her climbing out of the window and the sash rattling down with a crash on to her hands. Then the guard slammed her fingers in the train door. So she went back to the convent and hid under the dusty rafters bracing the roof. Damaged goods that no one wanted.

Marie-Angèle didn't stop me from going after the feather. Down in the convent garden she didn't take me by the hand and pull me back indoors. She wanted something to happen just as much as I did.

Sunday afternoon: the orphans out on a walk with one of the nuns, the day girls absent, the weekly boarders likewise gone back to their families, leaving the two of us, the only full-time boarders, alone. The curé, who would normally have come in to talk to us about the sermon he'd preached at Mass that morning, to make sure we'd understood it, was laid up in the presbytery with a bad cold. Mother Lucie had retired to the sisters' side of the house, shut their big black door. Not a peep from any of them until supper-time. We had our books to read: a copy each of *The Lives of the Saints*. Our other book was the volume of fairy tales Marie-Angèle had brought from home, but Mother Lucie had confiscated it and locked it in her cupboard until Monday: unfit for Sunday reading.

Marie-Angèle and I sat drumming our heels in the cold classroom on the ground floor. Whatever racket we made, no one would hear us. She leaned at one end of the bench and I at the other. High windows, their sills level with the crowns of our heads. Such a clean, tidy place you felt crushed. So empty you rattled in it and when you talked your voice came out in a squeak. Smell of ink, chalk dust, the soda crystals the novices used for scrubbing the floor.

I dared Marie-Angèle to come with me up to the dormitory.

But we're forbidden in there in the daytime, she said: what if they catch us? They nearly did last time.

I sang it out. Little Miss Mealy-Mouth, little Miss Preachy, little Miss Prim. I'll go by myself then.

What d'you want to go up for, anyway? she said.

Because. We could look out of the window and see if he's around.

'He' was the Hermit. The first time we'd peeped down at him, I'd asked: why do you call him the Mad Hermit? Marie-Angèle had said: just look at his clothes, stupid. To do his gardening he wore an old pink waistcoat flapping open over a collarless blue workman's shirt, shabby grey and yellow check trousers with the red braces showing, a green woollen cap, brown boots laced around his ankles. He grasped his scythe, raised his arm, swished at clumps of nettles, at ropes of brambles throttling bushes. Whack! Whack! Whack!

None of the townspeople down on the ground knew what his garden was like. Only Marie-Angèle and I, when we got the chance to climb up to our eyrie. You couldn't see his garden from the street, if you were walking past. It remained hidden, like a secret you've sworn not to tell. The bulk of his house reared up in front of you as you went by. The shuttered façade gazed back like a blind man wearing eyepatches.

While we watched him, that first time, Marie-Angèle had

pointed out she'd never spotted the Hermit in church. You didn't see him standing chatting on the square after Sunday Mass, then making for the café, as the other men did. Just occasionally she'd glimpse him going to buy tobacco, or bread. He carried a wicker shopping basket, as most people did, but the handle of his was bound with orange ribbon stuck with pink and red paper flowers. He was mad all right.

I heard his story for the first time on the day I started attending the nuns' school. My mother had to go into hospital, and Madame Baudry, Marie-Angèle's mother, organised for the nuns to take me as a boarder until Maman came home. Waiting for the iron to heat, Maman spat on it, to test it. Her spittle fizzed, water-beads dancing. I set up the ironing board, pulled its white cover straight. Why do I have to go? I want to stay here. Smacking the iron across her best nightdress, Maman frowned. It's an act of charity. Madame Baudry means well. So do the nuns.

Her mouth turned down. She looked pale without her usual red lipstick, her newly washed hair pinned back from her face showing her cheekbones too much. Her stick-thin legs ended in narrow feet in slippers. She turned her lips up again at the corners, to fake a smile. You'll just have to cope. As I do.

Before Papa's death, the three of us had lived in a flat over a jeweller's shop in the middle of town, and Papa had worked downstairs selling earrings for weddings and repairing watches and clocks. Maman sang a mocking song: we were poor but we were happy! Then Papa died. The lease on the shop ran out. The landlord gave Maman notice. We moved down to the bottom of town, and Maman went out as a cleaner. People like Madame Baudry felt sorry for her, gave her work, and parcelled up their old clothes for her to bring home. Maman said: I'm the poor widow, just like in the fairy tales! And now she's my fairy godmother! She held up a pair of bloomers, pink artificial silk yellow at the crotch. She snorted, threw them down. I suppose they'll make floorcloths.

That Monday, Madame Baudry wanted me at her shop in the rue de la Croix as soon as it was light, so that she could take me up to the convent with Marie-Angèle in good time and not be late. I couldn't eat my breakfast. Blackberry pips gritted my teeth. Maman and I had gone blackberrying together, and I'd helped make the jam. It hadn't set properly. It slid about, dripped from the bread on to my plate. The bread was snivelling. Purple-red tears. Maman said: you'll have to make up for it at lunchtime. She stuck two pieces of bread together with a smear of jam, wrapped them in a piece of paper and put it in my pocket. She kissed me, pushed me out, closed the door.

Greyness, with a hint of blue, as night turned into early morning. Wobbling spots of yellow light got bigger: people on bicycles rode past, making for the factory. One or two dark shapes waved, but I didn't return their greetings. I forced my feet to drag away, past the shuttered smithy and towards the bridge. Mist hid the water. I trailed my hand along the low stone parapet, dampening the fingers of my woollen glove, counting the slabs as I crossed. One mother two mother three mother four. My mother's face hard as a paving-slab. Be off, darling. I must get on. Away with you. With a stick I wrote her words in the dust on the far side of the bridge, in the dip before the pavement began. I threw the stick in the river. Then I headed towards the main road.

Blueness deepened as grey lessened. I plodded along the

blue-grey paving-stones. My route zigzagged under stumpy plane trees up towards the parish church and the town hall. White boulders set at the corners warned of more steep bends to come. When I was younger, Maman would haul me up this ascent: come on! Come on! No one to leave me with when she went out washing, so she took me with her. At the Baudrys' she'd sit me down with a basket of pegs, and I'd play with them while she worked.

Ste-Marie-du-Ciel squatted on a dumpy little hill. The oldest part of the town, with the château, convent and school, perched right at the top, streets and houses running down on every side. They pooled below, in the bottom town, where we lived, by the smithy and the river. Behind our building a shared yard let the women hang out the wet clothes. Over the wall, a waste-land made a space for the boys to play football. Beyond, the town allotments stretched to the factory.

The Baudrys lived over their grocery shop halfway up the hill, in a side street off the market place, near the cobbler's. The Baudry shop smelled of sawdust and ground coffee, and the cobbler's of leather, beeswax and oil. Monsieur Fauchon, the cobbler, kept his door propped open winter and summer. Inside, at the far end of what seemed a dark cupboard, he hunched over his counter, tapping at a boot propped upside down on a last. A bibbed canvas apron the colour of *café au lait* wrapped him. Linen strings tied in a bow at the front. Tools stuck out of his breast pocket.

His chin jerked up as I went by, and he nodded to me. A thin man, with a long face, big dark eyes and a beard, like someone in the Bible. He was a Jew, like my mother had been before she converted and got baptised. Maman had told me the tale of

7

Madame Baudry clasping her hand: I'll be your sponsor! She gripped her too tightly. Maman yelped in pain, which Madame Baudry took for delight.

Now Madame Baudry came out of her shop with Marie-Angèle beside her, both moving stiffly in their thick winter clothes. Look sharp, Jeanne! Stop scowling, Marie-Angèle! Madame Baudry's words puffed out as frosty clouds. She shooed us up the steep, narrow streets between grey buildings fitting together like teeth. From time to time we stopped, to give her a rest. Her navy-blue coat no longer closed over her belly. Her brown felt hat shaded her eyes. I clumped in my newly mended boots we had collected from Monsieur Fauchon the week before, banging my feet down as hard as possible on the transparent ice sheeting puddles. It cracked, shattered into dark glass stars, which sank. My wooden soles tapped morse code on the paving-stones I want to go home I want to go home.

We climbed up a series of stone staircases tucked in between tall houses. The town rippled down at us like icicles. A frozen grey waterfall. I hung on to the iron handrail and kicked each worn step. The grey morning, freshening with misty drizzle, smelled of horse dung. Church bells clanged somewhere ahead. I dawdled as much as I could but Madame Baudry tugged me along. Be good! You've promised to be good!

Hand in woollen hand, the three of us began to cross the Place Ste Anne just below the château, making for the door in the high façade opposite. Above this entrance, on a ledge, stood a statue of Sainte Anne, with her little daughter, the Virgin Mary, leaning against her knees. Sainte Anne held a copy of the Old Testament, so that the Virgin could learn to read. The New Testament ended with everything burning up. Everyone dying in flames. I had got to walk in under the statue, under the stone book. I crossed my fingers the end of the world wouldn't come yet; that we'd be saved. That Maman wouldn't die.

The convent and the school sheltered behind a granite veil pierced by peepholes. Square barred windows at ground-floor level, rows of tall rectangular windows on the upper floors, *œil de bœuf* windows right at the top. Round, sleepy eyes gazing out under stone eyelids. Where the wall of the school ended, the next building began, on the left-hand side. On the right of the school: the convent, and next to it the chapel, a gold cross on its roof.

Oh, my legs, said Madame Baudry, panting. Catching her breath, her hand at her side. We paused. She was gasping. Holding herself in. I could tell she didn't like our seeing how weak she felt, and so I looked away, towards the flat front of the building joined on to the school. Following my gaze, Madame Baudry pursed her mouth. She straightened up, adjusted her hat. Now her voice sounded strong again. He does all right for himself. All right for some. They know how to manage, those Jews. We let them in, we let them have jobs. And now, the money that they've got squirrelled away!

My nose was running. I fished in my pocket for my hand-kerchief. Maman had no money. Had she ever been a proper Jew? Marie-Angèle sang: squirrel squirrel squirrel! Madame Baudry glanced at me, then added: well, of course, as long as they try to fit in with us and be like us, they're all right. Live and let live, I say.

Marie-Angèle pinched my arm. I looked up. The door opened and a man emerged. White, gaunt face. Untidy black hair. He hunched inside a big overcoat. Madame Baudry

9

immediately called out, saluting him. *Bonjour*, Monsieur Jacquotet! She wished him good day, I knew, because she liked to be recognised by everybody, but he just looked from side to side, like a shy kid in the playground. Madame Baudry persisted, because she was used to everybody knowing she was there, and that she mattered. Serving in the grocery shop, she wasn't a woman who worked so much as a queenly mother who enjoyed the way people needed her provisions. Briskly she wrapped up their packets of macaroni, sugar, chicory, flour and salt. Sometimes, if I'd been summoned up from the bottom town to keep Marie-Angèle company, and we'd run out of games to play, Madame Baudry let us help her serve customers, dip the wooden scoop into the bin of dried beans, tip them out on to the scale, fiddle out the brass weights from their wooden box. The curé used to buy his sisters barley-sugars from Madame Baudry's shop and post them home. Once we started boarding, he'd bring some in for Marie-Angèle and me. He said: you two mopes need cheering up! On his Sunday afternoon visits to the convent he gave me news of my mother. He visited her in hospital, so that he could tell me how she was keeping. She's fine, Jeanne, never you fear.

Marie-Angèle poked me with her elbow. She whispered: look at his big nose!

He was pretending he hadn't seen us, hadn't heard Madame Baudry's greeting. He jerked his face away. He withdrew, back inside the house, and slammed the door.

The hermit, Madame Baudry said: the recluse. So unsociable! He thinks I don't know about him but I do. Everybody does.

Distracted from her aches and pains, she was in a better mood, so I could risk asking her a question.

10

What's a recluse?

So she recounted the tale. Marie-Angèle began smiling now, because her mother was keeping us company for five minutes longer, before delivering us in at the high wooden door. She could still hold her gloved hand, look into her face as she spoke. Coming from a foreign background, he was always a bit of a misfit. He and his wife didn't mix with their neighbours. They kept themselves very much to themselves. He kept his wife hidden away. Then, when she died, he went a bit crazy.

Marie-Angèle corrected her mother: he kept his beautiful young wife hidden away. Then, when she died, he went a bit mad.

Madame Baudry continued her recital. So now he pretended that he was gone too. He kept the shutters fastened in the daytime and took no notice when boys threw stones at them, rarely went out, crossed to the other side of the street when he saw people coming. Goodness knows what he found to do, alone in that house. He was certainly a bit peculiar.

Marie-Angèle said: you forgot to tell the bit about his eating such strange food!

Madame Baudry shrugged. I understood he might soon cease interesting her. A lost cause. Other stories would press in, replace his. But Marie-Angèle's eyes gleamed. She said: and nobody knows how his wife died. Madame Baudry said: well, let's say she died mysteriously. Marie-Angèle chimed in: Bluebeard!

I'd only dared read that story once. The young woman trapped inside the courtyard, no way out, the sun beating her head like a gong of death, the enraged husband, the huge Blackamoor, striding nearer and nearer, his upraised sabre about to whistle down, slice her skin, cause her unimaginable agony. He was coming to get you. You had no choice, you couldn't hide, you were powerless, your death advanced second by second, closer and closer. A gilded purple turban, a gold coat and gathered gold trousers, slippers with curled-up toes, his black eyes shot red sparks, his beard sprang out like blue spittle. He would hack at you and hurt you, his curved scimitar blade jabbing and slicing your flesh while you writhed and begged for mercy, he laughed, his blade twisting inside the mouth of your wound, blood every-where, blinding you, you'd slip in your blood and fall and he'd lean over and stab you repeatedly, your blood spurting out while you screamed. Then you'd die.

Jesus died in agony, hung from the cross, his flesh pierced by nails. The Jews' fault: they betrayed him. Was my mother still a Jew underneath? Was I? In church every Sunday we prayed for the conversion of the Jews to the One True Faith, and cele-brated the heroic martyrs who died defending it. The martyrs refused to marry pagans like Bluebeard. *The Lives of the Saints* listed the tortures: slashed with swords, breasts torn off, eyes gouged out, racked on the wheel, made to walk naked into brothels where soldiers waited for them. I wouldn't be brave enough to stand up for what I knew was right. I'd turn pagan and marry Bluebeard rather than be hurt so much. Then after death I'd be punished and burn in hell for ever more. You could shut all this away inside the slammed covers of your book but at night the book jumped open and red fire swept out and consumed everything.

Madame Baudry shook off her daughter's hand and tweaked her blue woollen gloves. She said to Marie-Angèle: you know, becoming a boarder costs a lot. It means behaving. Mind what I say!

12

Up until now Marie-Angèle had attended the state primary school, as I had. The nuns' school was a private one. Madame Baudry's pregnancy meant she became exhausted and could not cope, once my mother fell ill, and she had to do all her own washing as well as everything else. The nuns had agreed to take Marie-Angèle, like me, full-time for several weeks. Half rates for the Baudrys, because they were such good Catholics. I went free. Marie-Angèle had spelled it out: you're a charity child, other people have to pay your fees. I retorted: but my father was an educated man. Unlike yours!

The convent had sent over a lay sister to help the Baudrys. When she arrived they put her in Marie-Angèle's room. Supposing Madame Baudry died like the Mad Hermit's wife? Supposing Maman died too? I hadn't said a proper goodbye to her this morning. I wanted to run back home, not start living among strangers. Stop crying, Madame Baudry said: don't be so naughty. I cried louder. Her face reddened and she slapped me. Her woollen blow didn't hurt, but the shock of it did. Hot tears burst from my eyes and I bawled.

Marie-Angèle started crying too. It's just as bad for me! That nun's in my room! Madame Baudry cuffed her round the head. Stop this nonsense. You've got nothing to cry about. Jeanne lives in a hovel, her mother's got to go to the paupers' hospital. You should be setting a good example. I'm ashamed of you.

She seized my shoulder and shook me. D'you want me to tell your mother how you're behaving, when she's so ill? Do you? Do you? She'll feel so upset. After all I've done for her, too. I don't know why I bothered with that photograph. You don't deserve it.

To mark the occasion of our becoming boarders, we had had

our photograph taken outside the Baudrys' shop. That's nice for Jeanne, said Madame Baudry: people will see that someone cares about her. Monsieur Baudry took the picture. At nine years old, I was small and skinny, whereas Marie-Angèle was tall and well developed for her age.

I didn't smile for the picture. I refused. Once in their school I wouldn't smile at the nuns, either. You're hard-faced, Mother Lucie used to scold me. Dressed in our regulation pale grey pinafores, our hair combed back, posed side by side as friends, Marie-Angèle and I were supposed to look as though we came from the same sort of background. Alike as two dried peas. But underneath we were different, as the nuns recognised perfectly well. On their wooden board, with its list of weekly tasks painted in black italic lettering, our names, written on bits of white card, slotted into different places. On Saturday I had to mop the corridors whereas Marie-Angèle only had to dust the statues in our classroom. She didn't dare go into the larder in the convent-school kitchen, forage for leftovers. Always hungry, I stole food as a matter of course. My punishment, each time Mother Lucie found me out, was to clean the privies. These always stank because so many of us had to use them, and in such a hurry that there wasn't time for the cisterns to refill, and they often blocked because we put too much paper down, wanting to veil the yellow water bobbing with the previous user's business.

Sometimes I'd sit on the lavatory and read a square or two of newspaper before wiping myself with it. Marie-Angèle's father handed on his newspapers to the nuns. Sitting on the wooden shelf, one hand hoisting up my overall, I learned new words. Words about Jews, which hopped across the pages like toads. I wanted to spring up and chase them away. In the school we had silver-fish in the lavatories, and woodlice, and bluebottles, and ants. You had to squash them. Outside, on the garden paths, slugs and snails lounged along. You were supposed to squash them too. The words in my brain could not be squashed. They wriggled and squelched and inched back and forth.

Marie-Angèle said I might know lots of words but I was still a baby. I was afraid of the dark, and sometimes at night I wet the bed. Washerwoman's daughter pissing in the wrong place. All that gave me grace in her eyes was my capacity to tell her the stories I culled from her book of fairy tales. Reading bored her. She preferred listening to my oral versions. Chewing a fingernail. Sucking a strand of hair. The bloodthirstier the stories the better.

Now from the end of the bench in the schoolroom she hissed at me.

You're pathetic. First of all you dare us to do something and then you get cold feet. Are we going upstairs or aren't we?

She stood up, in front of the estrade and the blackboard, put her hands on her hips, stared at me contemptuously. She looked so exactly like a little woman that I wanted to laugh. She wasn't a child at all. You could see what she'd look like at forty. Her plump little face, with its apple-pip eyes, its tight mouth, wouldn't change. She was already complete and grown-up.

I didn't want her to leave me on my own in the downstairs classroom, too close to the front door on which passing tramps sometimes banged for food. If I opened the door to them, what would happen? They'd kidnap me I'd run away with them they might try to marry me I'd never see Maman again.

All right, I said: let's go.

15

As part of the dare, more chance of getting caught, we went up by the main stairs. This staircase wound about the great well in the centre of the school. It rose through layers of classrooms and dormitories, networks of corridors. The wide wooden treads gleamed, bare and highly polished. During the week, at recreation time, when the bell clanged, a flood of overalled girls would swirl down it, pour out into the school yard. Now only we two remained in the house.

No windows: we climbed up in semi-darkness. On the second half-landing stood a statue of Our Lady of The Seven Sorrows, her colander heart pierced by seven swords, all the love once in it leaked out like whey. A red gleam came from the votive lamp in front of her. I lifted my feet with caution: too much space around me. Not yet dusk: going upstairs in this half-dimness was more bearable than at night, when I stepped towards bad dreams. Dead mothers waited for me at the far end of the corridor with cobweb mantillas over their faces. They'd pushed up their tomb-stones and escaped. They were lonely in their graves, and so they'd come to the school to fetch some children to play with. They'd pull our bones about then eat us.

We climbed two flights and slid into the chilly dormitory. Here we fetched chairs, set them side by side, stood on them to peer out of the window on the left-hand side.

From this height, we could see over the high stone wall that separated the school grounds from the Hermit's garden. We surveyed a completely enclosed space. Between patches of melted ice the grass gleamed green. Inside his encircling walls he had allowed sycamores to seed wildly in little copses. These untidy saplings he had trimmed and pollarded in extreme fashion, stripping off all the lower branches and shaping the top ones into balls. The sycamores stood in groups: tall, slender ladies with round heads turbaned in brown twigs. Maidens who hovered, uncertain whether or not to walk inside the ogre's castle.

Bluebeard's fiancées, I whispered to Marie-Angèle, and felt her flinch against me.

A narrow gravelled path twisted in and out between the young trees, like a white ribbon tying them together. The school playground was all sharp angles; the nuns' oblong garden marched in straight lines, spotless paths bisecting rows of fruit trees and flowerbeds; but the Hermit's parterre undulated, all curves. Dark greenery glistening with wet. Clumps of laurels and bay, the narrow trees crowding between the high stone walls, ivy sprawling along the ground. Tumbledown brick sheds leaned together on one side, a few hens scratching about. A flight of steps led up to a terrace. At the far side of this: the back door to his house. No one visible. His shutters on the ground floor were open. Dark panes of glass.

From our high perch we watched the black and white feather twist down out of the grey sky.

Come on, I said: I'll race you to catch it.

Marie-Angèle hesitated. Supposing someone sees us?

I blew out my cheeks at her. Cowardy-custard. I dare you.

Hands skimming the slippery banister, we sped back down the coils of stairs, we fell down through the great, silent house like two pellets rattling out of a canister. We didn't stop to change our felt indoor slippers for boots. We unbolted the side door by the kitchen and ran out through the playground into the garden between the leafless rose bushes.

The feather had vanished. We searched for a while along the

gravel walks bordering the espaliered apple trees. We hadn't bothered with gloves or capes. Our noses ran with cold. The chilblains on my hands began to twitch. I distracted myself by noticing other things: the withered rosehips dangling from black twigs, thorny rosaries; the crusts of frost edging the dark earth of the flowerbeds. A few snowdrops stabbing up.

A ladder lay on the ground by a tall beech hedge, bronze barrier severely squared-off along its length. One of the lay sisters had obviously been trimming it. She would catch it if anyone found she hadn't cleared up her mess. Heaps of withered tawny leaves, like cut hair, dotted the ground at intervals. Sawn pieces of plait.

Rapunzel, I said, pointing.

Pick up the ladder, Marie-Angèle said: I'll help you.

Between us we carried it to the wall. I went first and Marie-Angèle followed. One rung at a time. Don't look round.

Marie-Angèle swung her leg over, edged close to me. We sat astride the narrow wall, clinging on with both hands, looking down. On the Mad Hermit's side a few stones stuck out near enough the top to offer footholds.

From there we can jump, Marie-Angèle said: go on.

I didn't want to move. I felt giddy.

No, I said: this is enough. I want to go back in.

The dare's not over yet, she said.

Halfway down, when the footholds stopped, we launched ourselves out into the air, thudded on to the ground, bumping sideways almost on top of each other. Ice-tipped grass against my cheek, the tang of earth, my arms around Marie-Angèle, the sour smell of her hair.

We clambered upright. A changed world. We had crossed

over. Now we stood on the other side, the convent and school inaccessible, vanished. Nothing to be done but go forward. Hansel and Gretel, abandoned by their parents, bravely approaching the dark forest.

We entered the copse of sycamores immediately in front of us. The trees pulled us into their company and surrounded us. Captives. Captivated. The sycamore fiancées marched with us along the narrow twisting path. Their heads drooped over us and nodded. Yes, you should go in.

We crept towards the house. We reached the bottom of the flight of steps up to the terrace. We paused, glancing at each other. A creak, a scrape. Our eyes shot up.

The door in the back wall of the house had opened. There he stood. Smiling. He leaned against the doorpost and lifted a hand. Between finger and thumb he twirled a black and white feather.

Welcome, my dears.

Afterwards, I didn't know what to say. A story they wanted me to tell, only I didn't feel clear which one. I improvised and put two stories together. Marie-Angèle made me do it. She wanted to. He made us do it. He wanted to.

What happened? they asked me repeatedly: tell us what happened.

I couldn't tell them everything I saw when the Hermit showed us around his house. Too much of it. Some bits and pieces I carried away with me behind my eyes and remembered afterwards, in silence, once I was back inside the school, with the nuns questioning me. Brightly coloured memories blurred past like flicked-over pages in a picture book. The book opened and the pages stood up and time stopped and the pictures

19

jumped out and came alive. Bluebeard-the-Jew's big blue eyes, his wild black hair, his indigo workman's shirt, red and white spotted neckerchief, emerald corduroy trousers. The bright bottles of *sirop*, green and pink and yellow, he brought out of the rose-painted cupboard and lined up on the blue and white checked tablecloth. We could choose: *menthe* or *framboise* or *ananas*. Black slabs of chocolate he fitted between pale lengths of bread before handing them to us with a courteous bow. *Mesdemoiselles.* The honey-tiled corridor, a dark yellow tunnel, silted with dust rolling light and silvery as fur, which ran through the ground floor of the house, connecting back to front. Cream-painted panelled doors, glistening like sheets of mother-of-pearl, opened off it on both sides. The bare, unfurnished *salon*, painted scarlet, stencilled with gold garlands. Oh, Marie-Angèle exclaimed: like a ballroom. She spread out her arms and spun, a grey-clad Cinderella.

The Hermit told us he preferred to sit in the kitchen. This pale green apartment, lined with old wooden *armoires* and *buffets* painted pale pink, pale green, pale blue, its rafters hung with wheels of dried apple threaded on strings, had a tiled floor patterned in small turquoise and cream squares. Above the fireplace he had pinned up three rows of small rodent-like animals, flattened, the grey fur and skin split open and peeled back, the tiny claws splayed out. Marie-Angèle shuddered: mice? Ugh! He said: these are voles. I walked over and stroked them. Soft. He said: don't be scared. They're dead. They can't hurt you. I like drawing them.

Scattered between the *sirop* bottles on the blue and white cloth lay photographs of fat, loose-haired women, in rucked-up pale chemises, lolling in armchairs. Big grins. Black bows in

20

their dark ringlets. Black triangles of hair between their plump legs. Outside, at the foot of the stairs, three nailed-up moles grimaced in a sort of dance, paw to paw. I've got lots more things like this. Come upstairs, if you like, and I'll show you.

The staircase was neater and smaller than the one in the school. It twisted up in a tight oval. Like going inside a snail's shell. Fragile and brown. You wanted to step delicately in case something smashed. Shallow treads tucking in around the corners, a curved wooden baluster. Men weren't supposed to have dolls' houses but he did because he was like a child. Smiling at us, hopping back and forth. The sort of child I'd have liked to make friends with, someone with a cupboard full of treasures who'd show me them and let me pick something out and take it home. He gave Marie-Angèle the black and white feather and that wasn't fair, I wanted it just as much as she did.

He opened the door to his study on the first floor, full of books and piles of magazines. Next to it, a smaller room containing a shiny black and gold cabinet in which he had arranged the bones of small animals in circles and rows. He let us pull out each shallow drawer in turn, examine the contents, touch them. With our forefingers we caressed the skulls of rats and squirrels, the dry wings of staked-out butterflies and moths, the clean white skeletons of mice, the transparent brown and white tubes of shed snakeskins. Wizened dark pellets he said were owl droppings. Iridescent blue feathers of tits, arranged in fans. Green-gold carapaces of beetles with black claws.

Up another flight to the second floor. He took us into his two bedrooms. One faced north, out into the *place*, and the other looked south, over the garden. One big and one small. One painted black and one white. One served for sleeping in during summer, he explained, and the other he used in winter. The small white room held a wardrobe taking up nearly all the space. Beside the black-draped bed in the big bedroom stood an ebony cot. That's where children sleep, when they come to stay. I love children. They love playing with me. Sometimes we play hide and seek. Do you two like playing games?

He escorted us back out on to the landing. His eyes burned blue. You can go anywhere you like, hide anywhere you like, but not to the top of the house. That's my studio, where I work, it's not a place for children. Understood?

He covered his eyes with his narrow, long-fingered hands. I'll count up to a hundred. Then I'll come and find you! Off you go!

Marie-Angèle jerked her head at me. I nodded. Our felt indoor slippers made no noise. So he couldn't hear us slide past him on the landing, holding our breath, and tiptoe upstairs.

Just a game. We wanted him to find us and we wanted him to play. He found us. In he stormed. Then he played with us.

Afterwards, when I tried to remember, the games came back to me in bits. The last one first. Marie-Angèle saying: my turn. My turn.

She arranged herself on the pink divan under the skylight. Hands clasped behind her head, knees up and apart, face turned, unsmiling, towards him. Her grey pinafore made her look young but her face looked old. A dip in the material between her legs. The feather rested in it. She brought down one hand and twitched her hem higher up, just above the edge of her bloomers. She picked up the feather and flicked it over the strip of white flesh showing between her black stocking-top and her creased-up overall.

Who am I being now? Guess.

Bluebeard's wife, of course. He frowned, looking at her, and stood still. He was stupid not to know, when Marie-Angèle was such a good actress.

I was wandering about, glancing at them from time to time, leaving them to get on with their new game. I preferred looking at the canvases propped against the walls. Shapes of colour that might be women or might not, which grabbed your insides and whirled them about as though you were cartwheeling. What seemed the same dark-eyed woman in a red frock over and over again. In the bottom right-hand corner of each painting he'd put a thick black squiggle: Jacquotet.

He'd found us easily. Crouching next to Marie-Angèle behind a big propped canvas, in the tent of dark air between its wooden stretcher and the wall, I'd willed him to make haste. End it. Too childish. I wanted to explore his room, see what he'd got. He'd stomped up the stairs, growling an ogre song fee fi fo fum. We heard him through the door. He drummed with his hands on the door and it flew open. We waited patiently. My thighs ached from crouching. Come on, hurry up. As he got closer we jumped up and ran out, squealing. Exaggerating a bit. A show we put on. Bad girls! I forbade you to come in here. What shall I do with you, bad girls? He swayed back and forth in front of the door so that we couldn't pass him and get out.

A forfeit, he announced. Now, what shall it be?

Was he pretending or wasn't he? We hovered. Marie-Angèle cocked an eyebrow, sizing him up. She wore a look I recognised: shifty, caught out, wanting to wriggle away from punishment, not sure how, putting on a pout. Not a look that worked with Mother Lucie, who knew her too well, you and your tricks, miss, tell me the truth now. It worked better with the curé, bored with testing us on our catechism, those Sunday afternoon sessions in the cold classroom, the three of us huddled against the lukewarm stove, desperate for a bit of warmth. He'd pat our heads, then his black soutane, thrust his hand through the slit in the side, searching for the bump that meant a bag of sweets, his pocket full of caramels: never mind, you'll learn the answer for next week, won't you? Have a caramel, my dears.

Marie-Angèle curtsied to the Hermit. You've won. We are your prisoners.

The Hermit beamed, bowed, handed her the feather. Your prize, *mademoiselle*.

The Hermit's wives, a red chorus, stood around the edges of the studio. They guarded us, making sure we'd not do anything we shouldn't. Women tried to keep children from getting into trouble. Marie-Angèle's mother droned don't touch don't touch don't touch you might break something you might get dirty you might make a mess don't touch. This lot weren't strong as mothers though. You could punch a hole right through them with your fist. If they came too close you could ward them off with a good clout. They wouldn't dare touch you after that.

Now he'd accepted us inside his studio, the Hermit took our arms and pulled us round it, showing it off. A cross between a workshop and a playroom; both messy and neat. He pointed out a cupboard under the eaves: see that? It connects to next door. Your attic is through there.

I said: liar!

The space we stood in was so completely unlike the space we'd left that I couldn't believe the two were anywhere near each other. I felt I'd entered a different country; utterly separate and distant from the bare, cold school. I said again: liar!

He said: once upon a time this and next door were all the same house, before the nuns divided it in two. It was too big for them, and so they sold off this part to my parents.

Was he teasing? Perhaps he crept through the door at night, slid downstairs from the attic into the dormitory, sat by my bed, watched over me while I slept. As Maman had told me Papa had done sometimes, when I was small. When she was too tired to rouse herself, when I cried at night, he'd got up to calm me. Did I remember that? I remembered her stories of how he told her he'd held my hand, recited me poems, promised not to leave me. I felt I knew his voice, golden-dark, but did I really?

Marie-Angèle leaned against me, put her head on my shoulder, whispered. Her breath smelled of boiled potatoes. Perhaps he comes hunting for children to kidnap!

In the olden days, Mother Lucie had told us, it was said that Jews needed little Christian children. They slit the children's throats, bled them dry, then used their blood to make Passover bread.

Marie-Angèle giggled. She said: he won't bother with you, because you're not a proper Christian. He'll want me!

The Hermit glanced at us. I flinched, pushed Marie-Angèle away. She followed me to the big table in the middle of the room.

He didn't mind us touching his things. He let us pick up black sticks of charcoal and find out what marks we could make with them on a sheet of white paper. When the sticks shattered in our clumsy fingers he didn't get cross. He let us stroke the soft, pointed tips of the brushes packed standing up in old tins, handle the stumps of pastel chalk, smear wax crayons along corrugated brown cardboard, try out hard and soft pencils. He let us open a tin of cakes of watercolour. I leaned over a piece of paper, hesitating. He said: just start! The brush leaped ahead and I followed its pink-red stream. Marie-Angèle tried to use the paint neatly but he shouted at her: no, go on, splash it on, don't be so mimsy, so niminy-piminy, the whole point is to spread the colour into the water, big bold strokes, get it really wet, look, like Jeanne's doing.

The wives looked on. They kept an eye on us. Doing their best, anyway. They were getting bored with guarding us. They twirled away, preferred to dance. Canvas ladies, rather like the ladies in the photographs downstairs with not a lot of clothes on. Curly dark hair spilling down over their shoulders, red frocks falling off their shoulders, arms arching into the air, hips swaying, skirts falling back over their thighs. The studio smelled of the paint he'd painted them with. Oil paint. I snuffed it up.

While we waited for the water paint to dry we tried to think up another game.

I know, Marie-Angèle said: let's act plays. And you have to guess what they are.

First, I did grocer's shops. The Hermit wanted to have a go next, but Marie-Angèle waved him back.

No, I want to do one, you be the audience. My turn.

She arranged herself on the pink divan. She wriggled her backside into the cushions and locked her hands behind her head. She parted her legs. She looked, somehow, as if she had no clothes on. She looked rather like one of those girls in the magazines downstairs.

A pause. He gazed at her.

Stupid pose, he said.

I turned round from where I stood at the skylight, writing my name in the dust on the glass pane.

Get up, he said. Stupid little girl.

He really did look like an ogre now. Cheeks flushed red, eyes snapping blue fire.

We could play a different game, I said: I know a game. Have you got any sugared almonds? Or caramels? You sit in the chair and hide them in your pocket and we'll come and sit on your lap and search for them.

The Hermit advanced on Marie-Angèle. She tried to look bold but I could see she was scared.

How old are you, for God's sake?

She jumped up and skidded towards me. I thought he was going to hit her. The wives shrieked. He was coming closer. In one hand he held a palette knife. He would stab us and we would die. I grabbed Marie-Angèle's hand and pulled her over to the door, pushed it open. I whirled her downstairs, slippered feet skating over the treads, out of the front door into the street. I pulled it shut behind us. He wouldn't dare follow us on to the square. Recluse. Out here we were safe.

Marie-Angèle made for the front door of the convent and tugged at the bellpull to be let back in. I ran away, into the dusk. I shot down the hill, making for home. I scudded through the dark streets. Locked front door a slap in the face, a slap to the heart. Maman wasn't there. I'd forgotten. She was in hospital.

The shut door and the blank wall smirked: keep out. I twisted back and forth on the pavement. The wrong place. I'd get into such trouble. I couldn't face going back up to school and explaining. I was locked out of everywhere. The world had turned inside out, like a pullover, and shaken me off like a ball of fluff. I started crying, keeping my head down so no one would know me. Where was the hospital? I couldn't remember.

I stumbled back on to the bridge. The shallow steps rose in a gentle curve. At the top, where the bridge flattened out, a young workman was leaning on the parapet, smoking. How would I get past him? I tried to run. Crying too hard to look where I was going, I stubbed my foot and fell over, and he caught me. Hey, little one, it's OK. What's up? Where d'you live?

He brought me back up the hill. He took me into the cobbler's shop, the only place with a light still burning. Monsieur Fauchon brought me back up to the school. In the parlour I had to tell what had happened. Marie-Angèle had already confessed and been sent to bed.

Black wooden chairs lined up around the panelled brown walls, listening. Mother Lucie pulled a chair forward. She stood to one side of it, gripping its barred back, and I on the other. The wooden paddle lay on the seat. I stuttered out the words that came into my head.

Mother Lucie handed me over to Sister Dolorosa, who thrashed me, because I was a liar who made up stories, and I was the ringleader, the troublemaker who led my friend on, she was too weak, she followed. And as for that Jew next door, she'd tell the gendarmes to keep an eye on him in future and no mistake.

Afterwards I shouted to Sister Dolly: it didn't hurt, so there! Hauling me up to bed, Mother Lucie warned me: not a word of this to your mother. Poor woman, she's got enough to bear.

She let Marie-Angèle off with a scolding, a fable by La Fontaine to learn by heart. She didn't want the Baudrys to find out how lax her supervision was. We all understood the bargain that we made.

Quite soon afterwards Marie-Angèle's mother had her baby and Marie-Angèle could go home. A bit later Maman came out of hospital, well enough to return to work. For the moment I stayed on at the nuns' school. Mother Lucie said: when you're completely returned to health, Madame Nérin, then we'll see. And in the meantime, heaven knows she needs the discipline.

We heard that the Hermit caught influenza and nearly died. It was a hard February, that one. Marie-Angèle's mother got the flu, too. But she survived, and gave birth in early March. She named her son Marc, and invited Maman and me to the christening. A new priest officiated. The curé had been posted to another parish, no one knew where.

Marie-Angèle acted as her brother's godmother. Standing at the font, she held him carefully on her left arm. In her right hand she held a lit candle. On his behalf she renounced the world, the flesh and the devil, and the priest beseeched God that Marc be kept from all harm.

Leaving church, Marie-Angèle and I avoided looking at each other. I wanted to ask her whether she still had the feather. I couldn't, because I'd have been overheard. I was supposed to obey my elders and not talk to anyone about what had happened. Had Marie-Angèle told anyone the truth about it? I didn't know. I peeped at her as she swept past with her parents, her mother carrying the fat white bundle in its shawl. Buttoning her gloves, she looked composed. She seemed to have put the event away into the past, like old school exercise books you shove into the bottom of your desk.

Perhaps one day far in the future she'd want to tell someone.

A grandchild, perhaps, whom she loved, and to whom she told stories of her youth.

I couldn't imagine us as old ladies. Anyone over sixteen was old. But I did try to imagine what Marie-Angèle's account might be like.

Marie-Angèle

Before the war we lived a normal life. That's to say: each one in his right place. My father wheezed back and forth in the shop on the ground floor, the shed and storerooms in the yard behind, wheeling sacks, boxes, crates. The wooden counter in the front belonged to my mother. Blue-overalled, upright on her tall stool, her fair hair netted in a bun, she served the customers, did the accounts, kept an eye on my little brother Marc running in and out. I'd stayed on at school to get my *Brevet*, so that I could earn good money as a secretary, but in between bouts of study I had to help with the housework. Maman told me each morning what jobs to do later: I want you to grow up capable!

Jeanne's mother came in once a fortnight, to do the washing. She flaunted herself in a navy cloth coat trimmed with brown fur: a relic of better days! She would peel off her fine leather gloves with a sigh: they're falling apart, but they've lasted a long time, they're of such good quality! She would grimace as she unpinned her hat, smoothed it. Her way of letting us know what a lady she was: not born to this kind of work. No daughter to give her a hand, either. Jeanne had skipped out of school as soon as she turned fourteen, and gone to work as a maid. No laundry duty for her.

She's doing well, her mother boasted: a decent employer, decent wages.

Madame Nérin paused from her hauling of wet sheets. She dropped her wooden tongs and straightened herself, eyes lowered, hands bracing the small of her back. She leaned forwards again, her lips puffing out a groan. The bulk of linen washing, sodden with water, weighed so much that when you dragged it up and started shoving it through the wringer you felt your insides might fall out. Jeanne's mother hadn't the sturdy build a charwoman needed. Skinny as a weasel, she wore a black overall, a blue apron tied over it. Her hands, plunging and rinsing, were red and cracked. Her black hair, escaping from its pins, stuck to her crimson face. She smelled of sweat, so I kept my distance.

And you go to Mass together every Sunday? asked my mother: which Mass do you go to? Not the early one, surely. I never see you there.

Oh, said Madame Nérin: both of us need our lie-in on Sundays. But Jeanne gives me most of her wages. She is a good girl.

So I should hope, said my mother.

I thought of Jeanne on those alternate Monday afternoons, straight after school, when I helped heave up the tangle of boiled sheets from the copper, twist out the worst of the wet from the long steaming coils of linen, feed them between the rollers of the mangle. Moisture coated my face. The skin on my hands puckered and wrinkled. Did Jeanne go out dancing? Did she have a boyfriend? I couldn't ask, and encourage Madame Nérin to waste time chatting. My mother talked little while working. No energy to spare.

She said: the devil finds work for lazy hands.

We did our washing in the backyard, even in winter, chilblains or no chilblains. We hung it to drip on tubs and rails, and then later on lugged it upstairs to the attic to finish drying, suspended from the washing-lines there. I helped with the ironing, also the mending. I had my own darning egg, my own paper of needles. Maman also taught me to knit. With lengths of leftover wool we made cardigans, which the nuns sent off to their daughter-house in London. The English sisters ran a home for delinquent girls, and it was nice for these young women gone wrong to be able to dress decently.

A stitch in time saves nine, said my mother.

She kept an eye on everything, tried to look after everything and everybody at once, fought non-stop against dirt and disorder.

A place for everything, she said: and everything in its place.

Her rules dictated that certain corners stayed out of bounds. The shelves in the little back room where Marc slept, which doubled as an extra storeroom, bore ranks of bottled preserves, not to be pulled about by childish fingers. The nook by the stove in the front room with the two armchairs belonged to Papa and her. My route from bedroom to kitchen involved steering well clear of the occasional table with its wireless set, tobacco tin, jar of pipe-cleaners. Papa sat here when the shop was closed, frowning over the newspaper. He would beat his fist on the arm of his chair and shout. They'll take everything we've got! We shouldn't be letting them in! He fitted extra bolts to the doors downstairs, front and back.

For her part, Maman kept her bunch of keys on her at all times. She guarded her best things locked up in the grey-painted flat-fronted cupboards on either side of the stove. I wasn't allowed to touch the mauve china vase with its lustre glaze, the porcelain soup tureen, her wedding wreath of pink wax flowers. For my Confirmation, she lent me this wreath, and her lace veil to go under it: I want you not to show me up!

Jeanne, poor thing, had nothing so fine. She fixed her cheap square of cheesecloth in place with two kirbigrips concealed under a strip of white ribbon. For the ceremony Maman wore her fur cape, with its two dangling paws. She kept this locked up in her wardrobe, shrouded by an old pregnancy smock. She brought it out just for best: unlike some people, I don't believe in showing off.

I copied my mother's housekeeping ways. Time-consuming practices of thrift.

Waste not, want not, she said: God helps those who help themselves.

The government certainly won't, my father would say. Thinking about the state of the country made him shake with rage. Almost anything could set him off. We tried to avoid upsetting him. Sweeping the floor on a Saturday morning, I'd carefully skirt his chair. If I banged too close, he'd jump, and curse me. His lid would fly off and he'd swipe his fist in the air. At meals, with a captive audience of three, he'd boil over. One Sunday lunchtime, shouting about the cost of living, he thumped the table with his tumbler of wine. Drops flew out and stained the white cloth red and my mother sprang up, crying out. He made to hit her and she cried out again. Calm down! Shut up!

Papa sat back in his chair trembling and wet-eyed. He poured himself more wine and gave me some, mixed with water. After lunch he took me in his arms and hugged me, pressing my face against his jacket. You understand me, don't you?

Maman put the cloth in soak. The stains stayed in, even after regular poundings by Madame Nérin. Pale purple eventually faded to pale blue. That was my one and only damask table-cloth, Maman complained: what's the point of trying to make things nice if people keep spoiling them?

Soon after that it wasn't a question of making things nice. Just of surviving. Making do. We patched and darned, turned sheets side to middle, knitted and unknitted and re-knitted, let down hems and let out side seams. I padded my boots with folds of cloth to keep my stockings from wearing into holes. All through the bitter, insecure thirties, with so many men thrown out of work, with rising prices, we managed. When war came, bringing even greater austerity, we knew how to cope. At the beginning, anyway.

Tighten our belts, my mother said.

War fell out of the sky. Planes nosedived, dropping bombs. The local bakery blew up, rose in the air, collapsed. The baker and his wife and their two children vanished under a pyramid of beams and rubble. Hauled out by local men, the bodies were placed in the cobbler's shop along the street. Monsieur Fauchon was away fighting but his wife opened the door and took in the dead family. Maman was distressed: they should have been put in a Christian house. She and I dodged in, with other neighbours, to say a decade of the rosary. Waxy yellow faces; like shells. Madame Fauchon drew the grey blanket back up over their heads: I suppose we shouldn't be able to bury them for days. Not until someone gives us permission. Maman and the neighbours prayed Hail Mary after Hail Mary. The prayers made the corpses seem less frightening.

When the church bells rang to signal that the Germans had

arrived we hid indoors, peeped through cracks in the shutters. A motorcade of metal giants on motorbikes, rifles stacked in their sidecars. Next, a parade of open trucks, each displaying a machine gun. Eight stiff soldiers to a truck, propping their raised weapon, ready to fire. The convoy rolled in smoothly, a machine made up of many moving parts, neatly synchronised. So solemn and so grand! Next to me, Marc chanted: nasty buggers! Buggers buggers buggers! Maman slapped him: quiet, you!

The bells clanged again to mark the Armistice. We gathered in church to pray for Marshal Pétain. High above us, the curé's red face peered over the edge of the pulpit. He raised the silver crucifix and said: the hero of the first world war has become the father of the nation.

We filed out of the pews in silence. At the door, the curé shook hands with my father. He said: you veterans suffered so much on behalf of us all. Now, again, you must set us an example.

Papa hurried us home so that he could stuff the louvres of the shutters with crumpled newspaper, against the blackout demanded by the curfew. We sat and gazed at the photograph of Marshal Pétain that Papa had nailed on the wall behind the stove.

Needs will as needs must, said my mother.

Posters went up: handsome German soldiers wagging forefingers, telling us what we could and couldn't do. They looked like kindly teachers. They did a lot of marching. Whenever you went out you saw them swinging past. No more colours: just a uniform khaki green. Green beans, said my little brother Marc: string beans! The Germans re-named our streets and squares in German, hung swastika flags from our buildings. They moved into our houses. Anyone with a spare room promptly got a

German soldier billeted on them. The German military band played German music in the park on Sundays. My mother sighed. Well. At least things have calmed down.

A month before, Belgian refugees had streamed through our town, making their way south. A chaos of people in cars, farm carts, on bikes, pushing prams, just walking with suitcases, bundles of possessions. We gave them food, as you had to. After the Belgians, a wave of people from Normandy washed up. More food had to be given away. People from Ste-Marie also fled south in panic. Then, gradually, they straggled back. What else was there to do? We ourselves had set out on foot for Bordeaux, pushing a handcart, got fifteen kilometres down the road. Journeying to nowhere. When Papa collapsed, we turned round and came home, like so many others. In her panic Maman had left behind in the back yard the basket she'd packed with her wedding sheets. The yard had been broken into, and the basket of linen had vanished, but we found the shop itself mercifully intact, unlooted.

Brace up, little ones, said my mother: life goes on. Everyone still needs shopkeepers!

The men who'd been called up to fight returned home. Not all of them. Some remained imprisoned in German camps. But Monsieur Fauchon from along the street came back. The Mad Hermit, too. Occasionally I spotted him going in to the cobbler's shop, which had opened for business again.

Though I'd passed my *Brevet*, I had not been able to find a secretarial job, and so I helped my parents behind the counter. On the days when we were allowed to sell sugar, the queue stretched round the corner of the block. People grumbled at risen prices. Maman would snap: it's not our fault! Customers came in with their food stamps and talked about little else but rationing, how hungry they were. We were hungry too. We stumbled through the harsh winter sawed from inside with hunger pangs. When I complained, my mother shouted. You're not a child any more! Grow up! You've just got to cope!

We crept through the grey-green months of the following year. You can't sleep properly when you go to bed hungry. I prayed for food. I prayed for the war to end. By my fingernails I clung to my faith that God would not fail us, that he would help us survive.

Maurice appearing in my life was my miracle. I wrote down the date at the back of my old school exercise book. Only I knew what it meant.

March 1942. Easter still far off. A dark, raw morning. Rain pattered against the window. Too cold to strip and wash. I got dressed under the bedcovers, put on two petticoats, two pairs of socks. I went out, hooded in an old grain sack, to take the shutters down, came back in and stamped about to try and get warm. We drank our morning broth, then my mother wrapped a shawl round herself and went off in search of bread, leaving me in charge. She said: I don't want you standing in a queue for hours. She didn't like German soldiers looking at her daughter. When we went out to church she made me cover my head and most of my face with a scarf. I had to keep my eyes lowered and not look at the invaders. Not give them that satisfaction of being feared.

In fact I didn't fear them. I peeped at them without my mother noticing. Inside their stiff clothes they were human beings, just like us. Many of them were young. The contrast between their severe grey-green uniforms and boyish faces made them seem vulnerable, appealing. Many of them must have seen comrades fall and die. They had suffered, just as we had.

We were allowed to open to customers only on certain days each week. Today we were closed. I sat at the counter on my own. Taking the shutters down had provided me with some light so that I could peer at the books. I was supposed to be checking the accounts. Shivering in the draughts, I hadn't started yet. Too cold to do sums. I huddled in my coat, my shoulders hunched up towards my ears and my hands tucked into my sleeves. We couldn't afford to light the stove down here. Oil cost too much. The only way to fight the cold was to try to shrink, to give it less of yourself to bite on. I wasn't going to let the cold win.

I wasn't going to let the shop win, either. Ill-lit, gloomy space, sawdust silting the corners, pockmarked brown lino floor, the brown walls hung with empty shelves. I'd spent my life in it. The shop was like the war. If I let it, it would eat my youth. It would go on and on and never end. Nothing would ever happen to me. I'd grow old and die with the war still going on.

The shop bell rang; the door scraped open. Large shoulders filled the doorway. Raindrops glistened on an overcoat of fine black wool. No: cashmere. A man with dark eyes, aquiline nose in a bony face, jet hair sleeked back. My eyes gobbled his coat. I'd never seen anything of such quality. The water just slid off it rather than soaking in. Raindrops ran from his shoes, polished brilliant black, puddled on to the lino. He doffed his hat. Soft black felt, looking brand new. His black eyebrows twitched together: he must have been expecting my father, not a girl. He grinned. Even white teeth under his black moustache. He came towards me. He smelled of lemon verbena soap. Such a fresh, sweet-sharp scent in our shop that smelled sourly of damp.

Bonjour, mademoiselle. Is your father in?

Papa appeared from the yard, coughing as usual, and took the visitor upstairs. I ran for the mop and swabbed up the pool of wet he'd left behind. My father yelled for coffee. I put on water to boil, ground a few roast barleycorns in the little coffee-grinder. It squeaked a dance tune and I hummed along with it. I took the coffee in on a tray, the cups set on a clean napkin, spoons laid in the saucers. The big, sleek visitor was sitting with my hunched father by the stove. Beside him, Papa dwindled. A fold of loose chin. A flap of stomach. He merely grunted as I set down the tray but the visitor looked enquiringly at him. I edged towards the door. I slowed, my hand twisting the doorknob.

My daughter Marie-Angèle, said my father.

I turned. The man gave me a nod: Maurice Blanchard, *mademoiselle*, at your service. He exuded aliveness, a smell of money and newness and cleanliness. Under his coat glossy and sleek as fur his muscles flexed gracefully, energetically.

He stretched out his hand for his cup. His signet ring glinted gold. My father gave the jerk of the head that meant: out you go. Downstairs in the shop I searched for the comb my mother kept on a ledge under the counter. My fingers brushed against woven straw. Maman had gone out with just her purse, leaving her handbag behind. Perching on my high stool, I opened it, got out her compact. Just a few grains of powder: enough to do my face. I ran her stub of lipstick over my lips, found her comb and tidied my hair.

When Maurice clattered downstairs, my father behind him, into the shop, I put my chin in the air and tried not to notice him. Putting on his hat, he nodded at me again: *au revoir, made-moiselle*. He looked into my face, winked at me.

That night, in bed, I hooked my exercise book out from underneath my pillow, found a stump of pencil. I wrote down the date, circled it and wrote a big M for Maurice. Then I hid the book under the mattress.

Maurice came again a few days later. From his coat pocket he produced a brandy flask: can't drink this foul coffee otherwise. No disrespect intended, *mademoiselle*. Into his and papa's cups went the golden drops. Papa seized his cup, drained it in a gulp.

To give myself an excuse to stay in the room, I got out the darning basket and started sorting through a pile of clothes. Shirts with frayed cuffs. My brother's grey woollen Sunday trousers, held together by darns, the darns wearing back into ever bigger holes. Papa said: what do you know about business? Maurice said: it's a question of seizing opportunities. Unwinding a ball of grey darning wool, I sat well back in the corner, so that Papa would forget I was there. After a few stitches, my hands felt too stiff with cold to sew. I tucked them into my cuffs, fingered my bare skin inside my sleeves. Good shivers now, not bad shivers. Maurice leaned forwards, his hands on his knees: I started at the bottom, and climbed up. A self-made man!

Papa grunted. Maurice sat back, absentmindedly stroked the arms of his chair, padded with blue material, now balding and shiny. Spotted with grease. My mother always meant to re-upholster the chairs, but never found the time. Now there was no material in the shops so no point fretting. Maurice sat back, looked down at his hands. He took out a big white hand-kerchief and wiped his fingers. Best thing I ever did was apply for promotion and leave Limoges. The job here gives me far

41

more scope. He glanced in my direction. Inside my sleeves I clasped my hands to my forearms. I'd never been to Limoges. I'd never been anywhere, not even on the annual church pilgrimage to Chartres.

Maurice turned his gold signet ring, polishing it. Papa said: so this new job of yours entails what, exactly? Maurice explained. From his office in our town hall, he managed the organisation of food coupons for the whole area. He said: everybody's food cards are on file. Everybody's name is there. Papa said: so you know who everybody is.

Maurice took to dropping in quite often. Papa liked him, because Maurice listened to him talk about politics, and treated him with respect as the head of the family. He would spread his hands: sir, I'm afraid I know nothing about war. Papa would say: so I'll tell you. Maurice's responsibilities at the town hall had kept him from being called up. Now, they meant that he could find things out, and stay ahead of the game.

One afternoon he arrived with a warning for my parents. The arrival of another detachment of troops meant more billets would be needed. We'd have a German soldier parked on us in the blink of an eye. Papa smacked his chair arm. *Merde*! Maurice said: don't worry, I know exactly what to do.

He came back later that same night, with Monsieur Fauchon and a couple of other neighbours. Together they demolished the wall between our sitting room and the back storeroom where Marc slept. A rough arch, edged with wood, now framed Marc's campbed in its newly prominent position near the dining table. The German officer, arriving to inspect the accommodation, admitted he'd been given faulty information about available space, apologised, and withdrew. My father wrung Maurice's hand.

42

Handsome is as handsome does, said my mother.

She said it to Maurice's face, challenging him. She'd given him, as her guest, her chair by the stove. She sat at the little dining table, patching one towel with remnants of another. All our towels were paper-thin, held together by my mother's tiny stitches. I sat opposite her, tearing a newspaper into squares to go in the lavatory. Maurice smiled at my mother, raised his coffee cup. Madame, I'm proposing a deal. She shrugged her shoulders, looked down at her work. Convince me. He said: you'll appreciate a bit more money coming in. Oh, I'm sure you were doing very well before the war, making a good living, you're both so capable, but who knows now what will happen?

Maman hesitated, then said: I don't want to be rude, but we know nothing about you.

Maurice spoke quietly. Unfortunately I have no parents. They were excellent people, of good family, who ensured I received a good education, but they died when I was very young. Papa interrupted. He addressed my mother: shut up! He's proved himself, hasn't he? He's a good lad. He wants to help us.

Maurice ferried goods in and my parents sold them on, under the counter. Maurice supplied anybody who needed what he could get for them, regardless of who they were. Everybody was desperate to obtain food. As shopkeepers we suffered alongside our customers. The peasants on the farms roundabout were grasping and selfish, reluctant to let go of too much produce. We had to shift for ourselves. Maurice simply had the wits to organise things. He knew how to bargain, what prices to pay. From the countryside he coaxed chickens, vegetables, butter, eggs, milk, which my parents discreetly passed on to customers.

Maurice didn't have time to organise sales; he needed my parents for that. Thanks to his capacious car he could ferry in not just food but also big bundles of firewood, bicycle tyres, laundry soap. He made daily domestic life possible for a lot of people.

Yes, we've all got to live, my mother said: we've just got to cope. My father added: the Germans aren't so bad once you get to know them. They understand fairness, discipline, they are polite, they are very clean.

Maurice would tramp upstairs, whistling, for his cup of ersatz coffee. After his first few visits, watching me hover near the door, he insisted I be allowed my own thimbleful. Tasting of dust. In my father's presence I didn't dare accept a drop of cognac. Maurice would catch my eye, shrug, open his palms.

He began to take me with him on his business trips to collect food. Throughout that spring of 1942 we worked together. Time began to exist for me again: no longer uncountable weeks of endless war but precise moments of intense life. I marked our outings in my exercise book; precious afternoons whose dates I wanted to encircle in gold. We were heroes, hoodwinking the Germans. A man and a girl in a car looked like an ordinary couple out for a spin in the countryside; less suspicious than a man on his own. Maurice knew all the back ways; how to avoid checkpoints. I asked him: how do you manage to get hold of petrol? He winked. Business contacts. I didn't ask for details. I trusted him to know what he was doing and to keep out of trouble.

Not just groceries and petrol. Information, too, if necessary. Papers. Documents. Whatever people needed. He provided cigarettes as well. My father had been reduced to smoking dried comfrey leaves, but Maurice snapped open fresh packets of tailor-mades. Once he brought a cedarwood box of cigars, the lid sealed with a paper stamp with frilly edges. He taught me to smoke. I smoked only in the car, with him, wanting smoking to stay secret. My mother had her locked cupboards; I had my packet of cigarettes. They helped kill hunger. Maurice feeding me cigarettes let me know he'd picked me out, that I was special.

One wet afternoon in late May, when we got stuck in nearby Ste-Madeleine, waiting for a delivery, a parcel of something or other, Maurice took me into the bar in the main square for a drink. We ran in out of the rain, into blessed warmth, acrid clouds of cigarette smoke, a shifting mass of grey-green great-coats. German voices: a vigorous music of conversation. Maurice ordered us a brandy each: it's time you tried this. It burned its way down my throat. I kept my coat well pulled round me, to hide my shabby linen blouse, with pale yellow stains under the armpits, and my old blue serge skirt. The soldiers' green uniforms, well brushed, seemed new. How well fed they were. Pink, plump faces above their high, stiff collars. They called out teasingly to the young *patronne*, who responded with tight smiles. They nodded at us politely as we left. In my confusion, I nodded back.

Outside, the rain had turned to drizzle. As we walked to the car, I noticed a young woman hovering in the doorway of a closed shop on the far side of the street. Pale triangular face. Wavy dark hair. Vulgarly bright clothes: a little red hat with a black veil, a thin red dress that flapped above her knees, a little red cape hugging her shoulders. She jerked out of her shelter. Her high heels slipped her away down a side street.

That furtive air: it could only be Jeanne. Maurice, busy lighting another cigarette, hadn't noticed her. I didn't say anything to Jeanne's mother, next time I saw her. Poor woman: I didn't want to shame her.

Maurice and I were both silent as we drove back. I was thinking about having sat in a bar with Germans. Both normal and strange. Germans were our enemies, yet had accepted me in their presence. They showed me no hostility. As Maurice's companion I had entered the German world. The soldiers made the bar feel completely German, yet it was French. You could criss-cross from one world into another and back again. I was a smuggler, smuggling my self. Or perhaps the worlds existed in layers, like a cake, the German one overlaying the French one. No. More like two soups: the green one had mixed itself so thoroughly into the red, white and blue one that just one soup resulted. Khaki-coloured. Muddled soups, muddled thoughts. Too much brandy.

I said: I'm drunk. Maurice laughed and said: you need more practice.

My face felt warm. My limbs relaxed against the seat. Maurice put out his hand and touched my knee. The brandy glow spread all over me. A couple of kilometres outside town, he turned off the road on to a track leading towards the forest. We swerved in, deep under the chestnut trees, into green silence. Once we were well out of sight of the road, he stopped the car.

He handed me a twist of white waxed paper. Go on. I know you love them. Chocolate drops: I ate the lot, while he smoked. You want to smoke too? He lit my cigarette from his, handed it to me. He sighed, blowing out smoke. With his free hand he pulled off my beret, pulled off the ribbon confining my roll of hair, tossed out my hair so that it fell down all over the place. He put his arm around me and pulled my head down on to his shoulder. The soft nap of his overcoat caressed my cheek. Like the friendliest of animals. I wanted a coat like that. I wanted a fur cape like my mother's. I wanted a new dress. I wanted the war to end. The impossibility of all of this tasted, despite the brandy and the chocolates and the cigarette, like a fistful of filth scooped up from the gutter and pressed into my mouth. I wanted to cry. I wanted more chocolates, and more cigarettes, and more brandy, to stop me feeling so awful.

Maurice began to stroke my hair. He stroked its surface, over and over, smoothing it, going from the top of my head to my neck. Sweetness fizzed up inside me, all over my skin, coursed up and down my spine. Gently he spread out his fingers and plunged them in, picking up handfuls of hair, moving his fingers through them, around my scalp. He played with my hair for what seemed like a long time. We said nothing. When we'd finished our cigarettes he drove me home. He stopped outside the shop, came round to my side of the car, opened the door. In you go, little one.

The next time we sat together in the parked car, a week later, his fingers slid around the edge of my ear. He traced my cheek, my forehead, my chin. I liked the way his hands felt big, holding my head. I felt safe as well as excited. Something to do with the way the strong metal body of the car curved round us and smelled so expensive, its clean leather and petrol smell, the lemon verbena and damp cashmere smell of Maurice. The good tobacco smell that we shared.

I blurted out: have you got a girlfriend? He frowned. He pitched his cigarette out of the window and drove me home in silence. He made me wait another ten days. All these moments I stored away in my memory. First meeting. First touch. First kiss on the cheek.

Mid-June, in one way, was just like midsummer in other years. In the countryside all round town the peasants got on with the haymaking, the cuckoo called from the woods. In another way, everything had changed: I had grown up. Maurice and I drove into Ste-Madeleine on business. We drank brandy in the bar in Ste-Madeleine again, and I'd had nothing to eat, and felt tipsy. I spotted Jeanne in the bar, sitting in the far corner, with a German. This time all got up in a dark blue crêpe de Chine frock with a tiny lawn collar, and a little blue velvet hat, and high heels with cork wedges. She'd painted her mouth dark red and rouged her cheeks. She shot us one anxious look then swivelled her eyes away. Maurice looked back in her direction for a second, then moved his chair so that he had his back to her.

I pretended not to see her. My stomach burned with brandy but also with scorn. The make-up made her look so common. That day I was wearing a skimpy dress made from two old ones of my mother's cut up and stitched together. Marks on my skirt showed where the hem had been turned down twice. I still wore my school coat, and my school shoes. Maurice had noticed me looking at Jeanne. He lifted an eyebrow. Just someone I thought I recognised, I said. Maurice said: my dear Marie-Angèle, you don't know girls like that. They're nothing to do with you.

In the car I shrank inside my coat collar and stared through the windscreen. My bare legs felt itchy and hot, my ankle socks damp with sweat. I forbade myself to scratch; stuffed my hands into my pockets and pressed my knees together. When Maurice turned off the road and stopped the car on the track through the woods I willed him to lunge at me, grab me, do anything: just kiss me. I wanted to snarl, to burst into tears. Just get on with it! I stared at him in silence. He had to make the first move. Then it wouldn't be my fault.

His mouth tasted of brandy and tobacco. His skin smelled of lemon verbena. Sunlight and green branches surrounded the car. We got into the back seat, leaving the door open. Maurice said: you're so beautiful, so sweet, I need you so much. He stroked my hair. He whispered: let me, please let me, you know I love you. The forest closed round us and Maurice's arms closed round me and I gave him what he wanted. It hurt a lot. He said I've got to, I've got to. He held me in his arms while I cried and kept on doing it and I knew he loved me.

Next day he brought me a ribbed silk scarf: blue, with a yellow stripe at the ends. The most sumptuous thing I'd ever owned. In return I gave him my photograph. The only one I had was the one posed with Jeanne, both of us aged nine, standing outside our shop. My mother had two prints of it; I persuaded her to part with one of them. I tore the picture in half, so that it showed just myself. Maurice burst out laughing. Darling, ridiculous little girl. I adore this. He stowed the photo in his inside pocket. Sweetheart! I didn't return the torn-off image of Jeanne to the box in the cupboard. She no longer belonged in a respectable house. I threw her half of the photograph into the waste-paper basket. I prayed for her. God might help her, but I couldn't. At school she'd had a chip on her shoulder about being poor, not having a father. She didn't accept help gracefully. I didn't suppose she'd changed.

Maurice held me, kissed me, caressed me. After the first time the pace increased. He'd seize me: now! The car became our little house: crammed together in it we were runaways, rebels, newlyweds. Afterwards we'd smoke. I copied his way of holding a cigarette, nipped between finger and thumb. I liked the way he wanted me so much, pulling me into the back seat, his hands unfastening my coat so confidently. When he'd writhed and cried out the first time I'd felt surprised, but then I got used to it. After our expeditions, he would give me gifts. A pair of kid gloves with jet buttons, a powder compact lidded in mother-of-pearl, a lipstick in a chased-gilt swivel case, a tiny pot of rouge. A bar of lemon verbena soap. I went out with him smelling as sharp and citrony as he did. My mother's powder compact, old and cracked, was empty, and her lipstick worn right down. I didn't put on my new make-up in front of her. I did my face once I'd got into the car.

He was so clever, so much more experienced than I was. I worried I wouldn't be able to keep up with him. I could hide my ignorance most of the time, because if he felt like talking he just wanted me to listen. One day, however, parked in the woods, he said: talk to me. He lit cigarettes and passed me one. I didn't know what to say. I offered him stories of my childhood. Memories of Papa making me a doll's house, of Maman stitching me doll's clothes, teaching me to read and to say my prayers. Maurice tapped his fingers on the wheel: you don't know how lucky you are, having a proper family, parents who care about you. Go on, tell me some more. I told him about the Mad Hermit, and his crazy studio, his secret door into the school attic. Tales of hiding and of playing charades, outwitting Bluebeard, escaping into the street.

Maurice whistled and flicked my cheek and held me close: I don't believe a word of it!

I left Jeanne out of these tales. We'd been thrown together as children, purely by accident, we'd had a sort of friendship for a certain time, but we couldn't mix now. I preferred to concentrate on positive things. That was how we were getting through the war. We tried to continue a normal life. Because of the curfew, we couldn't go out to dances any more: very well, girls down the street organised secret dances at home to the music of an accordion. I didn't go to these. Too juvenile. I preferred to wait in for Maurice. He and he alone transformed the difficult present. 1942: my year of grace, when I fell in love.

One afternoon, later in June, he took me with him to collect some paperwork from someone in Ste-Madeleine. I carefully did not ask him what sort of paperwork. I prided myself on staying calm and adult, showing no curiosity. He didn't need my help. He just wanted my company. After being held up in a roadblock we got back an hour later than arranged. Maurice dropped me off and I got in to find my mother pacing the shop, fretting about not knowing where exactly we'd gone. Wretched girl! Why had we taken so long? I fobbed her off with some excuse as I removed my beret and fluffed up my hair.

Everybody else in this house is longing for supper, she remarked, watching me take off my coat: except you.

I'm full up, I said: it's the chocolates Maurice brings me, I can't resist them.

You could still fetch some spuds for our dinner, my mother said: some of us are hungry, my fine lady. If dinner's late it will be because of you dawdling about and keeping us all waiting.

Her tartness was unfair. She benefited from Maurice's

51

generosity just as much as I did, and she benefited from my bravery in accompanying him in the car, too. She got some cooking oil out of one of these trips, or a packet of margarine, or a block of lard. I said nothing. I thought: when I've got my own house I shall do exactly as I please and you'll have to ask permission to come and visit me and perhaps I'll say no.

We kept the potatoes in a sack in the back shed, together with all the under-the-counter provisions stacked in locked boxes. I took down the big iron key from the hook next to the shop door. Out I went into the yard, bowl in hand. Twisting the key in the lock, I discovered that the shed door was already unlocked. How careless my father had become. I'd have to mention it to him and hope he didn't hit me for criticising him. I pushed the door wide open, to let in enough light for me to see into the darkness. Sunshine fell on to lumpy shapes of piled logs, barrels, crates. As I filled my bowl with potatoes rats rustled suddenly in the recess at the back of the shed, making me jump.

Not rats. Walking further into the shed I found not just potatoes but people too. A woman and two little children, dressed in coats and hats. Three suitcases, one big and two small ones, bound with leather straps, stood nearby. The sunlight blazed through the open door on to their very bright yellow hair, which peeped out from under their hats. Some sort of odd game? Hide and seek? Were they play-acting? They gazed at me. I opened my mouth to speak, to blurt out their names. Madame Fauchon put her finger to her lips. The children clutched her coat. I shut the door on them, locked it. I locked them back into darkness.

My mother called: hurry up!

I clattered back across the yard. I felt I needed to make a lot of noise, for some reason. Upstairs in the kitchen I scrubbed the potatoes, working the bristles hard. The muddy skin paled. I gouged out rotten bits of potato while my thoughts jumped about. Madame Fauchon and her two younger children were trying to steal our food. They'd crept into our house and stolen the key to the shed. Then returned it. Why? They'd brought suitcases to fill with our potatoes. Why had they bleached their hair with peroxide? Robbers needed a disguise? Surely she had four children? Where were the older two? Presumably it was harder to go thieving with four children in tow. Where was her husband? I chopped the potatoes into greenish-white slices, slimy with starch. The cold water in the tin basin rose up my wrists and made them itch. I put the potatoes on to boil. The water leaped up and down. My mind sloshed with uncertainty. I couldn't tell my parents, summon the gendarmes. We didn't want police poking around our shed, finding our secret supplies. I'd ask Maurice what to do. He'd know. Until then, Madame Fauchon and her two little ones were my captives and deserved reasonable treatment.

I said to my mother: next time I go to the shed I'm going to take a candle. It's so dark in there you can't see a thing, even in the middle of the day. She answered: don't waste good candles. Take an old stub if you must.

I made a large saucepan of potato soup, thinning it out with extra water. While my mother went next door into the living room to check on my brother, who was supposed to be getting on with his homework, I scanned the top shelf, on which my mother kept moulds and crocks she didn't use every day, and took down, from the back, a little tin flask. I ladled some soup into it, screwed the lid on, went downstairs and out to the shed.

I didn't speak to Madame Fauchon. I couldn't say her name. I needed her to remain at a distance and not come too close. I didn't want her to talk to me, and so I pretended not to recognise her under her disguise. Her eyes spoke to me. Her eyes told me that Maurice had hidden her and her children in our shed. Her eyes wanted to tell me more. I turned my eyes away and concentrated on putting down the flask on a wooden box.

I did my best for those Jews: I gave them soup, a candle-end, matches. I shoved in a bucket, too, so that they could do the necessary. I went back into the house and got back upstairs without anyone realising where I'd been. We didn't have a telephone. If we had had one I would have telephoned Maurice and said get rid of them, you've got to get rid of them as fast as possible.

I worried that my mother might notice some disturbance in the orderliness of her kitchen. She knew exactly how many plates, cups, pots, dishes she owned. She had too few things to lose any of them. She'd spot the gap where the tin flask had stood.

I needed to keep her out of the kitchen. I went back next door, into the living room. She was sitting by the stove, ticking off entries in an account book. My brother, perched at the table where we ate, was shifting to and fro on the straw seat of his chair. His shorts hardly reached to mid-thigh. He'd outgrown all his clothes, as I had. Dreamily he turned the pages of his stamp album.

He scratched the back of his bare leg. He said: perhaps if I make friends with a German soldier he'll give me some German stamps. My mother glanced across at him. Her brows constricted. She said: how can we lay the table for supper if you sit dawdling there? If you don't get on with your home-work and learn that poem, you little brat, I'll tell the Germans to come and take you away!

I spoke in a low, soothing voice: Maman, I'll finish getting the supper, you stay here by the stove and keep warm.

My brother folded his hands, put on a pious expression and recited his lesson: oh dear Marshal Pétain I'm such a good boy, if I'm top of the class will you give me a toy? He bent double with laughter. I tapped his cheek, pushed him out of the way, laid the table, brought in the soup. My father came in and then Maurice arrived, as I expected he would, to drink soup with us. He shook hands with my parents, handed Maman a couple of food coupons. She nodded at him to sit down in his usual place next to Papa. He had his own napkin now, his own raffia napkin ring.

Marc gazed at him with admiration. We all did. His clothes, as ever, looked expensive and new. His navy suit looked freshly pressed, his fingernails looked very clean. Who laun-dered his shirts for him? His landlady, perhaps. Or that saucy girl, whoever she was, who sometimes left a dark hair on his collar. A buxom landlady, with crimped blonde curls, a woman of the world. Her man away. Lonely at night, no doubt, lying awake, inventing excuses for calling Maurice into her room when he came back of an evening. Simpering at him, asking him to adjust the wireless set or fix the blackout more securely in place. Whereas the forward girl would be a blowsy brunette with a reddened mouth and cheeks. Whether blonde or brunette, the laundress was someone for whom he procured big packets of starch. His collar and cuffs, thick unfrayed poplin, gleamed crisp and white.

He glanced across the table at me, winking, as I passed the soup plates. Papa said: give me some bread. Maman offered him the basket. He said, as he always did: bread! *Putain bordel!* You call this bread? We all knew perfectly well that bread now meant a sawdusty composite scratched together from bakers' rations, bulked out with nameless substitutes. Papa made the same complaint at every meal. Maman said: why do you have to go on about it? Why remind us? Papa said: the word bread should mean bread. His mouth worked. His face flushed red. I clasped my hands together under the tablecloth, praying he wouldn't start shouting, and stared at the greasy water in my plate. Maman said: eat up! Don't let it get cold! My brother chewed his bread and read the comic laid over his knees, out of my father's view. Maurice fingered his moustache. Glossy black brush looking newly trimmed. I wanted to reach out a forefinger and stroke it. I pleated and unpleated my napkin in my lap.

My parents began discussing the news, that's to say Papa talked and Maman half-listened as she spooned down her thin soup. She glanced at the empty bread basket. Tomorrow she'd have to queue for hours again, and perhaps no bread at the end of it. She interrupted Papa: you spend too much time thinking about the war, no wonder you feel so dismal. Papa jerked, and frowned. The muscles at the sides of his mouth started to twitch. I braced myself for him to start bellowing. Maurice smiled at my father and said: so what's the news?

These days Papa's nerves were worse. He kept to his chair by the stove, leaving most of the work of the shop to my mother and me. We were the ones who had to put up with customers' grumbling whispers: we cheated on weights and prices, we watered the milk, we kept certain goods out of the window. Papa would shout: tell them I'll know what to do! An empty threat: he was the one who'd get into trouble. Now he threw down his napkin and started off. Usually, like Maman, I ignored his rants. But because Maurice was listening politely, I listened too. France, with enemies in her midst gnawing her like woodworm, needed loyal sons to restore her to vigorous and fruitful life. We'd been weakened by letting in too many immigrants, aliens, refugees. Now we were paying the price. That the Occupation could have happened at all demonstrated our rottenness. On and on he fulminated to the sound of our swallowing, the rustle of my brother's pages as he turned them. All undesirables should be rounded up and put into camps. For the duration. While we decided what to do with them. For the sake of France and her purity and her strength. Creepy-crawlies, said my brother vaguely: you just pour boiling water on to them. I kept my head down over my plate. The word soup still meant soup, just about. The word Maurice still meant reliable; true gold.

It wasn't yet dark, but the blackout needed putting up in good time. I swallowed the last of my soup. My father clattered down his spoon. Dishwater, he said to my mother. She snorted. What d'you expect! I got up. Maurice said: I'll give you a hand with the shutters. Down we went.

Sawdust felted the floor of the shop. It looked soft. I wanted softness. I wanted Maurice to stroke my cheek and stop me worrying.

He explained rapidly in a low voice. You could say, another form of contraband. Just a package to smuggle out.

I said: but why d'you want to get involved with these people? How come you know them?

Maurice raised his eyebrows. He stuck his hands into his pockets, clinked his loose change: they're human beings in need of help and so I'm going to provide it.

I pressed on: why our shed? We're not the only people living close to them.

Maurice sighed. He said: I knew where you kept the key. I've carried stuff in and out of there often enough. I left the door open so that they could find somewhere to piss outside.

We padlocked the big shutters at the front. At the back, the shutters were smaller. I watched Maurice's hands twist out the bolts, push them into place. Curly black hairs protruded from his cuffs, curled over his wrists. His fingers worked deftly, quickly.

But my mother's bound to discover them, I said: next time she goes to the shed to fetch something.

Fetch it yourself then, Maurice said.

I shivered. My stomach shook. My mouth shook. I already understood some of what was happening from the titbits of information Maurice gleaned at work and brought back. I didn't want to think about the situation too much, because it made me feel so hopeless, so helpless. What was the point of getting upset? But Maurice said: forewarned is forearmed! So, thanks to Maurice, I did know the Germans needed a large labour-force back in Germany, for the war effort. They'd been asking for French volunteers, and in return releasing French prisoners of war. The supply of volunteers having dried up, they'd decided to conscript. They would conscript where they liked. They were planning to take Frenchmen: fair enough they should take Jews too. First of all they were taking the foreign Jews, who didn't belong in France anyway. Those without citizenship were gradually being rounded up and deported to Germany to be resettled there. I felt sorry for the Jews, having to start again in a new country and work in factories, but I felt just as sorry for the Frenchmen who'd be taken away to labour camps. What could I do? French families all around us had already lost sons and husbands in the fighting; the families coped heroically. Soon they'd lose more. We couldn't stop the Germans organising things in their own way. We weren't in charge. We had to survive. People who made even small gestures of resistance got punished. A young woman down in the bottom of town who had embroidered a V for Victory on her blouse had been arrested and taken away to prison in Rennes for three months. Madame Nérin reported to my mother that a big crowd of her neighbours had gathered to see her go. The same neighbours welcomed her back. They hailed her as a heroine but I thought her foolish. She wouldn't have done it if she'd had children and had to consider them.

Maurice, however, I discovered, was thinking about the Jews and what he could do for them. Once we'd put the shutters up and come back inside the shop to pull the blackout curtains he said: don't go back upstairs just yet.

We pinned the heavy edges together. Maman had said: if we have shutters surely we don't need blackout curtains too? Papa had got agitated: not a single chink of light must show! The thick material smelled of dust. It hid us. We didn't turn on the light. We stood close together. Certain conversations were better had in darkness. A kind of test of love. When I couldn't see Maurice, but just feel his face held between my hands, I overflowed with trust for him. Darkness bound two people together. In the shadows, not seeing his face, you could concentrate more on what the other person said, just from the solemn note in his voice, and also he could tell you more of the truth. He didn't tell me all of it: I didn't expect that. I knew he protected me from knowing too much about the risks he was running, just as I was protecting my mother from knowing she had some Jews hiding in her shed.

The scrape of a match. Spurt of sulphur smell. Flare of blue-yellow lighting up Maurice's fingers as he lit cigarettes then handed me one. A red spot of light sprang out behind his cupped hands. I drew on my cigarette too hard and the nicotine hit the back of my throat and made me cough. He put his hand on my arm, hushing me, then talked in a low voice. My brave girl. I wanted to scream at him: I am not brave. I breathed in nicotine and breathed my words into silence and breathed them out as smoke. He said: I can't just stand by and do nothing.

I said: everyone knows how clever you are, how good your contacts are, no wonder they ask you for advice. But all the same you must get rid of these people quickly.

Not just advice, Maurice said: I'm running a taxi service here.

He stroked my bare forearm. He put his cheek next to mine. He said: I've started using your shed as a transit point because people know I often come and see you. No one will think twice about seeing my car outside your yard.

I shook more than ever. The Germans would punish us if they found out. We'd be shot. How can you imagine dying? You can't. But I was terrified of the pain before the blackness came. I couldn't allow my mind to get close to that.

Don't worry, Maurice said: they're leaving tomorrow afternoon, well before dark. Just one more night in your shed and that's it.

I asked: where are Monsieur Fauchon and the two older children?

Maurice said: there's been a bit of a hold-up with getting their new papers. Shouldn't be long now.

I didn't go back to the shed to check on the Jews. My mother might have become suspicious. I didn't dare take the Jews any more food. If they'd been sensible they'd have made the soup last. There was nothing more I could do for them. They'd looked quite well fed. They wouldn't starve. I went to bed early, to get away from my mother's glance.

Next morning, Saturday, my father decided to go to the men's fellowship meeting at church. Maman said: don't stay too long in the café afterwards. He snorted, brushed past her and out of the door. Maman said to me: haven't you got any work to do?

I could not settle to sweeping and dusting. Finally I took the basket of darning and sat in the shop with it, picking up one of my father's socks, lacking a heel, stabbing my needle in and out of the blue woollen weave. My mother, doing her books at the counter, shot me frowning looks from time to time but said nothing. Papa didn't reappear at midday. My mother struck her hands together in exasperation, and served our soup. Afterwards she sent Marc out to bring my father home, then sat down by the stove to take a nap. When I heard Maurice's car come along the street, go past the shop and turn the corner, I went down.

He parked behind the shop, on the far side of the yard, behind the gate there that led into the little back street. I threw on my coat and beret and ran to meet him, carrying my silk scarf and my kid gloves, so that anyone seeing us would think oh there she goes, off with her flash boyfriend, lucky girl.

Peroxide, I said: you need to get them more peroxide, though. They need to do their eyebrows.

No time for that, Maurice said.

The Jewish woman and her two children came out of the shed, holding their suitcases. She didn't speak to me. She should have said thank you but she didn't. So rude!

We hid the Jews in the back of the car, making the woman lie down on the seat and the two children crouch on the floor, and covered them with a layer of sacks. We drove them into Ste-Madeleine, to drop them near the station. I stayed quiet on the journey. No need to talk. Maurice had explained his plan before we set off. They were going to take the train south, armed with the false papers Maurice had had made for them, the tickets he'd procured. All part of the taxi service. We drew up in a side street, near a garage. Their three backs turned the corner and disappeared. Starting the car, Maurice said: up to them now.

As we drove home, I started chewing the fingertip of my glove. He reached across and pinched my cheek: don't ruin those. They cost a lot of money.

I said: I'm sorry. Maurice frowned. Don't make a fuss. It's all right. I know the dangers involved.

We bumped into Ste-Marie over potholes. I loved my town more than ever, because we'd got back to it safely. I loved every cobble we bounced over, every heap of rubble we passed, because they marked the way home. The rue de la Croix was shuttered and quiet. I ran indoors, looking neither to the right nor the left.

Maurice helped save quite a few people. I didn't know precisely how long he'd been using our shed, nor precisely how many Jews he helped reach the next step of their escape routes, nor where they came from. Paris? Not my business: I didn't ask. Nor did I praise him openly for his bravery. He was modest; he didn't want praise. He'd look at me with his dark eyes: those are very vulnerable people. We're all in this together. We've got to help each other.

He looked after me, and he looked after my parents and my brother too. He gave Marc boxing lessons, and he found a new battery for our wireless set. For my parents' wedding anniversary he gave them fine presents: a gold watch for Papa and a gold bracelet for Maman. He produced them one Sunday night, over supper at our flat. Casually he placed two little boxes on the cloth.

My mother wiped her mouth on her napkin. She looked carefully at the treasures, assessing them. She said: you've been given a rise, have you? You shouldn't be spending your money on us! Maurice smiled at her: but you've been so good to me. She got up. Well, I know where these need to go. She fished in her apron pocket for her keys, locked the boxes away in her cupboard. She made no more comments. Maurice's face fell. He didn't yet understand that that was just her way. And she didn't understand the full reason for his generosity. Only I did. It was a kind of wish: that Maman and Papa be protected from harm. Even if they didn't know it, my parents were in grave danger. It was their shed the Jews were hiding in.

Until the end of July Maurice ran his rescue operation. After that, he didn't seem to be needed any more. I didn't know why. In any case, to my relief, he stopped.

My mother appeared not to have noticed the comings and goings in our backyard. She tapped the side of her nose and repeated: ask me no questions and I'll tell you no lies. She did notice the way I'd changed. Throughout that summer we squabbled. She berated me often: you've become so cheeky! Stop answering back! What have you been up to, madam? I hope to heaven you've not become involved in any political nonsense.

August brought my birthday. Maurice gave me a string of pearls. I wore them every day, buttoning my collar over them when I went down to serve in the shop. In the countryside the peasants got the grain harvest in, the main benefit of which went, of course, to Germany. Our bread continued to be mixed with whatever was available. The maize crop, likewise, went to feed German cattle. That was just the way things were. We kept our heads down and continued to cope as best we could. September brought the hope of a good apple crop, the fruit reddening on the trees in the orchards lining the road to Ste-Madeleine. My mother didn't want to notice that my belly was swelling up round as any apple. She didn't want to notice that already I moved differently, my centre of gravity altered. She didn't want to let on she heard me throw up in the mornings. She regarded in silence my new patience with Marc. His kicking me under the table at meals or pulling my hair no longer had the power to irritate me. I just ignored him.

Eventually, one morning in October my mother cornered me. I was pulling empty dry goods bins into place. Maman stood between the shop counter and the door to the stairs. Hands on hips, she scrutinised me, eyes sliding around my waist. I straightened up and stared at the brown varnish on the doorframe.

You haven't had your visitor, have you, she said: not for months now. You've sent no rags to the wash. How could you do this to me, you wicked girl? How could you bring such shame on us?

I said: oh for heaven's sake, spare me the sermon.

She clouted me, burst into tears, took me to the doctor, who confirmed what both of us knew. The doctor wore a long white coat and gold pince-nez. His face was sunken and very tired. He looked me straight in the eye as I sat up on the cold leather couch, then turned his back to wash his hands. His cramped office smelled of rubber and disinfectant. His voice sounded disinfected too: I can't help you. Abortion is now illegal, a capital offence. I burst into tears that he could mention such terrible things.

The following morning, sitting in the parked car outside the shop, Maurice whispered to me: if you want to get rid of it I could find someone. I burst into tears again: abortion is a mortal sin! I'd go to hell! Maurice looked at his watch, shot his cuffs. He said: I've got to go now, I'll see you soon. Away he drove.

My coat pulled round me to hide my condition, I stood on the pavement, crying. I was afraid to go indoors. But I couldn't stay outside. The houses and shops on both sides of the street were shuttered and closed, but anyone might be watching. I couldn't bear to be looked at. I couldn't bear the thought of neighbours pretending to feel sorry for me. Being mean about my downfall. I forced myself to stop crying. I scrubbed my eyes on my coat sleeve and went in.

My mother told my father the news at lunchtime, once we'd eaten. He got up, pulled me away from the table. He slapped me twice round the face: count yourself lucky! Maman shouted at him: that's enough! He sat down, shaking. Maman pursed her lips. This isn't the way things should be. I wanted a proper wedding for you, with everything nice.

On the following day, the shop was closed. Papa, by the unlit stove, had his back turned to us. As soon as Maman went into the kitchen I put on my coat and beret and went out.

I met Maurice at the back of the church, as we'd arranged. I didn't want to go to the park, anywhere public. Maurice could no longer take me out in the car. No petrol. Was petrol scarcer than ever or did he not want to be seen with me? I didn't ask. I followed him into a pew. He dusted the dark wood with his handkerchief, then knelt beside me.

The heating was off. The church seemed solid with cold. Smelled of cold. Both of us shivered, despite our coats and scarves. I crossed myself, bent my head and stared at my gloved hands.

I waited until Maurice said: OK. Let's sit down. I heaved myself to my feet, settled myself on the bench. Too small for me: I had to concentrate so that I didn't slide off it. Maurice folded himself up next to me, his feet on the kneeler. He rested his black cashmere arms on his knees and gazed at his polished black toecaps and said: all right then, we'll get married.

Organ music pealing out, tall cut-glass vases of yellow gladioli, the choir singing, warm sunlight streaking the floor as I glide up the aisle in a white silk dress with a long train. Gently he'll put my lace veil back from my face and kiss me and slide the gold ring on to my finger and I'll carry a bouquet of white lilies and green maidenhair fern bound with white satin ribbon. Honeymoon in Paris. A huge pink and gold bed. Dinner and dancing at the Folies Bergères.

I said: well, you've always said you wanted a family. You've got one now.

Smile, I wanted to beg him. Say you love me. He glanced at me. He looked very young. Scared, sulky. He shifted on the pew seat and pulled his collar closer round his ears. I leaned my shoulder against his, put my hand on his knee. He said: well, I suppose we're business partners, after all, aren't we.

I said: you know, eventually I'll inherit half the shop. It's rather rundown but I think it'll be worth quite a bit, when the war's over.

I felt like crying. He should have been glad to marry some-one like me, hard-working and capable, with good prospects, from a decent family. And I knew I was pretty. He'd told me so often enough. I was much prettier than a shrimp like Jeanne. He ought to have been glad to find such a good wife.

Maurice sighed. We sat slumped for some minutes. The cold reached into me. We were the only people in church. The red sanctuary light burned in its gilt holder. I'd almost forgotten what church was for. In this quiet and dark you were supposed to pray. I said the Our Father in silence and waited. Eventually Maurice sat up and touched my arm: you're right, the future is what counts. He turned to me: you're the future.

I'd laid up my trousseau as a young girl, stitching away over the years at a stock of household linen. Even with the war, I'd managed to hold on to it. I'd refused to let my mother have it to replace her worn-out stuff, the sheets she'd lost at the start of the war, the tablecloth with indelible wine stains. Now Jeanne's mother came in to embroider my new initials on to my sheets, to sew new nametapes on to my drying-up cloths and towels. My mother threw a couple of thin, old sheets at me: you can have these! From them Madame Nérin stitched me a wedding dress. She did quite well. Over each darn she embroidered a white flower. She made buttons from bunched discs of leather snipped from the uppers of Marc's worn-out shoes then covered with linen. She cut strips of drawn-thread work from the top edges of the sheets and sewed them into a frilled collar and cuffs.

She fitted the dress in silence, pins held between her lips. She knelt at my feet, adjusting the hem. I said: how is Jeanne doing? She mumbled something. Looking at her bowed head, I felt a rush of pity. I said: I've been saving some hand-me-downs for her. Remind me to give them to you before you go. She mumbled again.

Maurice gave me a fur coat. Second-hand, obviously, but new-seeming. I hugged it and buried my face in it. Fresh, gleaming fur, tawny and gold. My mother had her marten cape, and now I had a long fur coat, its deep sleeves lined with rich brown silk. On our wedding morning in November the church was unheated as ever, but in my coat I felt almost cooked. The curé blessed us, shook holy water all over us, and said to me: have lots of children for the Church and for France.

On the afternoon of our wedding day Maurice and I lay together on my narrow bed, on the pink coverlet. Maurice embraced the curve of the child: I swear to take good care of you both. As a token he gave me a gold ring, elaborately chased, and a gold chain, and he gave my mother a gold bracelet. He gave my father a gold signet ring.

My mother hid Maurice's gifts, for the duration of the war, along with her other treasures in her cupboards. Maurice and I watched her lock the cupboard door, pocket the key. I stayed sitting at the table. My belly showed less that way. I had indigestion, and my legs ached, but I didn't want to make a fuss and draw attention to myself. Maurice got up and put his arm round Maman's shoulders. Her hand came up and gripped his.

He said: you've got plenty of storage space downstairs, mother-in-law, haven't you? Would you look after something for me? Just for the time being? Until I get settled?

When a big painting arrived, soon afterwards, enclosed in an old coverlet, Maman left it in its frame and propped it, wrapped in sacks, against the wall of the shed. Everybody had things hidden: their wine and spirits and cider; anything valuable. My mother locked away all my precious gold for me. She said: I'll take care of it until after the war. Then you can bring it out and enjoy it.

Hubert was born in March 1943. By then we'd moved into our new house. When I got back with the baby from the clinic, when he was a week old, Maurice gave me a gold ring set with tiny diamonds. He said: it's for eternity. You and Hubert, for ever. He began crying. He sat on the edge of our big marital bed, holding me holding the baby, and said: I will take care of you always. My darling, my darling. His tears wetted my face. I folded my arms closer around Hubert. My father cried when he was upset. Men weeping like babies: where was the use in that? Maurice had a soft heart where other people's suffering was concerned, all very well, but at this moment I needed him to be strong, so that I could depend on him. I still felt very weak, very tired after the birth. I said: this is supposed to be a celebration! Maurice apologised, got up, opened his bag, produced a bottle of Taittinger. I said: miracle!

He had found us our new home a while back, an abandoned house up at the top of town, which was going cheap; all the furniture thrown in. He kept the transaction a secret, wanting to surprise me. I wouldn't have chosen that particular house, but I knew Maurice needed to live somewhere dignified and spacious, befitting his good job in the town hall. He exulted in the elegant proportions of our *salon*, the graceful curve of our stairs. He'd had some preliminary works done on the house, the walls whitewashed and the floors re-sealed, as an extra wedding present. The day after we were married we moved. I put my few things in Maurice's car, kissed my parents: now the future could begin.

For the moment that meant cleaning and restoring. I scrubbed and scoured the shabby rooms, poulticed with dust, smelling of dead mice and turps, polished the shabby old furniture. In the wild, overgrown garden, Maurice dug a vegetable patch. Come summer 1943, I could pick big handfuls of spinach, cram them into a string bag, take it down to my mother.

Having promised me to run no more risks, to do nothing that would endanger us, Maurice concentrated, now, on his job, on us, his family. I ceased worrying so much about his safety. Life became simpler, centred on marriage, on home. We went on surviving. From day to day. You just got on with it. What choice had we? None. We were living under a harsh and vicious Occupation. Anybody who wanted to be a hero and defy the Germans got imprisoned, tried and then deported or shot. That was that. Communists ran the Resistance. We weren't going to get mixed up with Communists. We were just ordinary people, doing our best, trying to stay decent and kind. I locked up my thoughts about the war. For the sake of my health. You can make yourself forget if you try.

Jeanne, that poor, stupid unfortunate, was not allowed to forget. In November 1943 she returned from Ste-Madeleine and hid in her mother's flat. Madame Nérin began doing extra laundry and charring, to support her daughter. Jeanne took in sewing at home. I wanted to help her and so I sent her some mending to do for me. I didn't go to see her: I was too busy looking after my son and my husband, going to visit my mother and giving her a hand. Jeanne remained someone with whom I could not mix. Maurice preferred me to keep away. When I got restless, cooped up indoors, he would take my hand between the two of his and squeeze it. He'd hum some dance music, waltz me about, spinning, until we bumped into the furniture and got breathless. I depended on him to look after me. When I complained, he comforted me: what would Marshal Pétain say? Be brave, little soldier.

Jeanne's problem was precisely that it showed. Everybody could see her condition and everybody knew she had no husband.

We all know how she's spent the war, my mother said.

I'd come to keep her company for the day. I'd done her ironing for her, her sweeping and dusting. Now, in the late afternoon, we were sitting in the *salon* over the shop, wearing our overcoats because she'd no fuel. The clock sounded loud in the hush. Like a heart beating. The clock would go on ticking, and we would go on, and the war would end. We could allow ourselves to hope for that now.

Marc was out at his youth group. Maurice and my father were off on business somewhere. Little Hubert was tucked up in my mother's bed, the only warm place. My mother and I were knitting, making a jumper and blanket for Hubert with variegated wool from jumpers of our own we'd unknitted, working by the light of a candle as the electricity was off. I looked at my mother's wasted face, her jutting cheekbones, her fingers knotted with arthritis. Her deep-set eyes were sunk in shadows. At lunchtime she'd given half her portion to Hubert. Jeanne hadn't gone as hungry as my mother.

Madame Nérin came to do Maman's laundry as usual. As often as I could, I went down to help the two of them. Jeanne's mother looked skinnier than ever in her washed-out black clothes. Face seamed with wrinkles. One day, in early December, she began coughing into the wash, and my mother had to stop the mangle and make her sit down on an upturned bucket. She ended up recounting all her troubles, that's to say Jeanne's troubles. The child was due any day now and Jeanne hadn't been well. But she must go to the doctor, my mother exclaimed. Madame Nérin said: we haven't the money.

My mother clenched her fists and cast up her eyes at this fecklessness. *Nom de Dieu*! When she saw someone suffering, she couldn't abide it. She wanted to stop the suffering. It hurt her too much. Sometimes you had to drown kittens, if there were too many of them. Sometimes it was right a child died at birth, if he'd been born unfit in some way. Sometimes you just had to admit defeat with yellowing pot-plants and tip them into the dustbin. What could be done with Jeanne?

I felt obliged to visit my old schoolmate. The following morning, leaving Hubert with my mother, I wrapped up well in my fur coat, a woollen hat and scarf, and made for the Nérins' flat in the lower town. I walked briskly through chilly mist down towards the smithy, the river. I told myself: just get it over with.

The ugly tenements rose up around me. Rusty window-frames, broken panes patched with cardboard or tin, paint peeling off doors. I wasn't too happy to have to go into such a poor district, nor to have to be near Jeanne. Thinking about her made me itch, as though she were a flea biting me. She was like a flake of skin I longed to dislodge. I didn't want to be seen entering her flat, even though I was on an errand of charity. At the same time I felt a sort of fascination: how would she behave?

Madame Nérin opened the door. Thank God you've come. She had on her coat and hat. She pulled me inside the brown-painted entry. Quick, quick. Jeanne's waters have just broken. Stay with Jeanne, will you, while I go to fetch the midwife?

How familiarly she spoke to me in her urgency. She called me *tu*: I felt quite put out. She took no notice but banged out, and I went into the bedroom.

Light filtered under the lowered dark red blind. The poky little room smelled newly scrubbed. Cold air and cold bleach. Brown walls and brown floor. Little furniture: two iron beds, a chair, a chest of drawers. Jeanne without her gaudy make-up looked like a brown mouse. Sweating. Biting down on her lip with her little white teeth. I stood at the end of her bed. When she whimpered I flinched. I tried to be kind. I told her to keep her courage up. I felt frightened, being here with her all alone, having this unwanted responsibility forced upon me, and so I became the soldier self Maurice loved, dutiful, on guard, keeping watch. Jeanne seemed like my prisoner, but not one I could respect. She'd collapsed into the pains. They were rushing her away, like the current in the nearby river swirling debris under the bridge.

Giving birth is a lonely business. The nuns in the maternity clinic had been brisk, not kind. No one had comforted me. In the labour ward I was just left alone to get on with it for a night and a day. No visitors allowed. When I went in, my mother signed a cross on my forehead. Be brave! Then she left. I wanted to run after her but was felled by a pain. A nun gave me an enema and shaved me. I remember the shiny metal rails around the bed and the pale green lino floor, polished so clean they hurt. Steel rods everywhere, inside me and outside. Finally I tore apart and exploded. I felt I made a terrible mess. I didn't dare look. The baby existed outside me. The nuns whisked him off. To clean him up.

Jeanne gasped and screamed my name. I went round the bed and gave her my hands and she gripped them. She panted, she yelled good and loud. She didn't seem to care a bit about the animal noise she was making. Her pink nightdress was creased up round her waist and she'd kicked off the blanket and sheet. Her opened thighs, gripping the painful air between them, looked so strong. Her bare feet shifted, stamped. Don't push, I cried: I can see the head, you mustn't push, you've got to wait for the midwife. Fuck that! Jeanne shouted. She howled. A baby shot out as though greased, fat as a codfish. I cried out too. I caught the baby. A girl, red and creased, all slimy against the sleeves of my fur coat.

I studied her black eyebrows, her licks of black hair, her blue eyes. Jeanne, sunk in pillows, tried to sit up. She said: is she all right? I said: I think so.

The crimson, crumpled baby took a breath and began bawling. I put her into Jeanne's arms. Jeanne lay back, holding her. Mother of God, it hurts! Damned holy Virgin, why does nobody tell us what it's like? She pushed her nightdress off one shoulder, put the child to her breast. Immediately she began to suck.

What a smell in the room: blood and urine and worse. I disliked seeing Jeanne flopping so helplessly in her bed in her mess, floundering in her soiled bedclothes. I pulled the sheet back up and said: well, did you ask the Holy Virgin to help? You've left it a bit late, haven't you?

Jeanne said: I loathe you, Marie-Angèle. Her voice cracked. She glared at me, put up a hand and pushed her hair back. She was sweaty, pale as a pig, and shivering. The baby stopped sucking and began to wail. I didn't know what to do. The room seemed jumping around me. I couldn't quiet it. Hush, I wanted to say to the room: hush. I wanted to smash my hand over the room's mouth until it shut up.

Madame Nérin arrived with the midwife, a big, blonde woman in a skimpy grey coat and skirt. I didn't know her. She took over. I backed away, stood near the window. Madame Nérin started crying. She kissed Jeanne, over and over. I held on to the blind. My fingers found the little wooden barrel knotted on to the end of its string, and clasped it. Madame Nérin held Jeanne's hand while the midwife cut the cord, washed the baby, wrapped her in a towel and put her back in Jeanne's arms. She began to suckle again. Jeanne seemed to drift off then, to go elsewhere.

After a little while she opened her eyes, looked at me and winked and said: Christ, I could murder a cigarette. You haven't got one, have you? I bet Maurice keeps you supplied with fags, doesn't he, lovely treats?

She was babbling now. Hysterical. I said: calm down. Jeanne said: he can get hold of anything, can't he, that boy? What else does he get for you? That's a nice row of pearls you've got on. Maurice give them to you, did he?

Madame Nérin was wiping Jeanne's face with a damp flannel. Hush, *ma chérie*, she murmured: just hush. She turned her head, flicked a worried look across the room. I couldn't bear it that she should gaze at me apologetically, as though she knew a secret I didn't. I wanted to slap Jeanne. I should have. Instead, I stopped twiddling the cord of the blind, walked away from the window, held on to the back of the chair by the washstand. I looked down at it. What a mess! I began putting things into order: brush and comb, little bottles, sponge in saucer.

Jeanne said: you know, he used to love coming to the house in Ste-Madeleine. He couldn't get enough of it.

The midwife, four-square in her felted grey skirt, seated between Jeanne's splayed legs, stitching her up, swivelled her attention, looked up at me inquisitively. I said to Jeanne: shut up. Jeanne said: oh, Marie-Angèle and I keep each other's secrets, don't we, darling?

I said: I'm going now.

Outside I leaned against the frosty wall for a bit. Then I walked along the street with my knees feeling like india rubber, hands shoved into the pockets of my coat. My feet knew the way home, or else I don't know how I'd have got there. While I stumbled along I pretended to be a girl at school again. When people passed you nasty notes in class, under the desk, you tore them up. If necessary you put the tiny pieces into your mouth and swallowed them. Tiny papery bits, like tiny hosts. Then you could deny they'd ever existed. That was how you forgot words. Lick them, suck them. Ink swimming over your tongue and down your throat.

I concentrated on the approach of Christmas and the New Year, the approach of the birth of my second child. In April 1944 our daughter arrived. Little angel, I whispered to her. She flung herself into the world and gave us fresh hope. She heralded the Liberation. Joyful shouts banging along the street. Church bells clanging. More military vehicles grinding in. People bursting out of their houses and running along the square. I heard them rather than saw them. My world had shrunk to my bed, the baby in the cot next to it. I was sleepy and I was warm. I wanted to stay in bed for ever and never get up. I dozed, then fed the baby, then dozed again.

Everybody gave the troops the best welcome they could. My parents too. My mother repeated the story for years afterwards: a group of American soldiers, invited in for a drink, emptied their glasses of Benedictine at one go, then held them out for more. They finished the entire bottle in five minutes. My mother had guarded that bottle, well hidden, throughout the long war years, and now in the blink of an eye it was gone.

September brought the celebration of Liberation. The town councils of Ste-Marie and Ste-Madeleine decided to join together, to demonstrate unity and solidarity, to hold the festivities in Ste-Marie. They pooled resources: double the size of brass band, double the number of flags, two mayors marching abreast, two lots of choirboys and altarboys at the thanksgiving Mass. The gold-fringed velvet banner of Ste-Marie waved next to the silver satin banner of Ste-Madeleine.

Maurice and I, plus our two little ones, joined our neighbours to watch the victory parade. My mother stayed indoors. Papa, wearing his service medals, left early, to take his place among the veterans. Maurice and I, carrying the children, walked down all the way through town from our house in the square. We descended flight after flight of stone stairs cutting between narrow streets. Every step of the way resonated with memories of the last five years. I was not yet properly well again, and still very tired, but I wanted to be with my compatriots, to offer thanksgiving. We all wanted that. To be together, to merge into one another, all joined up, whole, perfect, full of light, a simplicity, a pure feeling, all united all part of one another part of the crowd. The old skin of unhappiness cast off, wrinkled, dirty, and the new beautiful self of France rising up reborn, intact, after so many years of deprivation and distress.

Maurice gave both children into my care so that he could stand like a soldier, heels together, shoulders back, as upright and erect as possible. People pressed three deep on the pavements, spilled along the kerbs. Tricolores tying up women's hair, worn as armbands, worn as sashes. Down the centre of the street marched the bandsmen, in braided maroon uniforms and gold-trimmed képis, carrying their golden instruments, followed by the mayors, all the local dignitaries, the military, the police, the veterans, the two church choirs, the nuns, the church youth groups. Then the crowd fell back, and made space.

Jammed up against the entrance to a shop, at first we just heard the cries, not the words at that point, just the angry shouts, the shrill jeers of children, and then we saw the bald creatures thrust forward through the mêlée of townspeople, men and women hollering and cursing.

No hair. Not just bare-headed. No hair. That made them seem utterly naked. Just the gleaming domes of their skulls. Whiteness of skin and bone where hair should be. All that was female ripped off them. Young ones. Middle-aged ones. One fat one seemed really old: sixty or so. Wrinkles. Mascara rather than eyelashes. Rouged, pendulous cheeks. The fat one and the thin ones; the old one and the less old ones. They staggered along, faces turned aside, eyes cast down.

The men propelled along the things they held between them. One gendarme on each side, gripping them by the forearms so that they couldn't escape. They were going fast, half-dragging them. They hauled at them so fiercely they seemed to be pulling them apart. The bald women stumbled in their high heels over the cobbles. They looked stupid as beasts being driven to market, terrified as beasts being driven to the abattoir. The fat, old one looked the most ridiculous, bosom bulging out of her décolletage. One young one seemed a kind of heifer, in a white coat like an overall flapping loosely over the dress beneath, her bald head bent down over the wailing child clutched in her arms. I knew her, but at the same time she was not a person you could know or name. Shaved, she was no longer human. Words whimpered in my brain. I couldn't speak the words I wanted to. I gripped Maurice's sleeve and held on. I heard my own bewildered voice crying: Jeanne, Jeanne.

They'd seized her and shaved off all her hair so that they could parade her, part of the procession of tarts, let everyone know she'd been with Germans. Baldness her sign of betraying France, her badge of shame. She was a repulsive sight and she was stripped of all disguise she was a mockery of a woman she was a disgrace to womanhood. The citizens of our town looked on triumphantly and judged the creatures: outcast; alien; lowest of the low. Filth. I felt sick. I swayed against Maurice, my handkerchief to my mouth.

Jeanne's child focussed the crowd's hoots and cries. Alone of the tarts, Jeanne blundered along bare-legged. Women, her own age and older, respectable, clad in skirts and blouses, ankle socks and sturdy shoes, their hair neatly pinned up, followed her, a chorus of good women staring and catching each other's sleeves and pointing, then joining in to scream insults. Everyone around her, a troop of little children included, pulled at her dress as she passed, got as close to her as they could to yell at her, to spit on her. She was lower than a cockroach. Really there were no words for her. I felt the crowd feeling all this and I was part of the crowd and I felt it too.

Two days later, when I had calmed down, I went to pay a visit to the Blessed Sacrament. The glowing red lamp recalled me to my duty. I realised that Jeanne needed help to get back on the right path. She'd come from a bad home, she'd been led astray, she'd fallen by the wayside, like a little sparrow. Now she needed a second chance, to be given a fresh start. I decided to take charge.

Through fine rain I went back to Madame Nérin's mean little flat. Madame Nérin didn't offer to shake hands. She said in a dull voice: oh, it's you. She didn't look grateful at all for my visit, but she could hardly not let me in. She told me Jeanne was asleep, with baby Andrée, in the bedroom. So I sat with her in the cramped kitchen, at the oilcloth-covered table jammed in between the stove and the sink. Madame Nérin's mouth set hard. I tried not to let her see how much her squalid surroundings depressed me. Brown oilcloth, brown lino floor. Nappies soaked in a tin bucket. A rack of damp clothes tilted against the food cupboard. The place smelled of milk, soup, soap, bleach. Not a crucifix or a statue in sight. Did her religion no longer matter to her?

How chilly it was in here. The mild autumn didn't seem to exist. I kept my coat and hat on, pushed my gloved hands into my wide sleeves. Madame Nérin, having observed me in silence for a while, roused herself, made me barleycorn coffee. She pushed away a pile of books, served the coffee in little cups whose stencilled blue and yellow pattern had almost completely worn off. How those cups affected me! I didn't want anyone I knew to have to drink from such cups, chipped and saucerless. Nonetheless I accepted and drank the coffee: Madame Nérin needed to feel she could give me something, so that she'd be less beholden. She pulled her sleeves down over her wrists, chafed her hands. She'd obviously run out of fuel. How cold it was! Much too cold for a baby.

I said: now, please listen to me. Beggars can't be choosers, you know.

I spoke as tactfully as possible. However well-meaning Madame Nérin was, with her shaky health there was little she could do to help. Better for everyone, and especially for Jeanne, if Jeanne went away for a while, far from shame and humiliation, to a place where no one knew her.

Madame Nérin frowned down at her folded arms. The fingers of her right hand tapped her woollen sleeve. She said: there was a man in Ste-Madeleine Jeanne mentioned, who I think wanted to marry her.

I said: well, he won't want her now.

The following day I consulted the curé, and the nuns. The convent in London, the daughter-house, was the obvious choice. Reverend Mother fetched a sheet of writing paper from one locked drawer, pen and ink from another. She peered round. Blotting paper? She put on her spectacles. She dipped her pen, hesitated: we've been out of touch for so long, because of the war. I can't be sure how well they understand French. I said: they'll have someone teaching French who can translate it, don't worry.

I took the letter away with me, bought a stamp, went to the

post. Two weeks later the reply arrived, written in bad French you could just about understand. The English nuns agreed to take in our little penitent, find her a job and a room. Maurice and I got Jeanne a passport, bought her ticket to England. Maurice had a discreet word with the town hall authorities, who let Jeanne off having to report in every week, and agreed she was better off moving away.

Andrée being weaned, Jeanne could now give her up for adoption without any problem. Unthinkable to keep the child. Unmarried mothers, and particularly one in Jeanne's situation, should try to bury their shame. Better by far to leave the child in the care of the good sisters.

Jeanne sipped her cup of tisane. She'd tied a gaudy yellow scarf around her head. From time to time one of her hands went up to touch it, explore the knot. Then she'd fiddle with the handle of her cup. I said: Jeanne, are you listening? She glanced at me but said nothing. She seemed stunned; apathetic. The ease with which she allowed other people to take over her responsibilities shocked me. I couldn't believe she really cared about the baby. A few weeks later she signed the necessary papers, relinquishing all maternal rights, swearing complete severance from the child, and departed without any fuss.

Madame Nérin proved the difficult one. She didn't want to let go of the baby. She insisted on keeping little Andrée with her. I was all for informing the town hall, consulting a lawyer, but Reverend Mother counselled patience: she'll come round soon, just you wait and see. No need to involve the authorities just yet.

Just as the nuns thought, the new arrangement did not last long. Small Andrée needed constant attendance, while the grandmother had to go out to earn her living. She took the baby with her, but this of course made her working life very difficult. Then, to make matters more urgent, Madame Nérin fell ill with some chest complaint. Confined to her bed, she could not properly care for her little granddaughter. She kept the baby with her in her bedroom. That was not hygienic.

My own situation made it difficult for me to give Madame Nérin the help she needed. Maurice and I had already decided to leave our house at the top of town. We wanted to start life afresh. We required money for that. So we sold the house to an elderly couple moving to Ste-Marie to be near their children. They appreciated the dignified architecture, the generous proportions of the rooms. We moved temporarily back with my parents while Maurice went down south to look for a new job. At night the children slept on makeshift cots in the living room. There was certainly no room for an extra child. I had no time to look after one: soon after the war ended my mother had a bad attack of nerves.

She crumpled; just let go. She became very forgetful. She denied all knowledge of the things she'd been keeping for me in her locked cupboards. She lost control. She would burst into tears and wail: *putain*! Everything's been taken away from me. You're trying to take everything away! She retreated to her armchair by the stove, sat in silence with her neck poking forwards, her head bent. In her lap she gripped her black iron ring of keys.

What could I do? Nothing. You don't ask your own mother for receipts. My father shouted from his chair opposite her: *merde*! Just leave her alone!

My mother's decline upset me so much that sometimes I

could not bear to look at her. I brought her meals on a tray, because she didn't want to sit at table. I tucked her napkin over her front, like a baby's bib. I kept her clean and washed her clothes. I did her cooking for her, and her housework. I found her radio programmes to distract her, brought home magazines for her from church. I told her: you've got to make an effort!

One morning I was so tired, the children having wailed and griped all night, that I lost my temper and cried out to her: why won't you try to help yourself?

She thinned her lips, said nothing. I shouted: no one helps me do anything round here. You're in no fit state to help me. I'm going to have to deal with this all by myself.

Maurice was travelling down towards the Midi, testing out business opportunities, factories, looking at houses. Before he went he said to me: just do whatever you think is right. He sent me cheerful postcards, urging me to hang on, everything was going to turn out well, I just had to have faith. When I wrote to his poste restante addresses telling him how exhausted I felt, begging him to return soon, he wrote back exhorting me to be brave, to stand fast.

I burst into tears. My mother shook her head at me. Her white skull gleamed through her thin grey hair. My father gripped the arms of his chair, turned and said: I can't stand nagging women. Show some more self-respect. My brother, head bent over his science textbook, stuck his fingers in his ears. His lips formed the refrain of his old song: bugger bugger bugger. I wanted to hit him but I restrained myself.

The following afternoon I left the children with my parents and walked over to the presbytery to consult the curé a second time. He said: the nuns are there to help. They helped with the mother and now they'll help with the child. It's all about timing. Now is the moment to act.

He accompanied me to the convent. Reverend Mother, with two of the senior nuns, received us in the parlour. Reverend Mother agreed: let's take the little one immediately. And then we'll have to have her baptised. I said: I'll be her godmother. Poor little thing.

Reverend Mother rang the bell for refreshments. A big black foot pushed the door open, held it wedged. In came a bulky black figure: Sister Dolorosa, carrying a tray. Her cheeks pushed out from her white coif. A smile split her cheesy face. Dear Madame Blanchard! I submitted to her kissing me on both cheeks. Her blistery skin repelled me. I said: dear Sister Dolorosa. So you're still with us. That's very good. She served us with a glass of Muscat each, a couple of macaroons. She stood back, feet splayed out, near the door, grinning stupidly; poised to refill our glasses and plates. She did indeed look like a big black Dolly. A sort of golliwog with huge dingy teeth.

The curé said: I myself shall inform Madame Nérin of our decision. And then I'll see that she goes into hospital. I'll be able to reassure her that little Andrée is in good hands.

Reverend Mother said: my sisters in England understand how to deal with delinquent girls. They'll know how to handle Jeanne if she becomes difficult.

The curé finished his Muscat. Such an unfortunate family! The child's far better off away from them. With one hand he flicked macaroon crumbs from his soutane and with the other he held out his glass: Sister, you spoil me.

I fetched the baby myself. For the last time ever I forced myself to walk through those miserable streets on the far side of the bridge. The wretched grandmother coughed into her handkerchief, turning her face away from the baby tucked in beside her, rolled in a quilt, fenced in by pillows. The damp flat shocked me all over again. Even wearing my fur coat I shivered. That confirmed my judgment: no fit place for a child.

I pushed Andrée through town in my own perambulator. When it began to drizzle I pulled up the hood of the pram. She gazed at me. Not really an appealing child. Pinched little face. Wispy brown hair. She didn't look like anyone in particular, which was just as well. Now, little one, I said to her, leaning forward over the handle of the pram: be good!

The walk from Madame Nérin's flat took perhaps twenty minutes. Plodding up through the grey back streets, I felt weighed down by indigestion. I kept hiccuping. Bending over the iron handle of the big pram, my stomach convulsed, twisted into knots. The road surfaces gaped with potholes, tarmac pocked with deep puddles after the recent heavy rain. I steered carefully around them. We reached the very top of town. I crossed the Place Ste Anne, the pram, its springs failing, jolting over the uneven paving-stones. A scarred and battered space. Someone ought to mend it. Do it up. In its ruined state it upset me so much I couldn't bear to look at it any more. I turned my attention back to the pram. The baby stared at me.

I halted outside the front door of the convent and rang the bell. The baby began whimpering. I jiggled the handle of the pram, hoping to hush her. Soon she would have to learn to comfort herself.

Jeanne

My thirteenth birthday began with a gentle tug on the ear: up, lazybones! My breakfast treat: coffee with an extra dose of sugar in, to mask the bitter chicory taste. Monday morning, the sunbeams showing up the dust on the kitchen window, shaming the bare yard outside, where our two skinny chickens jerked back and forth beside the rabbit hutch. Yesterday's stale bread: I dipped my tartine into my coffee, softening it. Maman said: what shall we eat tonight? We should celebrate.

I got down her cookery book from the shelf. Her Bible, she called it. *I Want to Cook*, by Brigitte Marisot, the title and author's name printed in well-spaced black capitals, tall and thin. As a child, desperate for something, anything, to read, I'd studied the recipes, night after night. Juicier than the poems I had to learn for school. I chanted these little songs about partridges, pheasants, capons, pigeons to myself. Other recipes told you how to make sausages from the blood. Madame Marisot, showing you how to dismember a duck, wielded a sabre-like chopping knife. Mrs Bluebeard.

Papa had given Maman the cookery book. For their engagement, she told me. He'd inscribed the flyleaf in brown handwriting: for Liliane, most affectionately, from Josef. The blue cloth covers had begun to work loose, parting from the spine. You could see where the pages had been stitched together with looped and knotted white thread.

Madame Marisot provided opening chapters on food science, hygiene, table manners, kitchen equipment, domestic economy. She adjusted her puffy white hat, her starched white overall, wagged her forefinger. She posed in the centre of a vast white-tiled kitchen hung with shining pans, her *batterie de cuisine* lined up in front of her on a well-scrubbed table. She inspected her troops for dust, for spots of grease. Look sharp! The ladle, egg whisk and wooden spoons stood to attention. The rolling-pin and cake-moulds saluted. The nutmeg-grater and cheese-grater wheeled round smartly.

Since we did not eat meat, because we could not afford it, I turned to the chapter near the end which proposed sample menus, suitable to particular seasons, for vegetarians. I read out the autumn one: *Délicieuses au fromage*, potato purée, Russian salad, pears with cream.

Maman wiped off her coffee moustache. She said: it all depends, doesn't it. What have we got?

Coughing, she got up, untied her apron. I checked the food cupboard: oil, flour, salt, sugar, a decent-sized heel of gruyère. No potatoes, pears, eggs, beetroot or cream.

I said: I wish I didn't have to go to school today. I wish I could leave.

Maman said: don't grumble. You should be glad you're getting an education at all.

I blew out my cheeks at her: you sound just like one of the nuns. Her hand whirled up. She frowned. Then she poked my ribs: behave!

That evening she came in smiling. She advanced her hand, her fingers petalling around two eggs balanced on her palm. Look what Madame Fauchon's given me. We'll have *Délicieuses* for supper, and we'll have pancakes as well. We'll be eating better than the nuns do, that's for sure.

She didn't want me to complain about being at a Catholic school. She'd been glad when the nuns proposed I continue to stay on, in return for helping with the little ones, because she wanted us to blend in with the Catholics. Just in case of trouble. What trouble? Wait and see.

She beat the Jewish egg yolks into the Catholic flour and folded and beat them together. She flipped discs of brown lace into the air and they looked identical.

She piled the sugar-sprinkled pancakes on a plate. Your Papa used to love these. Don't you remember? I shook my head. I hardly remembered him at all. A voice telling me stories at night. A blue trouser-leg. The scent of hot grass under a blue sky. Memory failed there.

Maman cleared the table, putting the cookery book back on the shelf: I really must mend it. On to the pancakes she poured a few drops of Liqueur 44: now that you're a young lady, you can try spirits.

Silly name, I said: why is it called that? Maman said: it's the recipe, everything comes in measures of forty-four.

Dark liquid, tasting both sweet and bitter. I swallowed my dessert as fast as I could: it's like medicine!

To begin our supper we ate the *Délicieuses*: the two egg whites beaten stiff then gently folded with grated gruyère, taken up in spoonfuls, dropped into the pan of boiling oil and quickly deep-fried. To test the eggs' freshness before she cooked them,

Maman held the bowl of beaten whites upside down over her head. Nothing fell out. She always did this, to amuse me, and I always gasped and laughed. One of our kitchen games, which blended us together.

Monsieur Jacquotet had blended in by retiring inside his hermitage-house. Going to and fro from school I would glance towards its façade. Closed shutters and closed door. He didn't know I'd had my thirteenth birthday and that I was nearly grown-up. I couldn't tell him. I wished I could.

When he and I met again, I didn't know what to say. Girls of thirteen didn't broach conversations with grown-ups they hardly knew. Not in Ste Marie-du-Ciel.

It happened by accident. I walked to school under a pale blue November sky spotted with grey clouds. In the afternoon rain spurted down, drumming on the high window sills. Cooped up in the airless sewing room with a child's blouse spread over my knees, surrounding the raw edges of buttonholes with tiny blanket stitches, I wanted the walls to crack, let in rainy freshness. My needle, stabbing through cotton, pricked my forefinger. A bead of blood welled. I sucked it. The metallic taste pleased me, gave me an idea. I put up my hand, went to the podium, mumbled to Sister Dolorosa, who supervised the sewing hour, that I had cramps. She swung her head towards me, pushing back her black veil. Under the dark muslin her white bonnet smelled of starch. Inside her coif her cheeks looked soft as ripe cheese and smelled of carbolic soap. She whispered: are you expecting your visitor? I nodded yes. Sister Dolly said: have you got a towel with you? I shook my head. She sucked in her spit with a hiss: dirty girl. Get off home, then.

Sheets of rain fell past my face. I'd forgotten my beret: I put my arms up to shield my head, ran into the square. Wetness hammered my shoulders and nails of rain pierced me. My feet squelched inside my flimsy boots. Water drove down my neck, off my nose, off my eyelashes, soaked through the front of my coat. No separation between me and the weather: I'd dissolved into the rain, become sludge, like melted sugar at the bottom of a cup. Sludge that wanted to dance and go a bit crazy.

The door in the façade of Monsieur Jacquotet's house swung open like the cover of a book, revealing the black oblong of a page. He stood against it, brightly coloured as a picture in a comic paper. He wore a blue coat, like an overall, flapping open, a yellow waistcoat, a red spotted scarf tied round his throat. He'd cut his black hair short. He seemed thinner. He beckoned to me. Come in and get dry – come into the warm.

The dark passageway smelled of vanilla. Through this tunnel of warm scent I blundered after him. In the kitchen he unbuttoned my coat, drew it off me and hung it up on a hook near the fireplace. He produced a rough towel, blue and grey stripes with frayed ends, threw it over my head and rubbed vigorously at my dripping hair. He took the towel away and considered me. Poor child, you're nothing but a puddle. Sit down.

I leaned my hand on the back of a wooden chair. The nearby table was littered with little glass bottles, saucers smudged with paint, yellow Ricard ashtrays, red stained corks, paper bags, boxes of matches, newspapers and magazines. Tables at home in our tiny flat did not tolerate such glorious mess. They invited hands to get busy sorting and piling, sweeping tides of rubbish into waste buckets. They urged dusters and polishing rags to approach. Then they breathed bare and silky for a moment before they got covered with oilcloth or blue linen depending on the day of the week, the time of day. Here, the table could not know whether it was a mealtime or a Saturday or anything. It obviously just got layers added to it. At one end a fluted green glass dish bore the scrapings of what looked like white beans in dried-up gravy. A half-empty pale grey coffee cup held dead flies floating in its scum. Tumblers lined up, crusted with yellow dregs of cider. A crumpled green and white checked handker-chief lay next to a hill of breadcrumbs, mixed in with blue glass beads, a broken string of pearls, bits of gilt, razor blades, slivers of pink soap, small pages with handwriting in red ink.

My mother would have put her hands on her hips, demanded to know who was going to tidy this lot up. Perhaps Monsieur Jacquotet's wife would have spoken similarly. Inside myself I felt the same confusion as the table did, words muddled together seeming to sway up and down. The table bore all the bits and pieces without complaint. Time vanished, meaningless: a fresh *pain au chocolat*, surely bought this morning, perched next to a splatter of black and white photographs obscured by dust.

The table turned into a mountain: to hold everything, so that the mass of stuff wouldn't slither over its edges and spill across the floor, it built itself upwards, a tower of used plates, railway timetables, dark yellow brass candlesticks branching like trees, squares of plum velvet edged with gold lace, a pair of reading glasses, a papery bouquet of dried honesty.

My still life, he said, with a little bow, smiling.

I hardly heard his words. I'd gone into a dream. I was warm, and colours jumped out at me from all around, caressing me. The wide cushion on my chair, worn cotton patterned in orange, red and pink paisley, plumped up around me. With my forefinger I traced the frill-edged comma-shaped curls of the design. I lifted my eyes and stared at his green brocade waistcoat, its silver buttons. Take your boots off, he said: and your socks too. He stood the boots on top of the range and hung the socks on the rail in front of the oven, in between two brown floorcloths, their coarse weave dyed by filth. He obviously didn't know how to clean floors. First you did them with a scrubbing brush, to get the worst off, and only after that with a cloth.

He looked at my bare feet, their cold whiteness studded with red chilblains. Dear little feet. He knelt down in front of me and clasped my toes gently, taking care not to touch the chilblains. He cupped my heels, one after the other, and massaged my soles. He said: wait here. He came back with a pair of grey woollen socks, some blue felt slippers. I put them on. They fitted exactly.

Silence opened up, surrounded us. Inside this quiet I could tell the truth, at least try to. I said: I'm sorry about before. What happened before. I'm sorry if I got you into trouble.

Would you like a bite of something? He opened a pale green cupboard and took out a battered tin, its dented sides patterned with red and white squares. He poured a stream of yellow biscuits on to a turquoise ceramic soup plate: go on, help yourself. The biscuits had sugar sprinkled on top and black speckles inside. They tasted of butter, cornmeal and caraway.

He took up a biscuit. He said: Monsieur Fauchon explained it to me afterwards. Don't you remember? You told him all about it when he brought you back.

What had I said? I remembered crying, down by the river,

and the young workman taking me by the hand and tugging me back up the hill. The orphanage, is it? I wailed no. No I won't. Lights burned in the cobbler's shop. Its door stood open. Monsieur Fauchon's voice called from inside. That's the Nérin child. Jeanne. Jeanne, what are you doing? The young man delivered me in to the shop, then left. The Fauchons asked what was wrong. They spoke quietly. I felt them trying not to frighten me. I choked; speechless. I felt ravaged by shame. People could see me but they shouldn't see me. That was my fault.

Monsieur Fauchon waved me towards his high stool. I shook my head. He scooped me up and perched me on the counter. He wore a brown linen apron tied around the waist with brown string. His fingers plucked at this hairy twist, fiddled with the frayed ends, as he hovered in front of me. His wife stood next to him, her black-haired baby, wrapped in a white shawl, curved in her arms. She had big dark eyes, glossy black hair swept back in thick waves. Little gold studs shaped like open flowers, a pearl in the centre of the petals, decorated her earlobes. She wore slippers, a pintucked blue pregnancy blouse. The baby rested on top of her swollen belly. Both of them gazed at me as I wept. They waited patiently for my tears to stop.

The shop smelled of leather. Rows of exhausted shoes had halted on the shelves, some with curled-up toes, some with holes in the soles. Bulging shapes of brown paper bags, pinned with numbered tickets: shoes awaiting collection. A silver till next to me. Tools with wooden handles. Gradually the warm smell of leather comforted me, calmed me down. Leather had been an animal once. A cow's hide. Living and breathing creature, giving milk. Spurting from teats, frothing warm into the pan. I leaned my head against the cow's flank.

94

Hide in the shed and watch a woman pull on the cow's udder, milking her.

Had I fallen asleep? I fell back into time: Madame Fauchon brought me a cup of warm milk and persuaded me to drink it. Her husband put on his overcoat. Come along, little one, we'd better take you back. His wife spoke briskly: nothing else for it, with your mother in hospital. You'll just have to try and make the best of it.

In his kitchen Monsieur Jacquotet and I munched our biscuits. I looked around. He'd put up more decorations since my previous visit. Now not just strings of dried apples but also bunches of blue-grey sage dangled from knotted cords looped all along the beams, mixed in with stiff plaits of onions and thinner twists of garlic, spiky little nosegays of dark green thyme. Along the mantelpiece he'd arranged a row of oranges with stubs of candles set in between. He'd covered the walls with paintings done on large squares of brown paper, which he'd pinned up in groups. Some consisted simply of thick lines of white and of black, zigzags and circles painted on to the brownness. Others were fat stripes of colour like mad rainbows. They made you see how beautiful brown paper actually was. How even more beautiful a brown paper bag might be if you painted the right kind of pattern on to it. Brown paper bags from the stationer's, plump with rubbers, pencils and pens, with twisted ears you spun; seized and swung up between your hands.

Bags didn't yelp with pain when you pinched them but children did. Bags of sinful mess the nuns gripped by the ear. Sister Dolly, paddle under her arm, had hauled me from the parlour into the classroom, where she thrashed me. I turned my head and watched her red hand whistle up and down. Afterwards she was angrier than ever because I denied it hurt. I'd won, and she knew it. Later, in the dormitory, I stuffed the sheet into my mouth so no one would hear me cry.

Monsieur Jacquotet's hands weren't red but brown. They knew how to make fine old messes in his kitchen, how to let the mess take care of itself, not get swept away. His were capable hands, which wielded awls, brushes, hammers and nails. He didn't like mops and brooms so much. I wanted to forage in his mess, find bits and pieces I liked, get him to make me something with them. I wanted to make something myself.

He said: so what shall we do now while we wait for your boots to dry? I remembered the attic studio, those big canvases stretched on frames propped against the wall. I know, I proposed: I'll pose and you draw me. I swallowed the last bite of the biscuit and sat up very straight on my wooden chair. Monsieur Jacquotet said: I'm going to draw your feet. I'm going to draw you wearing those socks and slippers. Stay still and don't move. He picked up a pencil and pad of paper from the table, where they lay on top of some cabbage leaves.

He encircled the pencil with his fingers, waited. The pencil quivered, zigzagged, jumped up and down, drew his hand across the paper, back and forth, feathering. I stopped watching and just concentrated on staying still. My muscles began to hurt. He said: that's half an hour gone. Your things will be dry by now. You ought to be getting home.

My socks, thin wool, bore black toecaps of the dried mud that had seeped in through the cracks in my boot soles. My boots had stiffened to husks of cardboard. I forced them on over my chilblains. Stepping into the street, I found that the rain had stopped. The wet cobbles glistened. I got home at exactly my usual time. My stomach-ache returning, I thought it was the caraway seeds in the biscuits.

My first ever visitor came on later that evening. Bravo, *ma chérie*! My mother patted my cheek, took me into our shared bedroom, showed me how to fold cotton rags into a pad held in a net of gauze. She foraged in her underwear drawer, produced a mauve silk ribbon: you can have this. She knotted the ends of the gauze on to the ribbon tied about my waist. The shreds of material pressed against me kindly and softly. They drank in my metal-scented blood and made me feel comfortable.

Back in the kitchen, my mother got out the two sponge fingers remaining in a tin, reached down the bottle of Liqueur 44 and tilted it over two tiny glasses. Just a sip. It's a powerful god! She toasted me and I toasted her back. This time the taste seemed less bitter.

In between drinking drops of the dark liquid we nibbled the sponge fingers, sugary and crisp. I asked: forty-four what? What d'you put in it?

She re-corked the bottle and recited the recipe. Forty-four coffee beans, forty-four lumps of sugar, forty-four small tumblers of squeezed orange juice from forty-four oranges given forty-four stabs, forty-four small measures of eau-de-vie. Leave for forty-four days then tap the bottle forty-four times.

Later that week I paid a visit to the Blessed Sacrament in the parish church on my way home from school. I wandered to and fro. I hung about in the side chapel dedicated to the Ste Vierge, rattled through a few Hail Marys while kicking the ends of pews. I was the fastest prayer-sayer in town.

I hovered near a prie-dieu set in front of the Virgin's statue. She stood on a lace-covered plinth, her bare feet level with my raised eyes. Not a woman: child-sized. She had a rosebud mouth, brown hair pulled back under a white veil, a crown of stars, a white cloak, its yellow revers painted with golden swirls. Her chapel, a baby church within a mother church, had a pointed, painted roof and held her inside carved and gilded panels. Shadowy place, smelling of incense and wood rot and dust and polish. Darkness clouded it like candle grease running and thickening. Red and blue glass glowed in the window.

The hush settled round my shoulders like an arm. He pressed us to him. One child on each knee. My dear little sisters. Let us pray.

How did prayer work? Why did no one explain? Like the telephone? A miracle: that was that. Second miracle: the Virgin could see through closed doors and knew everything I did. You hadn't to do anything that would upset her. Don't disobey your mother or turn Communist. Millions of excommunicated souls shrieked and writhed in hellfire and it was their own fault. To avoid that agony you kept on the straight and narrow. Not like my mother: she believed in workers' rights. One day, Jeannette, women will get the vote. I was brushing her hair for her, one of my treats. I tugged at a tangle: did you really have to convert, though? She said: it seemed the best thing to do at the time.

When she converted, my mother had changed her name from Nerinski to Nérin. Did that count as lying and deceit? Would my mother go to hell? Had the Virgin's blank eyes seen the curé stroke our necks? Her pinched lips couldn't name his favourite game. Darlings, oh darlings. He pressed our faces into his soutane smelling of old sweat, crusted with soup stains, and nearly choked us. Promise never to tell a soul or you'll be punished and thrown out of school. He set us down, made us stand in front of him. The sweets in his pockets came newly to life. Fat, squirming. With both hands I had to hold him, swollen up inside the black cloth. I tucked the soutane around it. Like dressing a baby doll which could wriggle and bounce. While Marie-Angèle watched, he pulled my knickers down. He gripped me in his arm, he panted and moaned, looking up to the ceiling. I can't help it! I can't help it! His black puppy leaped in his lap, barking and biting. I couldn't hold it any longer. Marie-Angèle reached out. Just trying to help? Curious? Mother Lucie told me that I invited touch. My fault: I was bold.

I stuck my tongue out at the Virgin, left the church, doubled back up the street and went to see the Hermit.

I led the way to his studio at the top of the house. He followed me up the curving wooden stairs. Milky sunlight leaked in through the square window set in the roof, flowed down the rolls of canvas leaning against the walls. I lifted some sheets of paper, testing their weight, ran my fingers along their sharp edges, and waited for him to suggest a pose. He wrapped me in a knitted blue shawl, arranged me on a low chair covered in a mauve and yellow bedspread: I just want to get the outline of a shape. He put one forefinger under my chin and the other in the small of my back, lifted with one hand and pushed with the other. I straightened my spine, tucked my legs down to one side. The next time I donned a little black silk cape, a black hat he pinned on to the side of my head. The clothes lay there ready, draped across a trestle. I just put them on over my school pinafore. He wouldn't let me look afterwards. It's none of your business!

I relied on his instructions. Just a fingertip touch on my knee and I'd spread out the long red skirts of my dress. I held up my head under its unaccustomed weight of combs, headdresses, feathers. As the days went by we experimented more. He'd roll my front hair over a ribbon and pull it back, put my back hair up into a chignon. He'd fetch the brush, combs and pins from one of the rooms downstairs. When I offered to help he pushed my hand away. He bent towards me and smoothed my hair and I smelled his coffee breath.

One afternoon he went downstairs and hunted for a scarf he wanted me to try. I heard him open a door on the landing below. So that was where all the clothes were kept. Had I seen that room? The shapes and colours of the house whirled inside me like a spangled cloak. A small white bedroom? A big wardrobe? Perhaps he'd changed things all around, moved the furniture, the beds. Perhaps I'd made it all up. I imagined a wardrobe big as a house, in which you could get lost, vanish, and then be found again. I imagined this wardrobe full of women rustling in satin, in layers of crisp petticoats, who'd draw me into their arms, wrap me up in a scented embrace. When they let me go again they'd stretch their arms lazily along padded hangers. They wore little bags of lavender, to repel moths, slung around their necks. High above their heads, on a shelf, perched their striped green and white hat-boxes, their handbags, their piles of gloves: woollen and lace and kid. A forest of women bending towards each other over my head, gossiping like the wind rustling leaves, and I in the centre of their circle in charge of the game.

Inside their wardrobe-house the wives wore different coloured negligees: red with black lace, pink with silver lace, black with grey lace. Perhaps he took them to bed with him one by one, night after night, his silky harem. Perhaps he chose a different favourite each evening, laid her down next to him, caressed her, murmured to her, hugged her close. Inside the wardrobe the wives struggled for power: choose me!

One afternoon, when he stomped off to the lavatory, three flights down, out in a shed at the back of the house, I descended, on stockinged feet, to the floor below. Which room was which? I chose at random. I seized an egg-shaped china doorknob in my fingers and twisted it. The door opened. In I crept.

Just a bedroom. Had I seen it before? Red wallpaper patterned with big golden vine leaves. A high double bed covered in a purple silk bedspread, a black cabinet on twisty legs near it, a low, red-upholstered chair with a dimpled back and no arms, a washstand set of bowl and jug stencilled with pink half-circles. Pictures, framed and unframed: blurs of colour. A tall, wide cupboard with a panelled door carved with flowers stood against the wall facing the bed. The key, a knot of black iron lace, projected from the black mouth of the lock. I turned the key and pulled open the door.

Behind me he said: those are her things.

His voice tickled the back of my neck like the point of a knife, teased down my spine. I turned. His face was flushed red. I said: you didn't tell me not to come in here. You didn't tell me not to touch them. I wasn't doing anything wrong.

My voice came out in a bleat. He looked at me impatiently: no, of course you weren't. But having got this far you'd better help me choose.

He plunged his hands into the concertina of material. He eased out the edges of skirts and frocks, caressed them in his long fingers, rubbed his thumb over the hems. He stroked a yellow satin cuff, a blue polka-dotted chiffon frill.

The clothes cupboard smelled of cedarwood. He plucked out hangers, scooped up trailing hems, laid his soft burdens on the bed. He left me alone while I changed and then I ran upstairs to join him in the studio. That day he drew me in a white poplin blouse with big black buttons, a three-quarter-length black skirt, black shoes with a buttoned strap. Two days later he drew me in a navy two-piece sprigged with cream flowers. After that in a frock of dark green crêpe de Chine. Each time I turned my face towards him I became someone different, not myself, yet someone who was always the same, the person he'd lost, whom he tried to re-capture on paper. She'd gone but he brought her back. I became her replica. He needed me as a medium, his contact with the world of the dead. I was her young ghost, thin and white as a sheet of paper. He drew on me to make her come alive. He outlined me in charcoal. I smudged where he touched me. He could rub me out then re-summon me, over and over. I rose towards him out of the dark of the wardrobe, the dark of the tomb. I did not speak. Sitting in his studio I composed my face to stay calm.

When I posed naked, I displayed my flesh like a coat. Another painted surface created by his brush. A rose-apricot satin cape. I stayed hidden inside it. His brush stroked the backs of my knees, stippled my shoulders, outlined my ears.

Sometimes he liked me to talk and sometimes he didn't. My occasional words drifted towards him like pastel confetti, and he flicked them off and let just a few fall into his pocket. My words hummed past him like bees, and he just left them to find their way, bumping around the room, out of the open skylight. He talked with pencils and paintbrushes. A skin language. Concentrating. One mark. Then another. Afterwards, in the kitchen, if he made us coffee, and found me some biscuits, he would talk to me. Fragments of stories, bits and pieces of information. His wife's name was Andrea. The baby who died with her he called Perdita. I whispered: she was going to have a baby? His face reddened and he shouted: yes! Then he described how to boil up glue and mix egg white into paint. He mentioned that when digging his garden he'd come across lots of bones of dogs and cats. Together we imagined children burying their cherished pets, marking the graves with pebbles arranged in patterns. He told me that the cornmeal biscuits were from a recipe of his grandmother's. I held the biscuit in the palm of my hand: it held his grandmother's life. I bit into it gently; kissing her. What happened to her? She was murdered in a pogrom. I put down the biscuit: what's a pogrom? His mouth twisted: little Jewish girl who doesn't know any history! I shifted: I'm not Jewish any more, really. He said: OK. I'll explain. Listen.

One day, wetting my forefinger and pressing it into petit-beurre crumbs, I said to him: I want to learn to draw and paint. He drained his cup then upended it, watched brown drops drip on to his saucer. He said: I don't know how to teach you.

I licked sweet grit off my finger. In that case, I'd better be off home.

I got up. His black eyebrows twitched together. He thumped his knee. Oh, for heaven's sake. All right.

Under his instructions I painted a colour wheel. I went on begging for lessons, and sometimes I got them.

After a few weeks I grew bored sitting. Instead I wanted to roam about the house and rummage, peep inside chests of drawers, perch at her dressing table and employ her scent bottle, her powder puff. Our solution: to return to the game of hide and seek we'd played years ago with Marie-Angèle.

He let me draw up the rules. I'd dart downstairs from the studio, select an outfit, don it, then hide somewhere in the house. He searched for me. If he found me before I'd counted up to a hundred, then I'd sit for him for an hour. If he didn't find me in time I'd go back into her room and play with her things or try to draw, while he returned upstairs and pottered about. After half an hour or so he'd make his way to the kitchen, shout for me, and I'd join him for our *goûter*. I spread a tea towel over my lap, in case I dirtied my clothes. Her clothes. While I ate and drank he'd watch me in silence. Then I'd go back upstairs and change before running home. On the days I sat for him naked, I'd wear her dressing gown down to tea.

I always left his house by the back door, crossing the garden in the opposite direction from the convent, then slipping out through the wooden gate in the wall on the far side. I emerged into an alley, whence I could hurry on to the street lower down without being spotted by anyone. I got home long before my mother returned from her various cleaning jobs. By the time she came in I'd be busy preparing the supper. Cabbage soup or onion soup or turnip soup or potato soup. You didn't need a cookery book for these. I learned by watching my mother cook.

If the state of Maman's purse meant that we had the ingredients to hand, she made special dishes for Sunday lunch: cabbage stuffed with onions, chestnuts and breadcrumbs, roast pumpkin with home-made pickles, potato pancakes, apple fritters, beetroot soup. Maman knew the recipes by heart; she'd learned them from her own mother. Occasionally, though, when I felt bored, or while I waited for the potatoes to boil, I still turned the pages of her cookery book. The title page promised 2,000 recipes for both exquisite and simple dishes. I recited to myself the names of sauces for white meat and for dark meat. What did *Sauce Crapaudine* taste like? *Sauce Raifort*? *Sauce Velouté ivoire*? I studied recipes involving bacon or shellfish. I tried to imagine eating croquettes of shrimps and prawns. *Moules à la marinière*, with white wine, parsley and chopped onion. I discovered sixty-two recipes for eggs, not including recipes for omelettes. Then I'd declare: Madame is served! and bring on the cabbage soup with a flourish.

While we ate we'd talk. Afterwards, I'd do my homework, and my mother would either sew, concocting new clothes for me out of scraps, or she would read. Political pamphlets, political magazines. The following day she'd tell me about what she'd been reading: you won't hear this from the nuns! I read too: the small collection of second-hand novels she kept on the shelf. These were your Papa's, so treat them carefully. Late in the evening, lying awake, I'd tell myself stories. Serials, that continued from night to night. Monsieur Jacquotet and I would never reach the end. There would always be something else happening; some new event. Our story could never finish. I could hide with him inside the story for ever.

His favourite of his wife's dresses was the red silk one. On the days when I wanted to keep him in a good humour, to make sure the game would go on, I chose to wear it and chose to let him find me. Eventually he used the sketches as a basis for completing a painting, a portrait of his wife he'd begun years earlier.

You could name her clothes according to the time of day. The clock struck, and the clothes changed. A morning dress, an afternoon dress, an evening dress. The best of her frocks, a white silk evening dress, I didn't dare wear for some time. It seemed too grand. When I riffled through the tight pleats and folds of material in the wardrobe I'd sweep my hands over it, then pass on to something else, softer and more ordinary, easier to get into; something I could cope with. Finally, one day, after we'd been playing our games for some weeks, I plucked out the queen. I felt ready for her, and that she was ready for me. In her unheated room, shivering, I took off all my clothes, lifted up her dress and dropped it over my head. Sleeveless, backless, it swept down to the floor and swirled about my feet. I fastened it together at the side. Tiny buttons, covered in white silk, like pearl beads, slipped into white silk loops. The dress captured me. It held me, stroked me, like two hands in silk gloves.

Sprays of artificial white flowers encircled the waist and scattered the skirt. On top went a close-fitting little jacket in matching white silk. I drew on white lace stockings and inserted my feet into white high heels criss-crossed with straps of thin white braid fastened with diamanté studs. I teetered a few steps. How did you walk in these?

Just concentrate. Shut your eyes. Imagine.

Now I was wearing her, my second skin. The other one. I'd searched for her; I'd got closer to her, week by week. We'd met at last. For these few moments she was my true self. Then I'd have to shed her and return to washed-out grey pinafores. We held each other. A calm and precise embrace. Can you waltz? Yes. I raised my arms and took a couple of turns with her around the floor. One two three one two three. I whispered in her ear and she whispered back. Her warm lips against my skin.

I shouted up to him to start searching and began counting to a hundred. I slithered under the purple silk coverlet of the bed and pulled it back up over my face. Smooth on my cheeks, it smelled faintly of dust. I buried myself in the bed. I flattened myself into the quilt, wriggling until I lay in a trough of down, as thin as I could be. I calmed my breath, breathed as shallowly as possible, so there'd be no telltale rise and fall of fabric when he came in.

His feet clattered down the stairs, across the landing straight to the door. Bang. In he came. Steps across the floorboards. Fifty-six. Fifty-seven. Halt. I held my breath. Fifty-eight. Fifty-nine. The cover ripped itself back like a wave of water. His blue eyes, faded no more, blazed at me. Blue water fire. I gazed up at him. He was crying.

I lifted the corner of the quilt. Come on. Get in.

He kicked off his shoes, lay down next to me. I pulled the quilt back up over his shoulders, so that it wrapped us both loosely, softly, and then his arms surrounded me and I tucked my head between his shoulder and chin and stroked his wet cheek with one hand. Trapping his tears on my fingertips, licking them tasting them then stroking his face once more. His bristly skin. Bristly paintbrush. He smelled of turps and soap. He sighed. His hand thrust into my hair, gripped it.

My hand left his cheek, rose up and began to draw him, first in the air an inch away from him and then closer, until I touched him again. I traced the angles of his jaw. I undid his collar, slid my hand inside, felt round, caressed the back of his neck. I unbuttoned his shirt, taking my time, while equally slowly he undid the buttons at the side of my dress, one by one, slipped his fingers into the silky gap, caressed my waist. Warmth began. He shut his eyes and I shut mine too. Black brilliance alive with tiny stars dancing on my bare skin. Our names fled; all the words separating us. Our ages melted; our selves. Dissolving. Held in warm darkness. Our joint breath, joint heartbeat. Rolled in the plump feather-filled quilt, satiny, a floaty cloud. Very light touch. Just brushing my side. My long, sloping curve. Our fingers our skin then time began again and we lay curled up two warm animals smoothing each other's fur.

We opened our eyes, lifted our heads from the pillows of each other, propped ourselves on our elbows. Distinct now: his messy hair, his nose. The air got in between us and I shivered. Suddenly he smelled sour and I wanted to push him away.

All right, then. Art lesson. Downstairs in the kitchen he gave me pencil and paper, tried to teach me about forms made by light and shadow. Blackness didn't mean what you couldn't see, didn't mean absence. It showed the shape of something on the other side of the light. I was the light. I looked at him, my gaze illuminating his flesh, his bones. I wanted him to take off all his clothes and sit for me naked. I wanted to use the pencil to trap him in outlines, but I couldn't. The line wavered, ran to the edge of the page, got away. Heavy pencil strokes crowded in, cramping his shape. Shadows rubbed him out. He shrank, vanished.

No good, I said in disgust: let's tear it up.

My dear little Jeanne, he said: everything's finished. You'd better not come here any more. It'll do neither of us any good. It's over.

No no no no no.

He refused to listen. He chased me off.

As a parting present he gave me some sticks of charcoal, some pencils, some oil pastel crayons. I hid them amongst my folded clothes at the back of my shelf in the bedroom cupboard. I

twiddled a stick of charcoal between finger and thumb. Its thin-
ness invited me to snap it in two. A stick in each hand, I'd beat
him until he bled. How dared he abandon me?

I turned fourteen and left school. I could begin to earn my
living, go out to work as a daily servant, like my mother. She
said: be grateful for what you can get.

If I was old enough to find a job I was old enough to have a
baby. If I had a daughter I'd call her Andrea. No, Andrée.

Once she got born she'd become herself. I'd have to study
her, learn her. She'd summon me, instruct me. She'd gaze at me
and tell me what she needed me to know. I'd listen to her
babble and translate it. What would she be like when she
reached the age I was now? Perhaps she'd sulk sometimes, as I
did. But I'd coax the words out of her.

Andrée

I didn't know anything much about my mother. Her name was Jeanne: I clung to that. Could you miss someone you'd never met? Sometimes her absence felt solid as lentil purée, pressed on my heart like a weight on pâté. Sometimes she sneaked up, just behind me, blew on the back of my neck. I'd whisk round, trying to catch her, but she'd melt away on to the flagstones. I'd try to melt with her, but I'd be shaken back to life by Sister Dolorosa clapping her hands, snap out of it will you, and I'd lurch back into the convent kitchen, soapy scrubbing-brush dripping suds down my skirt.

On the day of my Confirmation, when I was thirteen, Marie-Angèle Blanchard showed me a photograph of herself and my mother. The nuns left us alone together in the parlour while they went off to sing Compline: Andrée, you're to keep your godmother company. Madame Blanchard said: we'll have a little chat, won't we, and you can tell me how you're getting on.

She plucked out pictures from an envelope in her black leather handbag. Now, Andrée, which is which? A glossy shot of her seven children, lined up, tallest to smallest, their smiling faces turned to the camera. All dressed in sailor suits, hands on the shoulders of the one in front. Behind them rose a grand house, a high wall topped with spikes. Oh, Andrée, surely you remember all their names? Now, you know who this is! A picture of herself outside the front door of the big house with its rows of shutters, another picture of herself standing on her wide lawn set with flowerbeds like a park.

My godmother fished in the envelope again. Her red nails gleamed like enamel. Her cheeks too. Two glasses of dessert wine, two slices of Sister Dolly's buttered honey cake, sweet words from Reverend Mother and the curé: our dear benefactress! So good of Monsieur Blanchard to spare you to visit us!

That spring day, despite the sun shining my godmother wore her fur coat, I suppose to show how rich she was, and black suede high heels. Gold clips swept up her blonde hair. In the parlour she tossed the coat on to a chair, peeled off her gloves, dropped them on top of the coat. Her pale green dress, crisply ironed, seemed brand new.

She pulled out a small photo with deckled edges. Her brows drew together: I'd forgotten there were any copies left of this. I thought they'd all been given away. That's your mother and me. Goodness.

The black and white print showed two little girls in bunchy pale overalls buttoned on the shoulders and tied at the waist with strings. They stood on the pavement outside a shop. Fair curls bounced around Marie-Angèle's plump face. My small, thin mother had wavy dark hair and intense eyes. I knew her family name was Nérin, and that she had abandoned me as a baby and run off, and that soon afterwards her mother, my grandmother, had died of TB. Knowledge I'd always had, part of me like my hands and feet. In the photo Maman was a little pale ghost. There and not there at the same time. What was she like? I'd put this question before, and always got the same answer. No better than she should be, Madame Blanchard said: she turned out badly, I'm afraid.

My pudding mother, released from her mould and not standing up properly but collapsing, like a drunk. Smelling of rum and vanilla sugar. Madame Blanchard snorted: after all my mother did for hers!

She was reciting her part in the ritual, so I recited mine. I said: but where did my mother go? Madame Blanchard said: how many times do I have to tell you! She went off to England to get a job. She wanted a fresh start. Remember you're not an orphan. You're illegitimate.

The word rolled on my tongue like a ball of spit, slimy-sour. Did other people hear with their mouths? I thought with mine too. If only the school had been made of pastry I'd have eaten it all up brick by brick and learned something. That day Madame Blanchard gave me a rosary with brown wooden beads glossy as chocolate beans. Bite your way around the Sorrowful Mysteries, girl. Flagellation crunch swallow. Crucifixion crunch swallow. Spikes driven through your palms your feet crunch swallow.

Madame Blanchard nipped the photo back from me and tore it into little pieces. I cried out. She said: I don't need it any more. It's better that way. No use dwelling on the past. You've got to live for the future. You know I worry about you so much. I pray unceasingly that you won't turn out like your mother. The pudding erupted from its fluted tin, dumped itself over her head, cloaked her in hot batter buttoned with sultanas.

The door opened and the nuns came back in. I stood up, moved out of the way. Bits of talk fell on me, hot splashes of batter. Good Catholic home. Modern girls.

Confirmation marked the end of my schooling. I stayed on at the convent, working as a live-in servant, which Madame Blanchard thought best. I agreed: the outside world felt prickly. Everybody in town knew everybody else and so everybody knew me. They pursed their lips as I banged past with my basket of bread. I tied on a blue headscarf, knotting it behind my head as the postulants knotted their black ones, and tried to become invisible. My mother was a ghost. I wanted to be one too.

I hid in my stone shelter. Along stone corridors I drove lines of schoolchildren. Swing your arms, step out one two one two and try to kick Fatty Andrée in the back of the knees. Up and down the black tarmac playground enclosed by high walls, secured by a bolted gate.

Locked doors held us tight. Most people in town had put bars on their ground-floor windows straight after the war, Mother Lucie explained, to keep out the homeless and jobless men who roamed about. Groups of tramps, red-faced and shabbily dressed, silted up the corners of the park. Some of the homeless men lived in a hostel near the parish church, where they ran a *dépôt-vente*, selling donated furniture and so making a bit of a living. Others slept rough. As children we feared all of them. Ne'er-do-wells. Crazies. Thieves. When we went out for exercise we kept close in our neat crocodile and hurried past them. Wild men, who lived outside the rules, who might lunge at you and touch you. At least there were people worse off than I was. Nonetheless they claimed me: hello, little girl! Sometimes boys kicking footballs jeered at me: how's your mother, Fatty Andrée? Fatty batty Andrée! Your mother!

Now that I'd begun working as the convent servant, I had to go out in public whether I wanted to or not. I had to run errands. People nudged each other in shop doorways as I went by. Their sly glances said something, which I couldn't understand, about the war and about my mother. Against their nasty looks and hissed words I built a wall of family. I gave myself a gallant, eagle-eyed father, a hero of the Resistance. I gave myself soldier grandfathers, ranks of them stretching back and back. When anyone insulted them they kicked them up the arse. Take that, fuckwits.

I escaped the town whispers by scowling at the ground, pretending I hadn't heard. I took back routes down flights of stone steps tucked in between buildings. I dodged through narrow alleys. I hopped past bombed houses, open-fronted and roofless. I watched the streets change, as wartime damage was gradually repaired, rubble cleared, the clumps of old tenements beyond the bridge torn down. Three-storey blocks of flats, neat villas, reared up in their place, tidy and sharp-edged. A *Monument aux Morts* was built by the veterans' association, listing the dead men's names. Their children swelled the numbers in the orphanage. Rows of ancient plane trees were lopped, replaced by long beds of evergreen shrubs and bedding plants. Soon only the old people would be able to remember how the town had once looked and what had gone on in it.

When I prodded her, Mother Lucie sometimes dug up a few more memories. Car headlamps having to be painted blue. Eating animal food such as maize cobs and parsnips. But her mind was wandering now. She never reached the point of her stories. In the cupboard, she would say. Or: I thought they had such nice little coats. Her rambling tales trailed off into silence. Once she said: their mother obviously took good care of them. I asked: so what were they doing in the orphanage, then? Mother Lucie shook her head.

The convent rattled with nuns; a pepperpot with too few peppercorns. Sister Dolly pointed to a high kitchen shelf, a stack of white china bowls we never used. She had to make do with the helpers she could get: good-for-nothings like me. She sucked in a whistling breath through her teeth, turned back to the sink. Big enough to wash a cow in. The plughole gaped like a huge mouth. When you pulled the plug you might gurgle down the waste pipe along with all the dirty water. Then you'd swill along the sewers and drown, with your mouth full of turds.

Sister Dolly picked up a slimy-looking dishcloth, frowned, and wrung it out. She said: doubting Thomases, girls today. They want to go off and train for jobs. Her face sagged. She flung the dishcloth back in the sink: you haven't rinsed it properly. Kneel down and say sorry.

The cold floor struck my knees. I stared up at the little lumps on Dolly's nose, the red blotches on her pale cheeks. She picked up the saucepan I'd just scoured and put on the rack to drip, upended it, inspected its dented aluminium bottom: you call this clean?

Dolly kicked me into shape, gave me plenty of housework practice. Get a move on! Hauling my bucket I plodded along what seemed kilometres of shadowy pathways, vaulted and windowless. Everywhere was dimly lit, in order to save electricity. Stretching away into darkness, all the clammy stone corridors looked the same. Staircases rose at both ends, connecting them floor by floor. Thanks to my labours, they all smelled of polish and *eau de Javel*.

For daily Mass, I joined the black-scarfed postulants in their chapel. Most were local French girls. Just one or two arrived from England every year. A grille separated us from the altar, the golden tabernacle. Beyond this, an identical grille guarded the chapel opposite of the novices and the professed. At right angles to both these chapels, facing the altar, the schoolchildren and the orphans knelt in their rows the length of the nave. The postulants and the nuns formed the outstretched wings of a bird and the children its body, the rounded tabernacle its head. A dove, like the Holy Ghost in the picture on the kitchen wall. Rising up in the sweet smoke of incense, smashing its way through the roof and up into the sky, shaking off anyone who didn't cling on tight. I gripped its black and white feathers and flew with it. High in the sky the bird turned into a winged golden mare. Her name was Horsechild. She pranced past the women whispering over their shopping baskets, kicked at her enemies with golden hoofs and bashed their heads in and then took off with golden mane and tail flying and never got caught.

Coming out of chapel, I had to tail meekly behind those holy slugs, the postulants. I had to keep to the back stairs, the back corridors, use the back door, never the front. No short cuts allowed through the old part of the convent. The entrance hall here, with its twisting oval staircase, was out of bounds. Once a week I made an hour's visit to it, swiping at spiders' webs. The Bishop, visiting Reverend Mother, wouldn't want to catch sight of a fat, sweaty girl, with a red face and red hands, lugging pail, mop and broom. After I'd made the gold-brown parquet shine, after I'd dusted the white porcelain stand, with its pot of pink cyclamen, at the foot of the stairs, I had to retreat. The wrought-iron handrail and marble steps curved up out of sight.

What's up there? I asked Mother Lucie on one of her good

days. Sunshine seemed to help her get herself back. Light slanting in through the high windows knocked on her mind and re-opened it. Batty old Mother Lucie. Much battier than I was.

The nuns' recreation room had a bare floor, a black funnel-like stove at one end. We sat there on two wooden chairs, under a huge crucifix. Mother Lucie stitched at a black woollen stocking pulled over a darning mushroom. She stared at her needle, its eye threaded with black. Just lumber rooms, she replied: we haven't the means to restore them. All in disrepair. Nobody goes up there now. She held out the stocking to show me her neat, close darn. Now you try.

Her black woollen shawl looked as crumpled as the skin on her creased face. I wanted to bend forward and put my cheek against hers, lay my head on her knees and have her stroke my head. She reached out and gave me a push with her gnarled hand: come on, stupid child, concentrate.

At night the convent came alive and breathed, guarding a secret, holding me off, but I managed to slink inside it. In my dreams I wasn't fat but lean and nimble. I leaped up the curving stairs that rose from the convent entrance hall, arrived on the top floor, entered the attic. A long, narrow space, like a corridor, linking the convent and the school. Somehow it led into the attic of the house next door. Something unknown and nameless lurked here, blocked my way and trapped me. Fear stuffed itself down my throat, choked me. The convent and school buildings were separated by a thick wall from the house next door. Only at the very top could you get through. Each time I tried I'd wake up bleating and shaking in a tangle of coverlet.

The house next door was empty, its front door boarded up. The old couple who'd bought it at the end of the war had died and the family hadn't yet got round to selling it. The house dozed; our shuttered, silent neighbour. I told no one about my nightmares. Nobody to tell, except Jesus. I received him in holy communion every morning, bowed my head over my hands as I'd been taught. God the Son's body and blood. God fed you with Himself, better than any earthly mother. You hadn't to touch the sacred host. Sister Dolly told tales of Jews who'd stolen hosts from church tabernacles, torn them up and stamped on them. The hosts poured with blood and wailed in the street.

We were supposed to work in silence, but Sister Dolly couldn't do without words. You and your raptures! You don't fool me! She would scrape away at a blackened oven dish and address prayers to her knife: dear Lord, why did you send me this girl? She's ignorant as a beetle.

I was fat but flimsy. She knocked me out of the way like a bluebottle. She shut me up like a drawer. If she caught me eating stolen leftover crusts, rather than putting them in the pig bin, she'd make me kneel down on the floor, holding them in my outstretched hands. Sometimes, when she wanted her kitchen to herself, she sent me to join the postulants at Recreation in their community room. I plumped down on a stool by the door. Seated in a circle, the black-caped girls sang songs or were read aloud to as they sewed. Unpowdered noses red with cold. Thick, unplucked eyebrows. Those who liked each other sent half-smiles sailing across the empty space they rimmed. At least nobody pointed at me and hissed. If nobody spoke to me either I could tell myself that that was the Rule.

One afternoon the postulants grew very animated. One word repeated and repeated. Homesick.

Next day, watching Sister Dolly do the cloth-twiddling she called dusting, I asked her: do you ever feel homesick? Do you ever miss your family?

Homesickness smelled of warm candlegrease and dust and damp wool. Rags soaked in polish tied over my feet, I was working my way along the red-tiled floor of the windowless passage linking the convent to the school, a dark stretch of vaulted hallway sealed by black doors at either end. Dolly was working in the shrine that opened off this red passage like a big doorless closet. Opposite, a couple of steps led up to Reverend Mother's office.

Dolly straightened the vase of blue hyacinths on the Virgin's altar. She stuck her nose into the waxy flowers, sniffed, sneezed. She said: you know perfectly well that nuns are not allowed to talk about our pasts. Her voice thickened with catarrh. She said in a pious tone: my home is here, with the Lord. She fished in her sleeve, blew her nose. Her handkerchief, flaking with green crusts, bulged with fresh snot.

I jerked away, and made my cloth-bound shoes start rubbing again. I put my hands on my hips, to better my balance, and swerved my shoulders and feet forward, first the right and then the left. I hummed a tune, military time, to keep my feet marching. A polish and duster dance.

Dolly said: hoity-toity! Pretending you're better than you are! Like your mother, aren't you!

She'd hooked me. I was her fish. I turned round: what was she like? Was she pretty?

Dolly grunted. I'd asked her these questions before, and she always shook her head at me: you know I'm not allowed to say. Today, gripping a gilt candlestick in each hand, her face furrowed into red frowns, she said: in your mother's line of work she had to be pretty.

I stood still. My hands dived into my pockets and clenched biscuit crumbs, grainy in the seams. I said: what do you mean?

Dolly sucked her teeth. She was a tart. Everybody knows that. Don't pretend you don't know! She was a whore.

My mouth filled with acid bile. I kicked the rags off my feet. Redness patched Dolly's face. Her voice shrilled: she did disgusting things with German soldiers, she loved it, she got paid for it.

The walls of the passageway trembled, fell down, nails and timbers scattering around us. The shrine lunged towards me with spikes. I pulled my apron up over my head. Canvas; not strong enough. The convent was fragile as a cardboard box. We tore up old cardboard boxes to get the bonfire going in the kitchen yard, to burn refuse. I was the bonfire, the refuse, the box being torn up. I was a heap of black ash.

My hands over my ears, I lurched away over the red tiles. I got to the garden door, wrenched open the cupboard where the nuns kept their clogs and shoes, blundered in past the sharp edges of shelves. I plunged into the runny-cheese smell of sweat-soaked leather. Giant boots swung at me, kicked me in the belly. Eyes pierced my darkness. Voices slid under the door and poked me. We know all about your mother's history and you don't ha ha ha.

Horsechild drooped her golden wings, turned into Whoreschild who sat in the dark and hated Dolly. She'd ripped my mother out of me. Too much space inside. Fill it up fill it up. I could have stuffed down a whole loaf. I could have gone on to chew the air, the rain, the cold, to bite down on glass, splinters flying apart on my tongue, shredding me to bloody flesh. Words of blood.

God was useless. He did not exist. Next morning in chapel, when I received the host as usual, I did a test. I let the host stick to the roof of my mouth, licked it, chewed it a few times, spat it into my palm, put it back into my mouth, chewed it again, swallowed it. I did not pray. Nothing happened: no blood; no wailing. When we stood up to sing the final hymn I kept my hymnbook shut. The nuns' thin voices quavered out words insipid as watered milk.

Routines of work and sleep held me up like walking sticks by day. Towards evening they crumbled and snapped like stale baguettes. At night, Whoreschild grew her own red feathery wings, longer than Horsechild's, flew down, trampled Dolly with her red hooves. When Dolly squawked at me in the kitchen I put my finger to my lips. Batty Andrée can't talk!

Autumn brought the start of the new school year and the arrival of the new batch of postulants. They wore lumpy skirts and jumpers and clutched black cardboard suitcases. Later they came into chapel, awkward in their black serge dresses, their hands going up to check their headscarves, tug at the edges of their little elbow-length capes.

The dark convent sank into the pit of winter like a mouse drowning in a latrine. Every day I sluiced away muddy footprints from the cloakroom floor. Crawled on hands and knees to knock out spiders from the greasy black cave behind the range. They scuttled inside to escape the cold and I had to turf them out. I caught them in my palms and carried them to the back door. They scared Dolly. If she saw one scurrying across the flags she'd scream then stamp on it.

121

In the new year, my godmother summoned me. Dolly, loitering in Reverend Mother's office when the call came through, pieced together the news and passed it on. Her mother having died, Madame Blanchard was coming up north to clear out the flat and the disused *épicerie* in the rue de la Croix before putting the property up for sale. Her brother was too busy at his electrical goods factory near Amiens to help her sort things out. She needed a sturdy girl to do the heavy work and so she'd asked for me.

I went on dealing with a stack of used plates, scraping thick smears of grey slime off them into the bin. The cold scum reached up from the plates' undersides and clotted my fingertips. I shivered, wiped my hands on my apron. Dolly said: Reverend Mother wants you in her office right away. Jump to it!

I knocked, entered. The small brown room smelled of damp, and of unwashed woollen cloth. I hovered in front of Reverend Mother's desk. Hands hidden in her black sleeves, she peered at me out of the white frame of her bonnet. Jutting and stiff, it enclosed her gaunt face like blinkers. I'd ironed that bonnet myself. It didn't do much for her. Young women looked pretty in anything, even absurd coifs like frilled white paper cases in a *charcuterie* window. But old women ought to be allowed something less fancy. That was one of the reasons I liked helping Mother Lucie dress for bed. Seeing the white wisps of her hair curl out from under her soft white cotton nightcap. Smoothing them into place. Then she looked like the picture of a dear, sweet grandmother in a book. Even if she didn't behave like one. Fist hitting the air. Shouting rude words. Making brown smears on the sheets.

Reverend Mother said: how long is it since you cleaned in here properly? Months, surely.

Dust outlined the bookshelves, marked the angle of wall and floor. She never opened the window; no wonder the room smelled musty. Sour as old farts. She sat throned in a big wooden chair, its high back carved with pinnacles. Behind her on the brown wall a brown oil painting showed a brown palm tree, a hollow-chested Jesus droopily astride a brown donkey.

Reverend Mother said: that poor old woman. So proud, she didn't want people visiting, she wouldn't let people help her. It broke dear Madame Blanchard's heart, having to put her into the hospital.

I shifted from foot to foot. She glanced at me, as though I'd said something critical. She sighed: in the old days, families were able to take care of their own.

A bell rang: a handbell, wielded by someone in the passage just outside. Reverend Mother said: I'm due in chapel now, to speak to the postulants. Give this room a good clean. Tomorrow you're to go and help Madame Blanchard.

The morning smelled of fresh vegetables and horse dung and earth. I loitered in the marketplace, watching the stalls set up, then continued down to the rue de la Croix. New weeds, feathery and green, sprouted in the cracks between paving-stones, clung to crevices in stone walls. The wind flapped at my skirts, tugged at my headscarf. Cold air smacked my cheeks. A bitter green perfume sharp as a chisel was cracking me open. The longing for spring chipped at me and the wind pushed me and pulled me and I giddied along.

Though the black paint had faded and cracked, you could still read the legend stencilled above the lintel: *épicerie*. You're late, Madame Blanchard said, opening the door: we'll have to hurry, there's so much to do.

I stepped inside. She kissed the air in front of my cheeks. Waft of eau de Cologne. She had on her fur coat, a little red hat, carried her leather handbag slung over one furry arm. Deep, wide sleeve, revealing the rich brown silk lining it. She led me through the chilly shop, smelling of stale air and mice, and upstairs to the flat.

When I first opened the door to the kitchen and walked in, picking my way over the sticky lino, something whined and shuddered. I disturbed an atmosphere that was both cross and needy. It settled round me and clutched me. The place stank of sour milk and drains. Around the base of the stove flakes of loose plaster fallen from the walls mixed with mouse droppings, ancient crumbs of fried food hardened to spiky clumps, hair-coated balls of greasy dust.

Madame Blanchard's face twitched. Her skin, coated with pale powder, looked as though no dirt ever came near it. Her lipsticked mouth puckered into a moue of distaste. She pulled her fur collar up round her throat and patted her blonde perm. She frowned and said: she really did let herself go. You'll just have to do the best you can. She left me to it and went into the sitting room next door.

No broom or rubber gloves to be seen. I pinched up a grimy litter of old cardboard boxes and empty tins from the middle of the floor, threw them into a heap at one side. I forced myself to open the stained cupboards which looked as though someone in a fit of rage had poured soup down them or hurled cups of coffee at them. Sooty fingerprints smeared the surrounds of the doorknobs. Jammed inside were rusting pots and pans.

Eventually I found a bucket and approached the tarnished tap at the sink. Drips from long ago had left green-brown tracks down the enamel. I filled big pots of water and set them to boil, in preparation for scrubbing. I found scouring powder and soapflakes on an open shelf looped with spiders' webs, amid a clutter of broken lampshades and chipped *rillette* pots, but couldn't see a mop, floorcloth or brush anywhere. I went next door to ask my godmother what to do.

Had I approached the wrong room? The carpet had disappeared under a whirl of chaos, as though an earth tremor had caused a landslide and avalanches of rubbish had poured in through the windows. Madame Blanchard knelt in the centre of the disarray. Her red felt hat had flown off and perched on a chair. Her blonde hair crackled like straw in the weak light. Her fur coat flowed around her.

Not an earthquake. She'd turned into a burglar. She'd pulled open the cupboards set in the panelling of the walls and ransacked them. *Bureau* stood stripped. *Armoire* and *buffet* gaped, doors swinging free. The outside of the furniture was polished wood, carved and golden. The doors' insides, plain and unvarnished, seemed shocking as nakedness. Dark empty interiors. Stuff heaped up round my godmother's kneeling figure. A glass dome with a wreath of pinkish waxy flowers inside. A mauve lustre vase. Shallow cardboard boxes, albums, trays, bundles of papers and envelopes, clusters of jugs, ornamental baskets. Tall wobbling piles of plates, napkins, cloths.

She was consulting a list, ticking off items. So intent she didn't hear me. I stood in the doorway and watched as she put down her paper and pencil, untied a packet of pale blue envelopes. She opened a few, drew out what looked like letters scrawled in blue ink. She threw these down, then undid the little gilt clasps on a flat plywood box stuck with a colourful frilled paper label like a big postage stamp. She upended it and shook it out. Empty. Next she lifted the knobbed lid off a white porcelain soup tureen. She fished inside it, drew out a bulky packet wrapped in white tissue paper. She unfolded the soft white layers methodically. Her face concentrating. Her gestures very steady. A big white-petalled daisy lay in her lap. She picked it up, tipped out the contents.

Gold shone on her palm, streamed into her lap. A tangle of gold bracelets and gold chains. Gold rings. They glittered like the candlesticks in church. She sat back on her heels, very still, and concentrated, looking down. The white tissue paper billowed across her tweed skirt. Bowing her head so reverently, she looked like the priest at Mass, holding the gold paten and chalice. She breathed in, held her breath. So did I. Then, without closing the door, I retreated to the kitchen and coughed loudly, to break her reverie and alert her to my presence. I knocked on the half-open door, paused, and came back in.

Blank-faced, she looked round. Still red mouth; calm lips. Her hands shook, though, cupping the sheets of tissue paper. She squeezed them together, as though they were nothing but crumpled rubbish needing disposal. She looked up at me gently, just a nice housewife interrupted in her housework by the silly maid. She stuffed the billowy paper into the open mouth of her handbag, fished in her purse for money, sent me off to the *quincaillerie* to buy what I needed. In her confusion she gave me a big note. I pocketed it without outward comment. Silly rich bitch.

When I returned, she was sitting in an armchair, knees

together, head bent, dabbing at her mascara with her white handkerchief. She'd taken off her fur coat, revealing a pleated silk dress printed with a diamond pattern in navy and emerald. I clocked her little high-heeled ankle boots, soft grey leather laced with grey silk strings and cuffed with grey fur.

Oh poor Maman, said Madame Blanchard to her handkerchief. She cast the flimsy square of lawn to her lap, laid her arms along the arms of her chair, opened her hands wide, gazed down sadly like the *pietà*.

I'd never met the old lady who'd drowned in mess. I got to know her through rolling up the striped stained mattress, with its flat felt buttons, of her bed, emptying her shapeless skirts out of her cupboard smelling of camphorated mothballs, removing her tin of caked denture cleaner from the shelf over the sink. I folded her pink candlewick dressing gown, frayed and balding, her faded grey nightdress, collected up a pair of slippers and a pair of outdoor shoes. Why had she left these behind when she went into the hospital? Perhaps Madame Blanchard had bought her new things, so as not to feel ashamed of her. Perhaps the old people wore uniforms, like orphans and schoolchildren and nuns. What did whores wear? Gorgeous silk and satin clothes, like Mary Magdalene, to lure the men upstairs. Everything brand new, unwrapped from creaseless tissue paper, and smelling delicious.

The old lady had so much stuff. I wanted some of it. I wanted a souvenir. I waited until Madame Blanchard went to the lavatory then scrabbled through her mother's leavings. I picked up one of the scattered blue envelopes. I'd like a dress that colour. A cardigan to match. I stuffed the letter into my pocket. Now it was mine, and so I hadn't stolen it. Now it belonged to me.

At midday, Madame Blanchard released me: go back to the convent to eat. I nodded, but once outside the *épicerie* stayed in the streets. What was on the nuns' lunch menu today? Purée of split peas, black bread, half a tumbler of cider each. Hunger suddenly mattered less than roaming about, free because unseen. I halted at the entrance to the park, peered through the railings. No tramps visible, and so I dared to sit down on a bench. I was a respectable citizen, out taking the air, just like anyone else.

I fished out the blue envelope. A square gap at the top right-hand corner showed where the stamp had been torn off. Address written in blue ink. Madame Marie-Angèle Blanchard, care of Madame Baudry, rue de la Croix. Smudged, faint postmark. I pulled out the sheet of blue paper the envelope enclosed. The letter bore no date. Half a page of French words. My mother's name at the bottom.

The blue words leaped up and down. She loves me she loves me not. Warm sun pressing my face, cold wind blowing up my sleeves and down my neck, chilly fingers dressing me in a vest of ice. She loves me she loves me not. I folded the fidgety words back into their paper case, got up, walked briskly along the gravel path. I left the park, went back into the street. I studied the dishes of *pâtés* and *saucissons* and *rillettes* in a *charcuterie*'s window. The *pâté* was called: she loved me, she said send Andrée my love. The *saucisson* was called: she wrote to find out how I was, to ask for news of me. The pot of *rillettes'* true name was: she felt sure her letters to me had gone astray, wouldn't Marie-Angèle help, she begged her. A tray of jellied brawn spelt it out: had I received the handkerchiefs she'd sent me for my birthday?

All afternoon, Madame Blanchard kept me in the kitchen,

scrubbing. From time to time I peeped round the door, watching her sort good things from tat, pack china and small pieces of furniture, wadded by straw, into deep wooden crates. The blue letters had all disappeared. Looking at that empty space they'd left behind on the floor, I wanted to cram myself with bread. Stop up my mouth, stop myself yelling. My empty stomach growled and I told myself: later, just wait, it's all right, later on I'll find something to eat.

Madame Blanchard called me in to fill sacks of rubbish for the dustmen to collect. I nailed down the lids of the crates and she stuck address labels on them. Some of the crates were destined for her own house, others for her brother's home near Amiens.

A grey van arrived, parked. Like a large tin can, with metal pleats and fins. The driver loaded up, rattled off. I made up a bed for Madame Blanchard in the back bedroom, the one she said she'd slept in as a girl. Before leaving for the night I fetched her a fresh baguette from the baker's, and the greaseproof-wrapped supper she'd ordered from the *traiteur*. I laid out the dishes on clean plates: a big vol-au-vent stuffed with creamed mushrooms, a fat piece of poached salmon in shrimp sauce, some *salade russe* in mayonnaise. Back with the nuns, I stuck my spoon into my portion of Dolly's cabbage soup, to taste it. I pushed my bowl away. Dolly said: that's not like you. You're usually the first to stick your face into the trough! I said: pigswill is for pigs! Reverend Mother tapped the tabletop: Andrée, you're a disgrace.

Next morning I returned to the disused *épicerie*. Your final task, said Madame Blanchard, driving me up the stairs: is to help with the furniture. Goodness, you move so slowly! You really should go on a diet.

I was fat as the furniture she didn't want. Her mother's ugly, weighty pieces she was donating to the church *dépôt-vente* run by the homeless. A dark blue lorry duly rolled up the street. The driver, in blue work-clothes, was short and slight, with a bristle of grey-white hair, a bruised-looking brown-red face, faded blue eyes. Slowly he mounted the couple of steps to the front door, rocking a bit, stiff-legged. Like someone on stilts. He wore solid boots with metal toecaps. He smelled of tobacco, alcohol and sweat. Madame Blanchard welcomed him most graciously but flinched when he put out his seamed brown hand to shake her pale scented one.

Georges Duchamp, at your service, *madame*. You're the charity and I'm the homeless.

Madame Blanchard said: but I spoke to Father Duval about this. I was expecting him to send a couple of youth volunteers. However will you manage? These pieces of furniture are very heavy. Georges Duchamp said: we let Father Duval man the telephone but we run things ourselves. He winked at me, then scowled at my godmother: don't you worry, *madame*. I'm good and fit. Fit for anything! Madame Blanchard took a list out of her pocket, and a pencil: Andrée, stop gawping.

I said to Georges: I'll give you a hand.

Together we manoeuvred the dismantled beds down the narrow stairs. The *buffet* and wardrobe tilted between us, like little houses. Easy does it! We managed well, calling instructions to each other, swaying, lifting, the bulks of wood rising and falling as we nudged round corners. From time to time we rested, while Georges drew a breath. Fuck this leg of mine! We got the kitchen table downstairs, the armchairs, heaved them up into the lorry. Along the street aproned neighbours emerged into their doorways, stood with folded arms silently watching us. Madame Blanchard stayed invisibly indoors.

Georges closed up the back of the lorry. He said loudly, for all the neighbours to hear: thanks, Andrée, you're a good girl. I cringed but he gave me another wink. The neighbours withdrew, closed their doors. Madame Blanchard called from inside: hurry up or I'll miss my train!

Georges checked his watch: I'll be late. I'll cop it when I get back.

He shook my hand, tugged down his cap, opened the cab door. I stood on the edge of the kerb, balancing back and forth. I said: everybody in this town knows everybody else. Have you always lived here? Did you know my mother, Jeanne Nérin? Climbing into the cab, Georges glanced over his shoulder: sure. Just by sight, mind. Madame Blanchard shouted again from inside. Georges slammed the door. He rolled down the window: she left before the war. She went off to work over in Ste-Madeleine. See you! He revved the engine. Away he drove.

I helped Madame Blanchard transport her hand luggage to the railway station. She was too mean to pay for a taxi, so we borrowed the convent handcart and used that. I tugged it bumping along over the cobbles, while she tittupped next to me in her high heels. Before the train moved off she said to me: as your godmother, I've always done my best for you, I've done all I can, just behave yourself and you'll come to no harm.

The carriage window framed her. She'd pushed down the window glass and leaned out. Behind her, above the seats, her suitcases and boxes crammed the racks. She spoke her farewell then turned her face this way and that so that I could aim kisses at her cheeks. I seized the gloved hand that rested on top of the pushed-down glass and gripped it. Ridged seams of fabric fingers. The whistle shrilled. Madame Blanchard tried to wrest her hand away. I held on. The whistle shrilled again. The train jumped, jolted, began to glide past the platform. I stumbled along, keeping pace with it. I called: so where is my mother now? Madame Blanchard cried out: oh for heaven's sake! I let go of her hand. She shouted: I don't know, we lost touch years ago. And in any case remember that she didn't want to have anything to do with you.

She ducked back as the train moved off. I yelled after her: you're a liar! She slammed up the carriage window and disappeared behind it.

I started back towards the convent, my hands in my skirt pockets. I fingered notes and coins, the change I hadn't given back to my godmother after buying cleaning materials at the *quincaillerie*. She'd forgotten to ask for it. Just as well. I needed it for running away.

I heated up the nuns' leek soup, sawed slices of bread. These days the professed community comprised just twelve sisters. They used just one of the oak tables in the refectory, five sisters on each side, with Reverend Mother at one end and Mother Lucie at the other. The novices and postulants ate at the table opposite. A single bulb swung from the ceiling on a twisted brown cord and leaked pale yellow light. The nuns folded their hands and stared at their brown pottery bowls.

I stood at the serving trolley, ladle in hand. We all bowed our heads while Reverend Mother intoned Grace. She should have thanked me for that good soup, not God. The nuns tucked their brown linen napkins under their chins, picked up their spoons. Mother Lucie sang out to no one in particular: we worried we'd

132

not have enough to feed them, poor little things. But they didn't stay with us all that long, in the event, did they?

Clink of metal on earthenware. Click of someone's dentures. The older nuns dunked their bread in their soup, to soften it. They swallowed noisily. Another Grace. Scrape of benches pushed back. The nuns filed out, in the same order as always. I pushed the serving trolley, laden with empty bowls, into the corner of the kitchen. I'd do them tomorrow. Or not.

While the nuns went off to say Vespers I washed the kitchen floor. How many hundreds of times had I done that? I waited for Mother Lucie outside the chapel, helped her up the back stairs to the nuns' dormitory. One arm firmly under her elbow. Her fingers clutching mine. With her other hand she gripped the banister. She panted and wheezed, lifting one foot then the other. I felt her mind clench, instruct her muscles, I felt her will instruct her legs to shift, whatever the pain grinding in her joints. If I went away, who'd help her? Perhaps they'd just leave her to rot in bed all day. Over the slippery lino floor we lurched. I pulled aside her white cubicle curtains. I sat her on the edge of her metal bed and knelt in front of her to tug off her slippers. She gripped the bed with both hands, trying to keep herself upright. She closed her eyes, toppled into my arms, already falling asleep. Hey, come on, *ma mère*. I tapped her cheek. We're not done yet. Let's get these off. A docile old child, she raised her arms to let go of habit, petticoat, vest. She mumbled: we lost the children. She leaned back against her pillow, shut her eyes, began to snore.

I retreated to my own cubicle at the end of the postulants' and novices' dormitory and closed my curtains. They jigged to and fro. The draught whistled in from under the distant door, rattled the ill-fitting sash windows. I sat up in bed and wound the sheet around my hands lest the wind tug me forth. The wind won. Whoreschild neighed softly. This is your last night here. Your last chance to go exploring.

I got up, put on my dressing gown, glided out of the dormitory into the vestibule at the far end. Thick darkness. I didn't dare switch on a light. I'd have to find a candle. I slipped down the stairs, flight by flight, to the ground floor, passed the refectory, approached the big black door marking the boundary of the convent. I pushed through, entered the school, the red-tiled passage. A red glow from the shrine: a flame inside a red glass holder. I entered the shrine, lifted down the stubby candle in its red cradle, set off again, back towards the convent.

Beyond the big black door, I turned right not left. I crept into the convent's oval entrance hall. My red light gleamed on the columns bracing the front door, the porcelain stand bearing its pot of flowers, a marble lip of stair, the curled-over end of the balustrade.

I peered up into the darkness. Nothing up there, Mother Lucie had said. What did nothing mean? Heaven was always referred to as up there. You couldn't see it but you had to believe in it. At the top of the stairs might be ghosts, or monsters. There was something up there. If I didn't go up I'd not find out whatever it was. It waited for me. Did I want to meet it or not?

I ascended the staircase, pressing up into the dark, testing each step. Whoreschild spread her red wings and hovered above me. I held the votive candle in one hand and gripped the handrail with the other. The long, ornate iron curl spiralled upwards into shadows, tugging the wedges of marble to curve up with it.

I reached out, held on to Whoreschild's red mane, which twined round me.

On the first floor an oval vestibule echoed the shape of the hall below. It led, through two sets of double doors, into a *salon*. Curtains of mossy greyness, old hangings swagged with dust, let me through. I slipped across a curved, comma-shaped parquet floor, between walls of grey shadow. Lofty room draped with cobwebs, piled with spiky shapes of broken furniture, soft mounds of what must be yet more dust in the corners. Neglected spaces, smelling of rot. A girl in a long white robe advanced towards me, one hand outstretched. I jumped and squeaked and almost dropped my little light. The ghost-girl met me and struck me: my hand on a clammy mirror.

The steps to the second floor were of wood. They creaked under my bare feet. Now the house narrowed, shrank to a little panelled entry containing a single door. This opened into an oblong room, empty of furniture, the dust rolled into bolsters of fluff along the angles of floor and walls. I swivelled my candle-glass around, swept my glance up and down. Round dents in lino. Eight tiny punches. I bent closer, moved my flickery flame to and fro. The marks of little wheels. Trolleys? Beds? Perhaps the nuns had once used this room for an overflow of orphans. Mother Lucie probably knew the details, but I'd not get the chance to ask her now. She might have forgotten, in any case. She was no longer reliable. I could hear her quaver: they cried for their mother, but what else could we have done?

I retraced my steps back out to the landing. One more floor to go. I edged up a short, straight flight of ladderlike steps to a small wooden door. Opening this, I entered the open space of the attic. It ran off right and left, ends lost in shadow. Rafters reached down, bracing the sloping roof that skimmed my head. To one side, a low row of round windows faced out. I walked forwards over unpolished wooden boards, past a row of broken statues. Moonlight splashed on to battered, noseless Virgins, pale paint peeling from their moulded cloaks, their chipped hands clasped in prayer.

At the far end: a tall cupboard. I tugged at the white china doorknob, pulled it open. Two pairs of little wooden-soled boots spilled out. The cupboard was very shallow, its back a wall of raw brick, the cracks between blocks oozing hardened curls of mortar.

Perhaps the wall had been built to stop up an entrance. Perhaps my dreams had got it right: from here you'd once been able to get through, into the house next door.

I went back down the steep little stair to the second floor. I felt sleepy now, as though I were melting, part of the grey shadows. As I paused in the little foyer the place woke up, stirred, rustled. A kind of yawn took place inside me, outside me. Something, the fabric of my life, parted and tore, my skin peeled back and the world rushed in, I forgot how old I was, the wall cracked and something erupted through. Footsteps clattered on the staircase below, the steps creaked and shook, wooden soles bumping on to the bare treads, a child wailed, a young woman's voice whispered hush, be quick, be quick. I shivered. I felt I'd been slashed with a knife to the belly, I bowed over, wanted to cry, but knew I must make no sound. When I shivered again the crack in the wall mended itself, whatever had escaped went back in, the night folded back around me, I stood alone once more on the landing.

I returned to my cubicle, lay awake for the rest of the night listening to postulants and novices tossing on their hard mattresses, coughing and farting, one or two moaning in dreams. When the bell for rising clanged, I got dressed as usual, in grey blouse and skirt, blue overall and blue headscarf. I shoved the filched letter into my pocket, along with my money. I pushed back my cubicle curtains, joined the end of the short file of beginner-nuns processing past their stripped beds, sheets and coverlets all folded back. I stilled my breathing, bent my head, took neat steps.

The stone-floored chapel felt as chilly as ever. Kneeling to one side of the row of postulants, I blew on my hands, rubbed them together to try and warm them. Opposite me, beyond the altar, in their fenced-off chapel behind their grille, the nuns faced forwards in their stalls, fingers knotted on top of their prie-dieux. Backs as straight as they could make them. Faces turned towards God. Prayer stilled them to a black and white pattern of devotion. Like a photograph I'd take away with me. I was looking at them from a distance, saying goodbye. Set apart from me, suddenly they seemed holy, and powerful in their holiness. Not just ordinary women whom I knew well, their peculiarities and weaknesses, but so good. They accepted serenely what God sent them, whether he spoke to them or not. They had real faith, and lived their lives according to that faith, bravely dealing with loneliness, boredom and cold.

A voice growled in my ear. Sentimental rubbish. Why don't they ask questions? Perhaps they are scared?

I jumped. Sister Dolly would have said it was the voice of the devil but I wasn't sure. A puff of dust whirled up near the door at the back of the chapel as though someone had just gone out and let in the wind from the cloister.

I walked for the last time from the chapel to the kitchen. My convent-city: I could have strolled it blindfold. I laid a tray ready for someone to take up to Mother Lucie, who was still in bed. My fault: I'd not helped her get up. I was abandoning her. No other word for it.

Dolly stormed in, pointed at the trolley, stacked with unwashed supper bowls: leaving dirty crockery out overnight just encourages mice. Whatever's got into you? It's all this jaunting about. She grumbled on, while I ran water into the sink, kept one eye on the coffee urn, the big pan of milk. Washing up in a hurry, I didn't rinse things properly. Lifting crockery from basin to draining board, I dropped a bowl. Coated with soap, it slipped through my fingers and smashed on the floor. Smashed plate smashed mother smashed Whoreschild smashed me.

I knelt down to pick up the fragments. Thick pottery bits, painted with glittery brown glaze. I gathered them into one hand. Sister Dolly's big black shoes parked themselves in front of me. I ducked my head and studied the shining tiles, those old friends I'd washed last night. Suddenly I wanted to kiss them. I bent over, let my lips touch the cold surface. Smell of linseed oil and soap. Goodbye, floor. Peace descended on me. Thank you, floor.

For heaven's sake! shouted Dolly: no need to exaggerate! Stop showing off!

I got up, threw the broken pieces into the bin. Dolly jerked a greying tea towel between her hands and picked at its frayed edge. I was the tea towel. She wanted to give me a good shake but couldn't. Holy charity forbade it.

Sink lapping with warm water bobbing with slivers of onion. Rimmed with grease. The used smell of our woollen clothes.

138

Not enough air in here: windows all sealed shut. I said: I forgot the handcart at the station yesterday. May I have permission to go and fetch it?

Dolly folded the tea towel against her belly, smacked it smooth, hung it over the empty rack on the draining board. She blew out her breath and said: away with you. Off you go, you daft creature. You're in no fit state to serve breakfast. I think you've gone mad.

I lowered my head, started untying my apron. Why were warm drops falling on my fingers? Knots. Why were the strings wet? Dolly hesitated: sorry I shouted. I shouldn't have.

She made me cry so that then she could be nice to me. Stick the knife in then pat the wound. Shout more. Don't be kind. How will I manage to leave if you start considering my feelings? Whoreschild turned her head in anguish from side to side, neighing and trampling. Just let me out. I arched my neck and whinnied, reared on my back legs, striking my hooves on the door. I banged out so that Dolly wouldn't halter me with a soft word. Stay cold, Dolly. Stay hard as the floor. Remember after I've gone that I kissed the floor rather than you.

I'd turned Dolly to stone. I turned myself into a trolley on quick wheels. The corridors stretched ahead, very quiet and clean. I bowled down them. Another wave of my wand and I became the solitary ball of dusty fluff blowing along, the sole piece of grit fetching up against the doormat. I swung open the front door and the dustpan-house tipped me out into the square.

Behind me the chapel bell tolled eight o'clock. My scarf, fastened behind my head, felt too tight. I untied it, re-arranged it, knotting it loosely under my chin in the style of the women of the town. I pulled it forward, to shield my face.

139

The early air smelled fresh. Cobbles still wet with dew. A couple of men, holding newspapers and baguettes, stood on the corner. They took no notice of me. A dog trotted past, lifted its yellow leg to piss against a lamp-post, trotted on again.

I descended the steep street that led towards the parish church. Wind flipped up the point of my headscarf, chafed the back of my neck.

My pace began to slow. Such a cold morning. I had no coat and no jacket. Should I turn round and go back? They wouldn't have missed me yet. Dolly would simply suppose I'd flounced off in a huff. She'd be expecting me to return with the handcart sooner or later, once I'd had a good sulk, to get on with the vegetables for lunch. A hill of turnips awaited me. I could slip back in, no questions asked. Be safe again. I wanted a gendarme to tap me on the shoulder and demand to know my business. I wanted to scream: capture me! I've run away! Take me back!

I called to Whoreschild to follow me, stuck my hands into my sleeves and marched into the park. Dark flowerbeds put up ramrod stems. Evergreens dripped and gleamed. When I passed the tramps' bench, the shape slumped there stirred, spotted me and sang out. Hello! Hey, Andrée!

White-grey crewcut, creased reddish face, bald brown coat, brown scarf. Georges Duchamp patted the bench. Come on, don't be in such a hurry, sit down. Where are you off to in such a rush? His voice slurred and slid about. I said: I don't know. I've run away.

Georges patted his pockets. Dearie me. Hey, what's this? He proffered a squat bottle.

I took a sip, not wanting to hurt his feelings by saying no. Deep, dark taste. Sugared and fiery, it hit the back of my throat, made me splutter and cough. Georges dug his hand back into his pocket and brought out a broken bit of petit-beurre biscuit. He folded my fingers around its pleated edge. He laid his hand on my arm: *bon appétit*.

My lips began trembling. Words jumped up from somewhere deep in my stomach, flew out of my mouth: what happened to you? Why are you homeless?

He wiped the neck of the bottle on his brown coat sleeve and handed it to me again. I shook my head. He sighed, flattened his wrinkled eyelids over his eyes. People were supposed to be in charge of their own faces but his loosened far too much. His cheeks plumped, sponges to soak up tears. I whistled, summoned Whoreschild, who leaped over the park fence, trotted up. I murmured to her; she swished her tail, backed off, nibbled grass. He said: who wants to employ a *mutilé de guerre*? Who gives a fuck? No one. Then if you're out of work you can't pay rent. So you're thrown out.

I said: you've no family left? Georges shook his head. Let's say the bastards don't want to know me. Gone to the bad, haven't I? He mused for a while. I ate the piece of ancient biscuit, stale and soft. He said: I lost touch with most of my friends during the war. I've had to start all over again.

He opened his eyes, took another swig. His breath smelled thick and sweet. His mouth worked. He said: what with one thing and another. Thousands like me.

I waited for him to put some more words into the right order, tell them to look sharp, but his words wouldn't obey. His lips parted, but the words flew out soundlessly and escaped over the treetops. The spirit I'd drunk felt like a knife scouring my innards. I said: we need something to eat.

141

I could take Georges to a café, pay for breakfast with Madame Blanchard's money. Rolls with blackcurrant jam. Real coffee, not mixed with chicory, served in thick green cups with gold rims. Sugar cubes wrapped in paper. No need to rush. Bask in the heat of the café, the pop music on the radio, the sight of men's caps and hats on the hatstand, the smell of their tobacco as they lit up and inhaled. I'd wait as long as necessary for Georges to feel like speaking. Warmed and fed, smoking a cigarette, he'd tell me what he remembered about my mother. Perhaps he'd help me think of a way to discover where she was living. Someone at his hostel might know what you had to do. Where you went to find out. I could ask them to help me. Then I could write to her. Suggest a meeting.

I couldn't leave him just yet. His brown coat sleeve implored me to stay. At least twenty years old, that coat. Brown wool, shiny and rubbed. Smelling of tobacco. Perhaps she'd touched it once. I could touch the place where once she'd leaned her hand.

Georges said: you're a good, practical girl, aren't you. We could do with someone like you at the hostel. Want a job?

What kind of job? I was good at cleaning but I'd had enough of it. Laundry ditto. Nuns' vests, nuns' bloomers, nuns' bonnets: someone else could pound them, starch them, iron them. Never again would I have to plod out to that little back yard on a raw winter day, my cold slippered feet sliding in my clogs. In windy weather the sheets flapped and cracked on the line and smacked me as I tried to unpin them. Dolly's job to cope with the laundry now. Good luck to her.

Georges said: we could do with a decent cook. Someone who really knows what's what.

What was their kitchen like? Big enough to walk to and fro in, with a back doorstep where you could sit and feel the sun on your face while you topped and tailed beans. I could be in sole charge of it. No one bossing me around and ticking me off. I'd wear a smart white cap and apron and dip my ladle into the pots, tasting and testing. If anyone gave me grief I'd whistle up Whoreschild, get her to rear and kick and frighten them.

Then I would leave, when I was ready, to find my mother.

Georges said: you'd get paid. Not much, but something.

What did my mother look like now? If we met, what would we say to one another? Would we feel able to speak at all? It would be hard for us both. That would be our point of meeting. That difficulty. Would we get through it? I didn't know.

I said: I'll come and help you out for a bit, if you'll help me in return.

I pulled him to his feet. He said: for fuck's sake! All right, all right.

Jeanne

Just before the war broke out, soon after my eighteenth birthday, I found new employment; in a house in nearby Ste-Madeleine.

News of the vacancy zigzagged towards me like a paper dart. Neighbours picked up the dart, read its message, sailed it on. The fact of a job becoming available pleated itself into the way we learned of it. Madame Fauchon heard about it from her husband who heard about it from the man who had married the young maidservant in Ste-Madeleine. The newly-wed couple had moved to lodgings in Ste-Marie, where the husband had found temporary work at the forge. The husband brought his boots into the cobbler's soon afterwards, and fell into conversation with Monsieur Fauchon. Monsieur Fauchon mentioned to his wife that the young woman had left her housemaid's job. Madame Fauchon told Maman the job was going. Maman told me.

She shook silvery raindrops from her hair, stamped on the mat. She unbelted her coat, fished in her pocket. She unscrewed a scrap of paper. Here's the address. Near the rail-way station, I think.

I took the paper from her, and her coat. I hung the sodden

coat on the peg near the door, put down a wad of newspaper to catch the drips. The kitchen filled with the smell of damp wool. The cold came inside with the thick wet smell, muffling my mouth. I laid the draught-extinguisher against the bottom of the door. A patched bolster-cover stuffed with stockings past repair. Only just wide enough. You felt the wind trying to lift it aside at either end; whistle in.

Maman said: sounds like a lodging house. She bent, pulled on her slippers. Her dark hair showed grey threads. Write this evening.

I wrote on a leaf of paper torn out of an old school exercise book. My prospective employer wrote back on pink notepaper with deckled edges. A small hand, with neat loops and flourishes. Pale blue ink. The *patronne* suggested a week's trial. She offered me my meals, a bed, my servant's uniform. Maman said: you'll be able to save your wages every week. She tied on her apron, began scrubbing a celeriac root at the sink. She spoke to the basin of water: I wish you didn't have to go away from home. My mouth felt crowded with spikes. Bite down on thorns, on blood.

We didn't own a suitcase, so I packed my clothes, books and art things in the old basket we used for collecting firewood. I mended the handle with string, and salvaged a box from the Fauchons to hold our kindling. I waited in their shop while Madame Fauchon emptied out a stream of silver nails. Monsieur Fauchon said: I wouldn't like one of my little ones to go so far. Such times we live in! He handed me the box. But your mother's always had her own way of doing things. His wife folded her arms. Just you watch out for yourself, that's all.

The day before I left was a Sunday. In the afternoon we got

dressed up and went to the dance hall near the factory. I wore Maman's old yellow frock, taken up and taken in. Maman wore its sister frock, in coral. She put on lipstick and powder, pinned up her hair into a glossy black roll. The lights in the hall burned red and yellow and blue. Men thronged at the bar, while women and girls sat on benches at the side. I found a vantage point behind the benches, in the shadows, peeped out between bare necks, ridged hairdos. Bare, shining floor. Fizz of fiddles. Smell of fresh sweat, lavender, musky perfume.

Plenty of men asked my mother to dance. They whirled her in fast waltzes, as though she were a spool of ribbon they were unwinding and shaking out. They spilled my mother tumbling coral silk across the floor and she gripped them and gazed at them seriously as they spun her round.

Halfway through the afternoon, the band began playing country dance music and the crowd on the dance floor thinned a little. A clear space showed me Monsieur Jacquotet standing by a wooden pillar on the far side of the hall. A dangling bouquet of bunched blue, yellow and red bulbs illuminated his shapeless blue jacket and orange shirt. The older men and women formed up in lines like the spokes of a wheel. As they moved off, arm in arm, going round in strict time, his pencil began dancing across the page of a small sketchbook.

My mother ran up to take part, joined a row of neighbours from our street, fell into step with them, advancing, pointing her toe, jigging forwards and back. People were grave-faced, concentrating. Only my mother smiled. The country dance finished and the wheel disintegrated. People scattered. A polka began. Maman hovered near me, under a yellow light.

Monsieur Jacquotet got up, crossed the floor, held out his

hand to her. She flowed towards him, fitted herself into his embrace. A group of boys holding glasses of beer blocked my view. I pushed round them, peered past them. One of them glared at me, swore: mind out, big nose! His friend hissed: Jewish cunt! I ducked away. Couples merged into a mass of circling bodies. Maman's red frock kept flicking past. The music dictated the swerve of her narrow, spirited waist, her thin ankles. She was whippy and quick, her skirts twirling. She'd forgotten me completely. A chisel drove into my belly, twisted its point round. Tearing flesh. Spill of blood and guts. I wanted to howl. Hold in the howl, hold in the chisel. Gouged inside, chisel twisting to and fro like polka music.

The polka finished and movement stilled. The dancers became individual figures once more. Monsieur Jacquotet bowed to Maman. He smiled. Took a pace backwards, into the crowd. One face among many. A blur. He vanished into the dark jostle of bodies. The air closed on his absence, on the smell of beer and hot flesh and cigarettes. I looked down at the scratched, muddied floor. The tips of my shoes. I hadn't let my shoes dance, though they'd wanted to. Too shy. Anyway, no one had asked me. Anyway, I didn't know the steps.

Maman's lily-of-the-valley scent approached. Her light tap on my shoulder: time to go. Walking home, she hummed a polka tune. Footsteps clattered behind us. I said: hush! Someone might hear you. She said: so what if they do? She loitered. She just wouldn't hurry. I dragged along beside her, fists in my pockets. She said: what are you sulking about? I was trying to give you a treat. Don't go spoiling our last evening. I burst into tears: I'm not sulking!

A hulk of male bodies ahead on the street, blocking our way.

Drunken voices punched the dark. Jeering. Someone called: Jewish whores! Maman straightened up double quick. She grasped my hand, pulled me along. She thrust her key into the lock and we fell indoors.

In order to walk the ten kilometres to Ste-Madeleine and arrive on time I had to leave early in the morning, while it was still dark. I put on my old school coat. Maman held out her boots: wear these. They're smarter than yours. She held my face between her hands. I shut my eyes. She kissed my eyelids, my cheeks.

Entering Ste-Madeleine, I walked from the end of night into a grey day smudged with pink dawn, the sky runny and wet like a watercolour. I'd try to paint this freshness, this creamy crescent moon. Monsieur Jacquotet had chosen to paint me. Not my mother. He mixed the paint on a grey china plate. His fingers squeezed pink paste from a silver tube and I added the water. He'd do this landscape on cartridge paper. He was hiding behind a zigzag cartridge paper screen. He folded it into an origami bird and flung it at the sky and I followed a frilly-winged pink and grey pigeon swooping ahead and forgot to look at the street names and so lost my way. Riffle of paper, riffle of unfolding images. A fountain. A marketplace. A church. Tiny squares surrounded by tall houses. A bell chimed the hour and a whole flock of pigeons flurried up.

Narrow cobbled streets, seeming identical, led away in every direction. How to choose? Lured by the smell of baking bread, I turned left. Dark blue shutters hid the bakery. Street door closed, blind drawn down, gold light framing its edges. Next to it, a yellow oblong: a café, its door propped open by a wooden crate. Someone had just washed the floor and released a dark swirl of water, lacy with white scum, across the pavement, to flow towards the gutter. Smell of coffee and cigarette smoke. Clatter of aluminium. A woman's hoarse voice. At the edge of the kerb someone had dropped a matchbox with a red and white label. I put down my heavy basket and stretched.

A blue-clad workman came out of the café, clumped across the soapy wet. He had a lively expression, sharp brown eyes. Morning, *petite*. I said: I'm a grown-up, if you don't mind. I showed him the *patronne*'s letter with the address written in copperplate. Can you give me directions to the rue des Lilas? He gave me a quizzical look. New girl in town, are you? Working girl? He whistled. I said: what? He explained matter-of-factly. The tarts' house. The *patronne*'s not a bad sort. Everybody knows her. I'll show you the way.

Behind me the bakery door opened, letting out gold light, the smell of warm yeast. Soon, people would start arriving to buy their morning loaves. Take them home to their families. Eat breakfast with their mothers, just as they did every day. I wanted to dive into that yeasty scent, that shop full of loaves warm as mothers. I wouldn't find her. She'd gone. A warm dent in her bed left behind. Absence warm as a loaf. As a child I'd often shared her bed, my arms round her, my head on her shoulder. Snuffing up her warm bed scent. Too old for that now. I scrambled my hands into my pockets, found my hand-kerchief and blew my nose. The workman said: my name's Émile. Allow me to be your escort. He offered me his arm very grandly and I took it. I laid my hand on his blue sleeve. Workmen at home wore these blue jackets in heavy cotton, these blue trousers. A line of men, arm in blue arm, stretching all the way back to Ste-Marie. My mother in her blue apron at

149

the end of the line waving hello to me. Waving goodbye. I said: my name's Jeanne.

Together we walked through the town, Émile carrying my basket. He said: I remember you. The little girl who was crying, that evening near the bridge. Your face is just the same. He swivelled his glance over my coat, my hair twisted up under my beret. I said: it's rude to stare.

Émile pointed out a side street: I work in the garage down at the end there. You can come and visit me, if you like. Tell me how you're getting on. I said: I'll see. Perhaps.

The girls worked at night. They got to bed at dawn. On that first morning there I cleaned the downstairs of the establishment while they still slept. A non-committal building, it seemed, from the outside, in a non-committal street lined with tall stone houses with blue slate roofs. A small round woman opened the door to me. She wore a shiny blue rayon dressing gown, frilled with black lace, which waved round her ankles, pink high-heeled slippers with blue pom-poms, her hair snailed up in pins under a brown hairnet. Small dark eyes expressionless as currants, face glistening with cold cream. Her glance dug into me, checking, assessing. You're Jeanne Nérin? Take your basket downstairs. Your room's the little one off the kitchen. Leave unpacking for the moment. You've work to do.

She drew me inside and closed the door. We stood in a dim hallway smelling of pastry and fried potatoes. A rubbed green velvet curtain hung across a doorframe jutting forwards on the left. A varnished door with an elaborate golden-gilt handle led off to the right. The kitchen's down those stairs there, she said, pointing to the back of the hall: and the *salon*'s through there. Clean the *salon* first. Later on you can bring me a cup of coffee.

She pulled aside the green curtain and tapped away up the staircase it revealed. The curtain swung back into place behind her on its brass rings. Entering the *salon*, I inhaled; sneezed. Wine dregs, stale tobacco, musky scent, sweat. I pulled back the pink rayon curtains, pushed up the turquoise lace blinds, opened the windows. I piled a lacquer tray with dirty glasses, empty bottles and full ashtrays, took them down to the kitchen in the basement. I brought up an armful of cleaning things, then a basket of logs. I swept out the stove, brushed the rugs, collected up crumbs and shreds of tobacco, dusted the little occasional tables and the fluted pink china vases of mauve roses on the mantelpiece. I fingered the stiff crêpe-paper petals, blew on them, re-aligned the vases with the red-flowered porcelain cigarette box and black embroidered fan displayed between them. I swished a miniature feather mop over the ruched lengths of pink artificial silk, gathered in festoons tied up with gold braid, which draped the walls.

The pink brocade sofas were fat and plush. Cosy armfuls you'd call them if they were girls. They lolled about the room sleepily, brazen and half-bare, their covering tasselled shawls, gypsy-bright, slipped to the floor. I flung the shawls back over their tight upholstery, smoothing the purple folds scattered with crimson poppies, straightened their lacy anti-macassars, plumped up their yellow silk cushions, pulled their gilt fringes straight. Sprawling in the white sunlight the seats and divans looked tawdry and tired. They didn't like mornings. They blinked and yawned. I half-lowered the blinds, so that you wouldn't notice the armrests' worn patches and frayed edges. I coaxed footstools into tête-à-têtes, drew armchairs into friendly groups, patted fashion magazines into place near the radiogram. The sofas nudged up against each other and settled down.

I descended once more to the basement and rummaged about my working and sleeping quarters. My whitewashed room off the kitchen, little more than a windowless cupboard, seemed clean enough. A crucifix, threaded with a spray of palm, hung over the narrow bed. I unhooked it and threw it into a corner. I dumped my basket on the blue blanket serving as counterpane, pulled out my nightdress and placed it underneath the thin pillow. No chest of drawers, so I left my changes of underwear in the basket, and hung it on the back of the door. In the chilly kitchen I riddled the range, blew on the embers, put on another log, boiled water, made coffee in a long-handled metal pot. No milk anywhere to be seen. I poured myself a cup of coffee, found a heel of bread, sat down at the kitchen table, propping my feet on a second chair. I allowed myself to think about Maman for just five minutes. I poured the *patronne* a cup of coffee, put it on a tray and carried it upstairs.

On the small first landing a door stood open. Her voice called me: enter. A lamp-lit room. Pictures on the walls of curly-haired little girls playing with kittens and puppies. The drawn-down blinds fastened in the smell, choking and sweet, of violet face powder, violet scent. Seated, taking out her curl-pins, at her dressing table edged by muslin flounces, she was still only halfway between night and day. The bed the same, its tumbled pink sheets not yet put straight. Night-time at noon. Falling asleep at breakfast time. I soon discovered my role in the house: to connect night and day, darkness and light; for people who'd somewhat lost their way. A small brandy at six a.m.?

152

Certainly. A footbath at four in the afternoon? Of course. Massage your shoulders at lunchtime? All right.

The *patronne* liked the way I found my way about and got on with my work without needing her to stand over me, give me orders. After a couple of days, watching me upend a kitchen chair and dust underneath it, she said: your mother's trained you well. She made her sound like a boss in a uniform, not like my mother, who couldn't stand the scratch of wool next to her skin, who could recite the alphabet backwards, who told me the names of stars. Who'd snatch my man and dance the polka with him. Sometimes, before going to bed in my cupboard-sized room in the *patronne*'s house, I kicked my mother's boots, which stood on guard by the door. Sometimes I patted them. Around the house I wore canvas slippers, cast-offs of the *patronne*'s. The boots waited; ready. As long as they stayed in place I'd be all right. I tied their laces together in a bow. I was one boot and my mother the other.

After that first week's trial the *patronne* took me on. I didn't tell her the trial worked both ways. As an employer she'd do. I saw how to manage her. I learned what she liked, then provided it. Bathwater, sprinkled with gritty lavender crystals melting to slush, at just the right temperature. Hot coffee in her favourite green and gold cup. Sheets well aired, properly tucked in, pulled taut. Clean stockings dangling ready over the back of a chair.

On my first afternoon in the house I met the four girls who worked there. Puffy-eyed, yawning, tangle-haired, they thumped into the kitchen for their late breakfast. They erupted: a burst of stale scent, a pattern of pink and blue. Their red-nailed fingers clutched the edges of cotton kimonos sprigged with azure flowers and dotted with rose butterflies. They shuffled in grubby fur-trimmed mules, growled for coffee and cigarettes. Scratching their heads, they grunted to each other. Give us a fag. No, you owe me one. Give us a light, then. One of them, a plump woman of forty or so, started fluffing out her hennaed hair, combing her fringe with her fingers. She blinked as I brought the pan of hot milk to the table. Who's this chicky-chick? Another, younger one, with tired brown eyes, her mousy curls tied up with a length of green net, rubbed her nose. She said: the new skivvy. Fucking slow she is too. Leaning her elbow on the table she crooked her finger: where's the butter? Skip to it, skinnyskiv! A third girl, with a flood of yellow hair, massaged her forehead, groaned with headache. After a shot of brandy in her coffee she perked up. The fourth, olive-skinned and black-eyed, with long, crinkly black hair, a wide mouth, sat silent.

I learned their routine. While I cleared away the dirty crockery and cleaned the range they would play cards, tell fortunes, poke grumbling fun at the clients, do each other's hair, paint each other's toenails. The blonde, milky-skinned and green-eyed, her thick frizz bushing over her shoulders, was the youngest; sixteen or so. The others created youth with wigs and make-up. At night, Madame turned the *salon* lights down low and the girls put on their fancy names: Desirée, Hortensia, Violetta, Pivoine. I peeped at them from the doorway. Decked in skimpy pastel crêpe de Chine slips, arms and legs bare, feet swinging high-heeled satin mules, eyelashes brushed black, mouths transformed to sharp red bows, they waited to be bought. Sugary sweeties on a confectioner's shelves. The men paid, chose their bullseyes, their lollipops, took them upstairs. *Madame la patronne*, coiffed and corseted and rouged, wearing a high-necked pink georgette blouse and plain black satin skirt, pin-heeled black shoes, kept a businesslike eye on the goings-on. Ping! Her bell declared time was up. In 1940, when the Germans arrived, she gained extra customers and made extra money and swelled up with content.

Inside her establishment the girls tried to hide from the war. They lowered their eyelids like window-blinds, and blinked. They clutched each other, merged, like lengths of blackout stitched together. They became a sealed house, its eyes glued shut, which didn't have to notice rows of trucks rumbling past, people being beaten up, posters appearing overnight depicting devils with hooked noses and pendulous lips, slobbering over fistfuls of banknotes. They got on with business as usual: men taking their trousers off and demanding service.

The *patronne* would send me out to queue for food. Outside a grocery shop, a bakery, a butcher's, the lines of women waited. Waited. I crossed my arms and tucked my hands in my armpits, to warm them. I jiggled from foot to foot. I studied the bricks on the wall next to me, dark red veined with yellow and blue. Standing well back behind the press of people, I scratched at the edges of posters, lifted them, tugged them. The paper peeled away in jagged strips I screwed up and put in my pockets. The devil lost an eye, a thumb. The queue shuffled forward. Back at the house the crumpled paper came down to the basement with me and got stuffed into the range.

Sometimes, returning with the bread ration, my pockets plump with paper, I would make a detour to visit Émile. On the first occasion I hovered outside the garage until he saw me and came across the yard. Slender body in bulky overalls. Sharp features softened by his smile. Wiping his black, oily hands on a rag, he offered me just his wrist to shake. I'm finished with this in a couple of minutes. Want to come up and see my room? Inside the open kitchen door his landlady had her back to us. She lifted a pot lid and steam flew out. We slid past her, mounted the stairs. Lino with a worn pattern of red and blue squares. Both of us holding our boots in one hand. Émile's darned grey woollen heels.

Émile sat on the bed and I on a wooden chair. He produced roll-ups and we smoked. The *patron* grows his own tobacco out in the back yard, he sells it to friends, and I get it cheap for keeping my mouth shut.

Harsh stuff, which made me want to cough and spit. Shreds of tobacco stuck on my lips. D'you like music? I like jazz. Émile had been to Paris once and heard jazz in a nightclub. He tried to whistle some bars of it for me, to give me a taste. The radio didn't play jazz; only German tunes. In return, I told him about my attempts at drawing: would you sit for me? No way, Émile replied. He sprang up and walked around the room: I can't sit still for too long! Come on, let's go out. We crept back downstairs. Arm in arm we walked through the backstreets. Émile had a message to deliver.

Messages meant bundles small enough to slip into my bag: newspapers, pamphlets, small pocket-sized flyers, produced in someone's basement. We rolled up the flyers as though they were cabbage leaves and slipped them into people's shopping-baskets in food queues. We spread them out as though they were lost handkerchiefs and slid them behind the windscreen wipers of parked cars. We were correcting German propaganda; giving people the facts.

New facts punched in, winded me. All I could do was try to make sense of them.

One fact was the census being made of Jews. I knew my mother would refuse to sign up to it. In the night she shouted to me from far away: they'll use this against us. She hid in her flat, as I hid in the *patronne*'s house. So far, my mother and I had got away with our identities as Catholics. In the night my mother whispered: for the moment. Then we'll see.

My mother's words combined to form a dream-telegram; I filled in what her dream-message did not say. Strips of white paper, printed with black type, pasted on to the pale slip, delivered a warning. You regarded it fearfully. You read it over and over again. You translated it, tried to make it mean what it did not, put it on the kitchen mantelpiece, fenced in behind iron candlesticks. It glared at you, crouching, ugly. Finally you permitted it to growl, to bark. It alerted you to the future: the police banging on your door in the middle of the night.

Another fact was having to live by German time, set our clocks by Berlin. I marked times and dates keenly, a way of grappling with the facts of the war. You pinned facts down by noting the date. The summer of 1939 had meant the first time that women and old people got the harvest in by themselves, with the men away fighting. June 1941 meant Hitler invading Russia. For Émile and his comrades, this brought new clarity, new urgency. For the house, it worked as an additional layer of felt, denying the possibility of more bad news. For my mother, a tight-lipped wariness as she read the flyers I brought home.

On my rare visits, she spoiled me with caresses, little attentions. She stitched me new petticoats from old pillowcases. She gave me one of her geraniums, grown from cuttings, for my room. Put it on your window sill, water it well, and it'll have pink flowers. Lovely coral-pink.

I held the little green plant in its red earthenware pot, fingered the edge of a frilled, rounded leaf to release its harsh scent. I said: have you seen that man again? The one you were dancing with that time? She said: I bump into him sometimes, at the Fauchons', when I visit them.

She smoothed the table top, brushing off crumbs of earth. She said: we've begun holding meetings there. We're all in the same boat. We keep an eye out for each other.

I handed her the geranium: I haven't got a window sill. Let alone a window. She pushed it back at me: so put it somewhere else!

We sat at her kitchen table and drank weak, re-boiled water smelling of the memory of coffee. She showed me the toy animals she was making for the Fauchon children from wool scraps: the parents don't approve of me but at least now we talk more. She criticised Marie-Angèle: a great big girl like that, lolling around at home! She's so lazy! She accepted the gifts I'd brought her: two little blue and yellow coffee cups from a junk shop, half a bar of soap stolen from the *patronne*.

I asked her: what kind of meetings with the Fauchons? She clicked her tongue. She said: political meetings, of course. As Jews, we need to resist, we need to be organised. She didn't mention Monsieur Jacquotet again, and so neither did I. I wondered whether her group knew Émile's. You hadn't to ask. You'd be super stupid if you did.

All through the winter I worried about her; all through the new year. Worry scraped away at me: what would be the facts of 1942? Throughout the spring I waited for the moment when something decisive would happen, something that would force me to act. I was poised to recognise it: I didn't know what it would be.

In May 1942 the *patronne* offered me a rise. Masked in cold cream, her hair still netted and pin-curled, purple wrapper tied with a red sash, she descended to the kitchen pretending to do a surprise check. Larder shelves scrubbed? Range taken to pieces, scraped free of grease, re-assembled? Her apparent nonchalance, as she prowled about, opening a jar of knife-cleaner, re-folding tea towels, alerted me. I went on swilling out wet soot from ashtrays, waited to see what she really wanted.

She sat down at the table, leaned her bulk sideways, fished in her pocket for cigarettes. She said: I wouldn't say you're particularly gifted at housework. I would say your gifts could lie in other directions. Her fat little starfish hands grasped the match-box. She sucked, puffed, blew out the match. Lipstick from the night before leaked faint red stains into the fissures radiating from her mouth. She smoked thoughtfully. Was she going to sack me? My toes flexed inside my slippers. Ready to make a dash for it.

She said: you'd look a whole lot better if you had some decent clothes.

I stacked the last ashtray on the draining-rack, wiped my hands on my apron. Every morning I donned this enveloping grey garment, similar to my schoolgirl's overall, tying it over my blouse and skirt. Pulling it as tightly as possible around my waist and hips, I controlled my hunger pangs. Like armour the stiff apron gave me courage to attack the cleaning. In the afternoons, when I played lady's maid to madame, I put on a little white apron edged with lace. Her stupid whim, which just added to the pile of laundry. I punished her for that by stealing her left-over bits of brioche and sharing them with the girls. In return they gave me cigarettes.

Madame picked at a thread on her cuff. She said: don't you get bored down here night after night, all by yourself?

She didn't know that I read the books I'd brought with me, that I practised my drawing. Her old newspapers salvaged from the waste basket met my sticks of charcoal. Over reports of politicians' speeches, over announcements about rationing and troop movements and our young men about to be sent away to work in Germany, I drew the curé's cock dancing out, his cock spewing Latin words, his cock fucking the Virgin Mary, his cock first fat as a sausage then curling up like a shrimp. I drew my mother, sitting at the kitchen table in her dressing gown, hands round her bowl of broth. I drew the curve and strain of her back as she scrubbed, wrung, lifted. I drew Monsieur Jacquotet standing thin as a stork on the roof of his house, the town in flames beneath him. I drew Émile, wreathed in jazz memories, lying, feet crossed, on his bed, hands clasped behind his head, roll-up pasted to his lip. The pictures were my witnesses. I was theirs. They were facts.

I turned to face the *patronne*. Mound of purple crêpe. She stubbed out her cigarette, took a gilt-lidded pot from her pocket. She stroked her forefinger against her cheek, rubbing in the cold cream. She massaged her double chin, her thick wrinkled neck. Old, fat, unattractive woman, even though she dyed her hair and rouged her face and cramped herself into corsets and high heels. I was assessing her, judging her, just as one of the clients would do. Ageing meat, marbled with fat, giving off a whiff of corruption. Ghost of plucked moustache on her upper lip. Moles on her neck. I was looking at her with unsentimental eyes. No: with the eyes of dislike. I might try drawing her again, see if a new picture could turn out differently. She'd have to be kinder to me first.

She couldn't be. She'd forgotten how. And I'd turned into someone like a client, who couldn't be kind either.

She plaited her fingers together. Dark liver spots on the backs of her hands. So what would happen to me when I grew older? What would I be like? Fat or thin alive or dead? The *patronne* said: why don't you come and work for me upstairs? I've been given a change of licence. I'll have more business than ever and I need a new girl.

Her gaze measured me. Her eyes ticked down a list: face, breasts, hips, legs. She said: you're too thin, but you're young and fresh, still unspoilt, and that's what they like. You could learn how to do it. Easy.

The women in Monsieur Jacquotet's collection of photographs had been plump. Grinning. What made them so happy? Told to smile? I might have liked to pose for a nude photograph taken by a lover: an astonishing pose, dreamed up by him and me together. Privately, though. Just for him to see. Not for anyone and everyone. Monsieur Jacquotet had never photographed me. When I sat for him nude, he didn't require me to smile. The women in his pictures, half-veiled by their red clothes, looked both haughty and abandoned. Bodies swirled in a wild dance. The nude women in the photographs sat still and spread their legs and grinned. The same poses and gestures repeated again and again. The pictures' layers of paint replicated layers of clothes. You might try to scrape them off and in the end you'd be left with bare flesh, bare canvas. Holes in canvas. Tiny holes. Women embroidered on canvas. They stabbed their needles into tiny holes. The clients stabbed their cocks into the girls. Pierce people enough times and their blood would leak out and they'd be dead.

I said: no thanks, it's not for me, I don't want to.

The *patronne* frowned. Her face puckered into powdered folds. She lit a fresh cigarette. She said: you're a foolish girl.

I folded my arms. Sponge, soap, scrubbing brush, bucket. You gripped your cleaning implements, subdued them to your purposes. When you were done you put them away. You were finished with them. Whereas the girls were the soap, the brush, the bucket of water, and the men said what they needed, what cleaning had to be done, and the girls had to be exact and if they weren't they got into trouble and anyway they had to repeat their housework over and over every night. Scrubbers, everybody called them.

The *patronne* snorted. Goody-goody! Prude! She got up. She said: well then, in that case I want you to start working as the greeter in the hall. I need someone to welcome the clients and show them in. I'm going to engage a daily servant to come in and do the kitchen work and you're to help me upstairs.

For my new duties she fitted me out in one of her old frocks, taken in at the waist: dark blue crêpe de Chine with a lawn collar, an embroidered yoke and three-quarter sleeves. I donned black stockings, high wedge heels. She insisted I fasten on a corset, to give myself the right flowing shape. Thick canvas and rubber skin smoothed my sharp angles. She donated a second frock: dark red. It waited for me, flung across my bed. I did up my hair in the chignon I'd learned from Monsieur Jacquotet. The *patronne* yanked out the pins, raked my hair back down, brushed it up again, into swoops and rolls.

Wearing my new clothes, I tested out becoming a stranger. Sitting for Monsieur Jacquotet I'd been shape, form, texture; the memory of his wife; a sort of daughter. He'd seen me and also he hadn't seen me. Ghost-hunting our game. Secret. No witnesses. Now I took a step away from all that. The short, clinging dress made me visible to anyone who came in; the first doll you saw when you entered the toyshop.

The job entailed smiles and politeness. I listened for the bell, opened the door, showed clients into the salon. The *patronne* prided herself on making customers feel special. I had to pretend to each regular who turned up that he was our favourite. Oh, sweetie, it's you! Oh, do come in! The *patronne*'s new licence meant that now we catered for Germans. Unbuttoning their uniforms the soldiers turned back into ordinary men, and like them had to be put at their ease.

Unable to understand their language, I studied the clients' behaviour, sized them up. Their blushes and bashful sideways looks, their loud laughs, their smug smiles. Their nervous or eager mounting of the stairs. Their noisy bravado, arms around the girls' waists. Their relief as they trotted back down. Before I went to bed, in the early mornings, I seized a pencil and committed the men's expressions, their gestures, to paper. A flung-out arm. A belly bulging over the waistband of trousers. A hand tugging an earlobe, smoothing an upper lip. Also I drew myself, wearing my costume of lies.

I went on drawing Émile too, from memory, head under the bonnet of a car, or flat on his back right underneath the engine, just his feet, in their patched boots, sticking out. I drew Maurice as well. Officially he wasn't a client but the *patronne*'s old friend who'd helped her get her change of licence. He was a special case; his pass for breaking the curfew waved in his hand. The *patronne* explained to me: he comes when he's in between mistresses. He's a good customer. Be nice to him!

He arrived late; outside official hours. The air in the house grown stale, my feet aching from running up and down stairs in high heels, I was shrinking. The tired walls leaned in on me, and I had to prop them up. Brown wallpaper patterned with pink roses. Smell of snuff and our breakfast soup of boiled onions. Rat-tat on the door. Blur of sleek black overcoat, black moustache, black hair. He threw his outdoor things at me, shouldered past into the salon. I peered after him. Hands on hips, legs wide apart, pelvis thrust forward, he posed for his audience. Big laugh showing white teeth.

His hands dived into his pockets, tossed out paper-wrapped packages. He'd brought impossible luxuries: a chunk of *saucisson*, a pat of butter, a pot of *rillettes*. The *patronne* tried to keep her face impassive but her smile broke out as she darted forward to accept these gifts. Maurice's mouth curled as the girls fell on his bounty. They exaggerated their gratitude, trying to please him I suppose, they put on high little voices and jumped about, exclaiming: Oh, a real country breakfast, just like in my childhood! Their lips glistening with pork fat, they lisped out their praise while he smiled scornfully. Next day I drew Maurice's hands offering these goods, the *patronne*'s accepting them, the jangling space between ringing like a till.

He departed at dawn. The *saucisson* he'd left us sat on a blue plate. We regarded it solemnly, calculating the number of slices it would yield. The *patronne* said: I can't remember what *saucisson* tastes like! She eyed me: you won't want any of this. Jews don't eat pork. I shrugged: I wouldn't know.

She let her face sag. She groaned: I'm exhausted. She dropped her bulk into an armchair, kicked off her high-heeled shoes, burped, farted. The girls and I were all yawning. I said: may I go to bed now? How often will I have to stay up this late? Surely it's not worth it, just for one client. The *patronne* tried to flex her toes, winced. Mind your manners, you.

Desirée stirred from her slouch on the sofa. She said: but he's too rough, that fucker. You have to handle him just right or you're in trouble.

Violetta dug in her pocket, offered her a cigarette. The *patronne* said: he's a moody bastard, that's all. You mustn't provoke him.

Handling the men right meant studying them, deciding on tactics, being kindly with some, teasing and playful with others. At the beginning of the night, this was possible. But as the hours wore on, the girls grew tired, bored, brisk. They yawned behind their hands, and sulked. They heaved themselves to their feet when required and stomped off upstairs to get on with it.

One hot night in early June, when business was slack, I sat downstairs in the kitchen and worked on a drawing of an empty sawed-open tin of pilchards. Madame shouted for clean glasses. Up I tramped with my tray. Maurice, the sole visitor, lolled on a small sofa in between Hortensia and Pivoine, waving a photograph. Isn't she sweet? They were giggling dutifully, teasing him shrilly as required, arching their plucked eyebrows, poking him in the belly. Beside him, on a little what-not, Pierrot the china harlequin, masked, pointing one black ballet slipper, hoisted his lamp. A gold flex trailed down like a tail. On the other side, on a matching spindly-legged stand, the china dancer flung up her stiffened, sequined net skirt to reveal her stocking-tops and drawers. Hey Janny-fanny, hey little Columbine, said Maurice: take a look.

Small girl, aged nine or so, curly-haired and plumpish, wearing a pale school overall tied at the waist. I recognised Marie-Angèle. The torn right-hand edge of the photo showed it had been ripped away from a wider one. You could just see some pale folds of cloth. A second child, in an identical overall, had stood there once. Who'd torn the photo in half? Where was my image now? I'd have liked to have had it, to show to Émile. Marie-Angèle's mother had promised to give mine a copy of the picture but she'd never got round to it.

I said nothing, just nodded, and carried my tray over to the sideboard. The *patronne* said: so you like little children, do you, naughty man? The girls squealed and squeaked, as required. Ooh: naughty pervert! They tossed their ringlets and raised their hands and pouted. Maurice handed out cigarettes. The girls lit up, began sighing, talking about their parents, their homes. From the side pockets in their slips they produced their own photographs to show Maurice: look, my baby brother. And this is my papa. And this is my little daughter. The air in the salon seemed to soften. Doves cooed in unison. Maurice looked bored.

Violetta had a hole in the side seam of her tight rose-coloured slip. Her flesh bulged through it. Maurice prodded it. Fatso! She stuck out her lip: don't be mean, darling! He pinched her. She yelped, and he smiled. The bell in the hall rang. A party of Germans clattered in. Back to business.

Later on, the bell rang again, summoning me to the hall, and I ran up from the kitchen. Maurice was leaving. When I handed him his hat and coat, he thrust an arm around my waist, pressed his mouth on to mine, stuck his tongue between my lips. I jerked my head away. He pinched my neck. Little tight-cunt! So chaste and superior. The girls are more honest than you. Come on. A quick fuck. Just five minutes.

The *patronne* called me from the salon. I pushed him out of the door and went in to her.

The following afternoon, as usual, I helped the *patronne* dress. I gathered up her belly and laced her into her corsets, put a net cape around her shoulders, released her hair from its curl-pins, one by one, and began to arrange her coiffure. She lit a cigarette and smoked in silence for a while. I could feel her enjoying the hit of the nicotine. That was my pleasure too, whenever I got hold of a cigarette: the drug stroking me, soothing me. When you felt lonely, cigarettes filled you up, gave you something to bite on, suck on. You were the baby, in charge of your cigarette mother. Also the fags stopped you feeling so hungry. You didn't bawl for food.

I started working out how to draw the *patronne*, the muscles deep beneath the flesh. She said: he's a good friend, that one. So don't go being rude to him. Be pleasant.

She caught my eye in the mirror: I hope we shan't lose him once he's married. Much better he should come here than have affairs.

I peered at Madame's grey roots. I lifted a fistful of hennaed curls, coaxed them to lie on top of each other and disguise the whitening hair underneath. I combed some tendrils into a fringe on her forehead. The *patronne* lifted her hand mirror and studied the effect. She bent forwards, groaning and puffing, to roll on her stockings. She said: help me on with my shoes. I didn't like touching her deformed, bent-over toes, even under their veil of silk. Nonetheless I knelt in front of her and eased her misshapen feet into her high heels. She groaned theatrically: oh my poor corns! She heaved herself up: you should have another day off sometime soon.

I said: I'd like to go home and visit my mother.

She shrugged. All right. Behave yourself properly with my visitors, and you can stay the night at your mother's.

She forgot about her offer, and I had to prompt her. A week later, she let me go. I walked home to Ste-Marie-du-Ciel under a blue sky. We were moving towards midsummer: the air smelled of ripe grass and warm earth. The fields on either side of the road showed the high green of wheat. Buzzards circled overhead. En route I got stopped twice by German soldiers at checkpoints. Once they recognised me they grinned, didn't ask to see my papers, slapped my backside. Fräulein Johanna! I shut my eyes and counted one two three. I opened my eyes, smiled, walked on.

My mother in her black widow's dress looked lean as a vanilla pod. Older. We hugged each other, sniffing. Look. There's a cup of milk. I saved it for you specially. Her thin arms, reaching around me like string, looped me to her; a parcel of love. Madame Fauchon had given me a cup of milk. She'd been pregnant with her third. Four little parcels by now to care for.

I drank the milk. Maman sat opposite me at the kitchen table. She'd spread a clean tea towel over the oilcloth, to protect her work. She fiddled with her sewing scissors, a little heap of children's grey woollen coats and jackets, and watched my every gesture. She said: how's the job? Her hands teased a spiky shape of yellow material.

I said: what's that you're sewing? She answered: it's for Madame Fauchon's children, you know we've become better friends these past months, we try and help each other out. She began to fold up the coats: now, darling, tell me about how you're getting on.

I said: may I have something to eat? I'm very hungry. She jumped up immediately: there isn't much.

Where before she'd saved the outer leaves of lettuces and cabbages as greenstuff for her rabbits, where before she'd nourished her hens in the backyard with the tops and peelings of carrots, the skins of onions, now she simmered them all for soup. The hens had been boiled long ago. The starved rabbits, very lean, had been killed and eaten the winter before. Two rabbits, roasted, stewed, potted, had stretched to many meals, their picky sharp bones then seethed for bouillon. I shelled a fistful of haricot beans. I soaked the pods in hot water, added them to the vegetable stock. I'd stolen some peppercorns and some coarse salt from the *patronne*'s kitchen, hiding them in separate fingers of my glove. One fingertip could dip into salt and lick it; one into pepper. The soup could be seasoned.

My mother and I argued over what to do with the two small potatoes she possessed: whether to add them to the broth or save them for tomorrow. She pardoned the potatoes, put them back into the hanging wire cupboard outside the back door; they could live another day.

She cleared away her sewing things, laid the cloth. She winced, sank back into her chair at the table. My asthma's worse.

Her shoulders drooped and her back humped. Suddenly I could see how she'd look as an old woman. Steam issued in clouds from the saucepan, beaded the wall. Living in this damp flat, she was prey to the moisture that seeped up from the lino covering the earth floor and through the flaking plaster. Sunshine leaked around the small window, reminding us it was summer outside. Nonetheless I kept my coat on: the kitchen felt chilly as well as damp; the cooking-stove gave out little heat. Maman grimaced: the landlord comes round for the rent all right, but he won't do any repairs, the bastard.

I tied an apron over my coat, pushed up my sleeves, began scouring the sink. My mother's voice jumped up behind me: I know what goes on in that house where you work. One of the neighbours told me. I want you to leave the job and come back home.

I turned round. Crossly smoothing the oilcloth, filling the pepper pot, the salt shaker, she looked small as a child. A child I could punish. When you've got a child you've got power over her. You can hurt her. You can ignore her, try to have all the fun. You can push her away, flirt with her man, dance with him, leave the girl out.

I said: I'll make my own decisions, thanks. You don't know what you're talking about! And we need the money, you know we do.

My mother said: I'm ashamed of you. Letting yourself be degraded like that. Where's your self-respect? Her face quivered. I could not let myself feel tender towards her. Instead I felt tender towards the sink, which was something I knew how to deal with. I wiped the white enamel as though it were a child's face. I wriggled a cloth into the ends of the taps and cleaned the green slime from them as though they were a child's nostrils crusted with snot. My mother set out plates and spoons, a jug of water. Glancing at each other, tacitly we agreed a truce. She opened the cutlery drawer, rattled her hand inside it. She produced a new subject of conversation. Marie-Angèle had a boyfriend. She'd heard all about it from Marie-Angèle's mother, when she went up to the rue de la Croix to do the washing. She said: a good job, wonderful prospects, apparently. If she gets married she'll probably need some sewing done. So that could mean a little extra money coming in.

Maman began inspecting the cutlery. She looked up from polishing a spoon. She said: I'll manage, you know.

Steam from the cooking pot cocooned her. I couldn't reach her. I wanted to jump up and down like the lid on a boiling saucepan. She lined up the spoons with her fingertips, patting them into place. She said: why should I leave? I'm not a refugee Jew. I'm a French citizen, I've lived here all my life and my parents before me. Across the kitchen the yellow scraps bundled on top of the sewing-box rose up: tiny gendarmes thumbing their noses. I said: you know as well as I do, if the Germans decide to de-naturalise you, that's that. Maman said: where would I go? And what about you?

I chopped up the moment into a collage. Two white soup plates, fluted rims stencilled with worn green chevrons, on the red and white checked oilcloth. A pair of brown hands. Stars of yellow material. Her gold wedding ring. I studied the bits of images as I ladled out our watery mush. Later on I'd draw them. I said: other people you know must be leaving. She agreed: the Fauchons are going down to Spain, but they've had to get new papers first, it's cost them their life savings. I haven't got money like that.

Other people. Fauchons, Jacquotet, Nérins. Names on papers, on cards. A long silver nib reaching down, marking them with indelible ink, then long silver tweezers plucking them up, lifting them out, dropping them into a hat. Pick a card. Any card. This one will live this one will die.

I said: how are they getting hold of the papers?

Maman said: someone who works in the town hall,

apparently. She stood the salt pot and pepper pot side by side, like a bride and groom. She glanced at me: obviously, they don't know his name. Sleek as a seal, Monsieur Fauchon described him, very well-dressed. Black hat, black overcoat. Sounds a pretty sharp customer to me.

The long summer evening would confine me to the same room as my mother. Night would pack me into my narrow bed in its corner. My mother seemed to think I was still a child she scolded, forgave, tucked up. She was clutching at me. I wanted to clutch her back and also I wanted to break out, break the curfew, run up and down the street, shouting, just to prove that I could. My mother sewed. I watched. She bit off the end of her thread, wrapped up the children's clothes in a piece of brown paper tied with a length of old string: you can take these across in the morning. Make sure you ask for the paper back.

When darkness fell we moved niftily around each other, checking the blackout was properly in place, undressing, extinguishing the lamp. I was imprisoned by anxious dreams in which I lost my way home. I kept kicking the coverlet off and waking up sweating. Over and over I dreamed that Monsieur Jacquotet was calling for me from where he balanced, trapped, on the roof of his house. If I reached him in time I'd be able to put out the flames. He gazed at me sorrowfully. Where are you? Why have you abandoned me? I burst into tears. But you told me not to come back!

I woke late next morning. Maman had gone off to work in a hurry, leaving an unmade bed, a toss of clothes. When I took down the blackout yellow light spilled across the room. Too bright. Noisy, like the blare of a military trumpet. I couldn't control the light, the noise. Instead I tidied the room, did up my hair, smoothed the creases from my clothes.

172

I'd run out of books to read. The kitchen shelf was bare except for the cookery book: pamphlets and magazines all gone. I searched for Maman's store of novels, at length discovered them hidden under the bed, wrapped in a dustsheet. I picked out a couple and shoved them into my coat pocket.

Maman had put out a piece of bread for me on a plate. A jug with the last of the milk. I covered them with cloths, against the flies. Childish slop. Let her have it for supper. I wanted a slice of *saucisson*, a tot of eau-de-vie.

More than that I wanted to see Monsieur Jacquotet. My soft parcel under my arm, I took the back ways to the top of town, hurrying up the stone staircases fitted between buildings, scurrying up the steep alleys. The town was quiet, the shops all closed. I met nobody. My path was deserted, as though everybody had left in the night.

Emerging into the Place Ste Anne, I began to cross it in the direction of the school. Monsieur Jacquotet's front door stood open. Wood panels fragile as a biscuit. Ste Anne and the Virgin stared down from their niche next door. Just outside the high gate of the convent, a group of townspeople had collected; a small crowd standing to one side, watching. A band of children loitered on the pavement, shifting and shoving. Why had they come out of school? Some of them clutched what looked like pieces of paper. I went closer. The gutter was scattered with torn-up photographs, little white bones, dead mice, dead voles. The lid of a cake tin. A string of dried apple slices. The children poked each other, giggling. They darted forwards and picked up more scraps of paper, waved these talismans in the air. One boy said to another: they found lots of bones buried in the garden. The corpses of children! The second boy said: they need little Christian babies. They need their blood! They hissed dramatically, stamped their feet and waved their arms, mock-roaring. A third boy said: once he kidnapped two little girls who were never seen again!

Voices called in German inside the house. Two German soldiers emerged from the dark opening of the front door. They shouted at the children, who ran away, letting fall their spoils. Drifts of torn-up black and white photographs. A breast. A triangle of fur. A hand. The Germans bawled at the silent group of men and women. They averted their heads, dispersed. I turned away, pressed myself into the school doorway, tried to vanish.

The Germans came back out, carrying paintings. They threw the canvases into a pile on the ground beyond the gutter. Some framed, some just on stretchers. A big, jagged heap. A higgledy-piggledy tower, like a sculpture of a star. The soldiers poured liquid from a can on to the stack of wood, set a match. Flames roared up, wavery scarlet, transparent in the still air. Painted canvas flared and crackled as the fire bit into it, and smoke billowed out in thick grey clouds.

Maurice came out of a side street, his black coat folded over his arm. He stood still for a moment, swivelling his gaze about, taking in the scene. He skirted the bonfire blaze, walked up to the open front door of Monsieur Jacquotet's house, watched by the children from their safe distance. He spoke to the two soldiers: a few French words, a few in German. They nodded, stood aside. He went in. The soldiers followed him, banged shut the door.

I waited a few minutes, then strolled off as casually as I could. Once I was out of the square I ran down to the rue de la Croix, to the cobbler's shop. A large sign hung over the window: Jewish establishment. The drawn shutters sealed the shop away from my gaze: look all you like; we're not here; we've gone for ever.

I rapped on the Fauchons' door, pushed at the handle. The locked door pushed back. Go away. Leave us alone. Madame Fauchon's voice whispered: who is it? I tried to magic my voice into a key: it's Jeanne. Her indrawn breath. Silence. A scrape of iron. She let me in.

She'd turned into a blonde with bright yellow hair. She wore smart clothes: pleated wool blouse, woollen skirt, highly polished shoes. She stood back, gesturing. Come in, quick, quick. She bolted the door behind me. We shook hands. She looked pale, and almost as thin as my mother. The shop was bare: someone had cleared out all the shoes. Run off with them. The shoes had run away. No rows of brown paper bags on the shelves, no scuffed boots toppled in heaps on the counter awaiting mending. Three brown leather suitcases, one big and two smaller ones, secured by straps, stood to one side. Madame Fauchon's glance followed mine. Her hand went up to her earlobe, touched the red spot where her earring had been, then flung away.

I held out my parcel: here's the sewing from my mother. Madame Fauchon put her finger to her lips: the little ones are having their nap. She picked up a broom and began sweeping sawdust out of a corner. I put the parcel on the counter. I smoothed the brown paper, pulled the string straight. My lips formed shapes of words I couldn't utter.

If you asked a question you risked getting an answer you couldn't bear. I managed to whisper. Do you know where

Monsieur Jacquotet is? She said: he's staying with us. He's been ill with bronchitis, but he's getting better.

Hide him in the house of your friendship. Your fragile house. We were small as mice, ants, birds. We tried to hide in our houses woven of straw, our houses of feathers, our houses of twigs. The Germans saw through our walls and could smash them any time they liked. Just one blow of a fist. They'd do it deliberately, as a punishment. Coldly. Not losing control. They'd calculate the force necessary and just beat the house until it collapsed, broken and bleeding. Marie-Angèle's book of fairy tales fell open at the page of the big bad wolf. Huff and puff huff and puff and I'll blow your house down. The wolves spared some houses because they could be useful. They appreciated the graceful proportions of Monsieur Jacquotet's *salon*, the elegant spaces upstairs: they were civilised wolves. What would they do with all his furniture? Chop it up for firewood, perhaps. What would they do with his garden? Dig it up for vegetables.

I said: can I do anything to help? Madame Fauchon didn't bother replying. She worked the shavings into a heap in the centre of the floor. I skipped out of her way as her broom knocked against my feet. I looked around, saw a dustpan behind the door, stooped to pick it up. She said: it's kind of your mother to help me. Say thank you for me.

She clutched her broom as though it were a child she were trying to calm down. You held on, steady and tight, while the child thrashed in a tantrum. No. Herself she was holding on to. Studying her broom's sturdy handle, its clogged bristles, she spoke in a low voice: the two little ones are coming with me and the older two are staying with their father and Monsieur

Jacquotet. Just for the moment, until their papers come through. They'll catch up with us as soon as possible.

I crouched in front of her, holding the dustpan steady. With one strong push of the broom she swept the pile of debris into it. *Voilà!*

From the room above came a child's wail. Tuneless music of distress. A moment's pause before a second piping cry joined in. Wobbling, then insistent. Madame Fauchon said: I must see to the children. Go up to Monsieur Jacquotet if you like, but don't stay long. He's still very tired. He's in our room, at the top of the stairs. I said: I've got to get back to work, in any case.

Dark wooden bedhead, white pillow. White sheet pulled up to his striped flannel collar. His eyes opened, saw me. I tiptoed forward. Hello. He wasn't asking for anything. He just lay there. I said: pyjamas. I didn't ever imagine you wearing pyjamas. I sat down on the bed, took off my shoes, swung up my legs. We lay on our sides, holding each other. He felt frail, as though he'd been wounded, then mended. If I embraced him too hard he'd shatter. He was light. If I didn't hold on to him he'd float out of the window, away away. Perhaps that was where he wanted to go. Away away. Behind his shoulder, on the night-stand, a white plate bore a small green apple, a brown-handled knife, saw-edged, laid across rim to rim. A tumbler of water, a folded newspaper.

His breath smelled syrupy, medicinal. He whispered: I gave him a painting as payment.

Ironed white linen cloth, lace-edged, on the night-stand. Tiny brown stain. In one part of my mind, time collapsed. We'd always be here, together, and we'd find our way towards each other clumsy sure silent confident. Why did language break up when I most needed it why couldn't I speak why didn't I know what to say? In another part of my mind someone warned: two minutes left to us, perhaps, before the rap at the ceiling: time to go, be off with you Jeanne. If only I could have known him longer, loved him longer. If only we'd had more time. I wanted to heap love on to him, give him everything I hadn't been able to give before, make it up to him, rescue him feed him happiness tell him how much I'd always loved him, but it was far too late for that indulgence, I had to hang back, just meet his gaze, tell my fingers to remember for ever the touch of his cheek. Under my hand his heart beat steadily.

I walked back to Ste-Madeleine. In the early evening I joined the girls in the *salon*. They sprawled around the room. Their faces seemed anonymous and closed as shops. I asked them if I might do drawings of them. They sat up straighter. Suit yourself. It makes a change from cards and manicures.

Monsieur Jacquotet had once described to me Degas's prints of tired whores posed thighs apart on couches, their rucked-up chemises showing their private parts. Drooping shoulders; frizzed hair; battered expressions. Pictures for other men to look at. You fucked the whore, all brightly painted up for you, and then afterwards you looked at her picture, her dead eyes, the exhausted slump of her face, and mused: oh poor girl. Or you praised Degas's brutal, uncompromising honesty. Whereas the girls in the *patronne*'s house wanted portraits that made them look their individual best, just like anyone else, done up in Sunday frocks and hats with their hair nicely set and waved. Photographs were good to give to their families, but who could afford the photographer's studio? Anyway, a pencil sketch, coloured in, was proper art. And done by me it was free. So I set to with pastels, rubbing and smudging.

Oh, you're so good at drawing, the girls exclaimed. My pictures were as skewed as those of Monsieur Degas, perhaps; but in the opposite direction. He painted girls looking pathetic and desperate; I drew them looking prosperous and well dressed, rosy-cheeked. I drew them as they wanted to be seen.

That night, in the hall, I let Maurice kiss me and fondle my breast. I stroked his cheek smelling of lemon verbena and said: why should I give it to you for nothing? You pay the girls, after all. Maurice said: little miss cock-teaser. Little miss hard-to-get.

Did Marie-Angèle guess what he got up to on his visits to Ste-Madeleine? What did he get up to with her? What would he look like with his clothes off? I put on a schoolgirlish voice: I'd like to get to know you a little bit first, that's all.

His arm tightened around me until I gasped. He let me go: skinny ribs! He pinched my thigh through my frock. We arranged to meet next day in the local bar. Late morning, the girls and the *patronne* still fast asleep, I took a chance and slid out.

Later on I'd try and turn it into a sketch. Maurice's black hat on his black knee. His hand on my red crêpe thigh. The Germans packed in around the little tables, drinking tall glasses of golden beer. Grey-green legs stretched out, blocking the space. Blue spirals of smoke. Blue eyes summing me up: Maurice's bit of skirt. I'd draw the scene very correctly. I was behaving very correctly, according to the rules of the *patronne*'s house. A knowing, come-hither smile. Legs crossed, feet pointing in parallel, one curled-over hand tipping my chin. I'd draw my gestures: tilt of head, crook of finger, flap of eyelash.

The scenes I'd lived through with Monsieur Jacquotet had been freely invented by us both according to no rules. Was that

179

true? How could I know? Anyway, those images had to be cut off, kept invisible, safe inside me. Perhaps one day I'd go back to them. Anyway, that had been love. Nothing to do with sex. No. Don't lie. Both. I didn't know what to call it. Why weren't there words for it? Words were no good. They separated everything. They could not possibly explain what you felt. Red-hot wires pierced me. Don't think about him. He's absence, he's got to depart, I love him, I'll never see him again. I wriggled my shoulders at Maurice and simpered and said: it's so nice to get out of the house sometimes. Life in there can be so dull. This is a real treat.

He ordered us a small glass of white wine apiece, gave me a cigarette. We eyed each other and smoked. Around us sonorous German voices lilted. Words melted together into long, warm sentences. Golden as gingerbread. The gingerbread house in the forest. The witch was dead. Cut up for stews long ago. Her gingerbread house ransacked. Ordinary men ordinary speech. Soft and melodious, unlike the abrupt, barking sounds you heard on the street. In here the German language became a rich flow, rising and falling. Their laughter sounded just like the laughter of Frenchmen.

Maurice said: those hand-me-downs don't suit you. You could do with some decent clothes. He touched my forefinger with his own. He stroked his fingertip across the back of my hand. Smooth touch. Surely one finger was just like any other. One skin touching another. Hundreds of fingers all feeling the same. If you shut your eyes you couldn't tell one man's finger from another. Maurice put his hand over mine and smiled at me. So, little Janny-fanny, wouldn't you like a new dress? Is that what you'd like? Or something else? Tell me.

180

A man in blue jacket and trousers walked in, glanced at me. Émile. I glanced back, away. He went up to the bar, murmured briefly to the *patronne*. Maurice asked: friend of yours, is he? All the men here know you, don't they? His eyes sneered. I shrugged, twirled the wine in my glass. I put on an indifferent voice: never seen him before in my life.

Émile left me alone. He understood me as I did him: business. When he and I made love in his room it wasn't business, and he wasn't a customer but a friend. The first time, with just twenty minutes before the *garagiste*'s wife would shout up to Émile that his supper was ready, we hurried, bumping and struggling on the slippery quilt. Émile took over and I let him, he fumbled and shoved. I wasn't myself but his pocket and I hated him as he thrust and yelped. Afterwards, he lit us roll-ups and said: I blew it, didn't I? Sorry.

Our bare shoulders were touching. I wanted my clothes back on. I composed a polite little speech. Never mind, everything's all right. I stubbed out my cigarette and flung back the sheet.

The second time, on a Sunday, the *garagiste* and his wife gone foraging in the woods towards Ste-Marie, and their flat empty except for us, silent except for our breathing, the chime of the clock outside, we took longer. Time for a long, wandering conversation. Sex flowed out of talking, into talking, in and out of talking. Émile wetted his finger and smoothed my eyebrows: they're lovely, Jeannina, thick as caterpillars. All furry and black. When you frown they go all wriggly. He kissed me, put his fingers into me, stroked me. I stroked him back. We found our way: rhythmical, rocking. Then an invented irregular dance. We both burst out laughing at the same time: jazz! Then rhythmical again. He waited for me: we went on for what seemed a long time, steadily, then time vanished, I lost myself, cried out, and then he did, which made me cry out more. Diving into the sky; a great golden parachute expanding, blooming, plummeting down; falling silk collapsing over us.

The sheets tumbled about our legs, we smoked. Émile said: we'll have to be careful. Just make love at the right time. We don't want to be making a baby. I watched a tiny spider abseil down from the dusty corner of the ceiling, pick its delicate way across Émile's belly. An acrobat spider waving its slender legs. I put out my finger and the spider balanced on it. I said: don't we? Why not? Émile rolled away from me. White shoulder blades dusted with freckles. He said: I don't know how much longer I'll be around. I may have to go away quite soon. I touched his back. The spider wrote on his skin. Émile brushed away the spider-words, scratched himself.

Maurice clapped on his hat. He said: until tonight, then.

While the *patronne* and the girls were busy with clients, I took him downstairs, to my cubbyhole off the kitchen. Looking at the cramped space, the narrow bed, he grimaced and said: it's like a convent cell. Are you a nun, darling? I'd love to fuck a nun.

Diagrams for gestures and poses existed. I remembered the photographs in Monsieur Jacquotet's magazines. I remembered Degas's tiredly expert whores. Maurice knelt astride me. He whispered: say something filthy, show me how dirty you are.

His big hands pressing my shoulders. His cock soft. I wasn't sure what to say. I blurted out bits of bawdy I'd heard from the girls gossiping off duty. He pinched my breast. Make it more exciting.

The pornography kept in the *salon* upstairs for the clients to flick through was all pictures, not words. I had to make up my own. I recited all the swear words I'd ever heard used in the street by brawling men, all their insults they could fling at each other like stones. Cunt cunt cunt. Big rude boys shouting in the playground. Next I took up all the prayers that priests had made for the Virgin, their sexless perfect darling who had no cunt at all. I twisted together these two hymns, turned them topsy-turvy. With every half-sentence I uttered Maurice hit me, staccato, his blows on my backside punctuating my tirade. I heard someone whimpering like an animal. Who is she? Where is she that animal? Not here upstairs up up up, I flew up to the ceiling and looked down at a picture. Red black brown white. Her white tits, his brown buttocks lifting and falling, brown shoulders with a black mole, a red cock, cocked, a gun cocked, the man's cock rises, he shoves into the girl, his redness splits her white. Now just shut up! He increases his speed, fucks her harder. He gasps. You love this don't you? Ask for it. Ask for more. The girl cries oh yes yes I love it give me more give me more. He leans forwards resting on one elbow slaps her hips plunges thrusts twice ready to fire his shot jerks out of her yells triumphantly shoots across the sheets.

I fell down from the ceiling, landed back on the bed. I wasn't there, I didn't do it, I wasn't there. We both lay still. Winded. He stirred and said: I'm not wasting my come on you. You weren't a virgin, you little tart.

I brought him a bowl of warm water, soap and a clean towel, washed him. He stood shivering and gasping. Big brown body. Curling black hair. He looked bewildered. Wide dark eyes. The boy waking from his bad dream. He put out a tentative hand and touched mine: you understand me. I can't control it. Soft towel blotted his words, the tears that stood in his eyes. I handed him his clothes, helped him dress, flung on my dressing gown, escorted him back upstairs into the hall, handed him his hat and coat.

He brushed his hat lightly on his sleeve, stroked his moustache. He said: if you don't want a new dress what do you want? I said: get rid of my mother's food card in the town hall. Make her records vanish. So that the Germans can't find her if ever they come looking.

Don't ask for too much. Don't ask him to lose my food card too. Anyway, I was well hidden here. Just a piece of the furniture: a footstool, a doormat, a drinks tray, a chamberpot. Germans saw me every day, knew my name, took little notice of me. On Madame's orders I kept out of their way. They got drunk with the girls, not with me.

Maurice smiled: what's the little word? I said: please please please. Looking into my face, he pinched my cheek. Tears started up in my eyes and he squeezed my hand: did I hurt you? I'm so sorry.

He flicked my nose: is your mother's hooter as big as yours? No good getting rid of a food card with a nose like that.

The following night it rained. He arrived carrying a bulky paper parcel under one arm. He thrust his streaming umbrella at me, his damp hat. He made a fuss about his black cashmere coat, insisting I hang it up extra carefully so that it wouldn't be pulled out of shape by the wet. Tonight he'd become the wolf on two legs. Covered head to foot in thick dark fur. Those fairy tales I'd read as a child: I fitted Maurice in amongst the book's pages. I'd illustrate his story. A black-haired prince in slashed sleeves, slashed breeches, who turned into an ogre once midnight struck. Outside in the dark and the rain he prowled on all fours;

starving and nameless; lonely. He longed for company. He was cruel because he didn't know whether or not other people felt pain and he wanted to find out and also he wanted to give them his pain to keep for their own. His blonde fiancée, dressed in white organza, sat at home drinking hot chocolate, toasting her bare feet on the fender, approaching her soles to the red scorch of the flames.

The fairy stories mixed into the girls' gossip about their clients. Four grumpy princesses discussed the prince clad in black fur. At the drop of a black felt hat yes he could turn into a wolf. He could turn into an ogre. Except you didn't realise he was an ogre because he looked at you with tenderly shining eyes. What's wrong with you? Why won't you trust me? He enticed you in to play with him because he made you feel you could help him, rescue him. Then he hurt you. No, but he doesn't really mean it. Underneath, he's just a little boy lost. So you shouldn't sulk at the things he wants to do. Stupid girl! You should get out of there! No, he told me he had an awful child-hood, his foster parents made him sleep in a shed, even in winter. Yes, and they beat him, I do feel so sorry for him. And who amongst us didn't get beaten, may I ask? No, but for him it was worse. No, one day he'll go too far and then you'll feel sorry for yourself, idiot. And who'll take any notice of that? Idiot yourself. Just close your trap! Get lost go screw yourself!

Once out of the dark, wet street, indoors in the warm house, Maurice turned from glittery-eyed wolf back into charmer. He preened himself as I watched. Raindrops sparkled on his black shoulders, slid to the floor. He dumped his parcel on the floor, pulled off his ogre-skin, threw it at me. I caught it, slung it over my arm, took his hat. He took pieces of torn-up paper and card

185

from his wallet, showed them to me, slid them back. I imagined him eating them, chewing them between his strong white teeth.

He said: you had the right idea. The Germans often wander in and search through the food cards. Looking for Jewish-sounding names. They've got good memories.

The shapes of typed letters hanging in the air even when the cards disappeared. Crisp and black, like print on a poster, like a sign over a shop, there for everybody to read. I felt breathless. He was watching me. He said: careful with my coat! He took out his cigarette case, lit a cigarette. I slipped a hanger inside his coat, hung it up on a brass hook. Water dripped from it on to the floor. Names were like coats. You put on new ones and disguised yourself. But Maurice watched, a sharp couturier, pointed a finger: those name-coats don't fit.

His voice stayed casual. Musing. How a husband might sound, home from work. Preoccupied, shrugging off the working day along with his coat, not quite arrived yet, still in transition, still thinking about the office. He said: they're very methodical. Checking numbers at the moment. New orders. I don't know. Lots of activity.

His words translated themselves: fists battering doors frailer than matchboxes, voices wailing. He dropped his match on to the floor, looked at me with kind eyes: do you want help with anything else? I'll come down later, shall I?

The hallway air shivered. The rainy night pressed at my back like hands. Perhaps he'd just come from seeing Marie-Angèle. She and I had been sort-of friends once. No longer. She had too much of everything and I didn't have enough.

The girls and I had that in common. When we couldn't steal, we bartered. Having got to know each other, we made exchanges. Cautiously. With reserve, with our own forms of politeness. In return for my sugar ration they did my hair for me. Plucked my eyebrows. Lent me shoes. They called me the little old woman, they called me monkeybaby, they called me cinnamon stick. I preferred fags to sugar, so parted with it easily. Marie-Angèle's glossy name stuck in my throat, like a boiled sweet. I'd choke. I said: all right.

Through the crack of the *salon* door I watched him untie the string, fold back the brown paper wrappings. Master of ceremonies. Jump to it! Shouts and laughter from the sprawled Germans watching, drinks in hands. One by one the girls rolled off their slips, stripped, put on the costumes Maurice handed out. Fancy dress party, shrilled the *patronne*: on parade, everybody! A white poplin blouse with black buttons. A green crêpe de Chine frock. A red silk dress. A white silk evening frock. The gramophone spat and crackled, the needle bounced then scratched out a waltz. The girls strutted up and down, chins in the air, hands flaunting their rustling skirts. The clients clapped, seized at the swirling material as the mannequins marched past. Hands plucked at sashes, hems. Hortensia fell over, dutifully waved her legs in the air. Pivoine yanked her back on to her feet. Stand at attention!

At the end of the working night Maurice came downstairs. He and I rehearsed our play again. He watched me strip, step out of my unstrapped pink canvas-rubber skin. I tried to smile at him. He caught my wrists, pouted. You're a rotten actress.

His lip sticking out, he sounded like a hurt child. Did he want me to pretend I loved him? I jerked my hands away, pushed him back on the bed. He whispered: fat greasy dirty Jewish cunt! The girl flew up, hovered just below the ceiling, wore the ceiling on her back like wings. An exquisite blonde angel who only ever felt chaste love. Down below, the little dark-haired devil lowered herself on to the client, leaned forwards, she rose and fell over him, rode him, she pumped away like a machine, he lay back eyes shut arms flung wide, the fuck could have gone on for ever in her tiny room in the lemon-sweaty half-dark with the footsteps going back and forth just overhead, the faint noise of the radiogram drifting down, she felt thirsty, she longed for a drink of water, she wondered if she had some clean stockings to wear in the morning, she wished he'd finish, finally he twisted round, got on top of her, arched up and back, groaned, and she leaped away from him and he shouted out and came all over the sheets as before.

His long cry roped me, hauled me back down. Sticky thighs. Bruised lips. Soreness. I lay in a cold puddle. He bit my neck and pushed me off him, sat up. He pinched my breast, my nipple.

When, at school, I cried in public, the nuns used to command me: pull yourself together. So I did that. My unravelled self. I picked up my dropped stitches. Hands piled with emptiness. I wanted my mother. I wanted kindness wrapping round me soft as new knitting wool. Everybody in this house needed so much kindness but they didn't get it and never would. Everybody's mothers were too far away. Gone. Lost. The girls wanted to receive true caresses, just like anybody else. Fat chance. After work ended, they'd run into the kitchen, search for something to eat. They'd fall on their late supper, stuffing themselves with whatever they could find. Usually thin soup, bulked out with stale bread. Madame ate well, but the girls didn't. They gobbled in silence, serious as cats.

Maurice said: so what do you want now?

I said: a ride in your car, please, please, please, Maurice.

Again I washed him, dried him, helped him to dress. He put his good self back on with his clothes. Dark eyes glowing, he looked at me tenderly. He stroked my cheek, said: I'll wait for you in the hall. Hurry up. I drew aside a corner of the blackout in the kitchen, craned my neck to squint up at the dark grey sky above the houses opposite. A glimmer of sun. My eyes stung with lack of sleep. I stripped my bed, bundled the sheets into a corner. Washing-day not for another week. I'd have to find myself some clean sheets from somewhere upstairs. I stood in my tin basin, shivering, poured a jug of water over my shoulders, reached for my flannel and washed Maurice off me, got dressed again. I wrote a note for the *patronne*, telling her that my mother was ill, and tucked it under her door.

Curfew was just ending; we slid through silent back streets. In Ste-Marie-du Ciel Maurice dropped me near the parish church. He touched my knee, smoothed my dress to lie neat and flat, as though he were my mother tidying me up for school: sorry I can't drive you back. I've got business to do.

But my mother wasn't here, was she? She didn't understand my situation. She'd start droning about right and wrong and the rights of women. No time for that now. Shut up, Maman. I slammed her shut up in the cupboard, along with the empty crocks that used to hold flour, sultanas, coffee, sugar, macaroni.

My mouth was watering and that made me feel furious. What was the point of feeling hungry when there was nothing to eat? I started to clamber out of the car. Hand opening door, foot searching for kerb. Maurice held on to me. His brows contracted. His dark eyes gazed at me. He flicked my nose with his leather

189

fingertip. He said: better not ask me for any more favours, little Jew-girl. That's enough. Silly child, you don't know how dangerous it is. For you and for me.

I was six years old, with scabbed knees, pigtails tied with tape, fists and elbows jabbing, dancing to and fro on the pavement throwing down marbles in front of the bullies you can't catch me you can't catch me! The words shot out of me like marbles. You should be helping people for nothing, not screwing them for money and sex. Maurice's leather hand drew back then swiped at me. I dodged. His words caught me full in the face. You offered me the sex, you little hypocrite. Nobody forced you. You just can't admit you wanted it. You enjoyed it.

I didn't try to visit my mother: she'd be out at work already, and anyway, I didn't want to involve her. She'd have started arguing with me, insisting on going through her political group, trying to take charge. She thought I was still a child but I wasn't. I could make decisions for myself. There wasn't time for meetings, for group discussion any more. I had to act on my own initiative. If I didn't hurry, it would be too late.

I walked to the rue de la Croix, knocked on the door of the cobbler's shop. I put my proposal to Monsieur Fauchon. It's urgent. You know that. He fiddled with a length of string. His eyes were red. I spoke in a brisk and practical way. I was able to sound so businesslike because he seemed a stranger. He'd shaved off his beard. His face looked raw and bare, like the shut-up shop. The semi-darkness in which we stood smelled musty and stale. I had a sense of time stopping, a clock falling on to a tiled floor and breaking, this moment lasting for ever. His wife and the two little ones were gone and so words were gone too. He'd put his words on to a piece of paper inside their pockets: I love you always. Inside my silence rose a cry I seized and strangled. If I let it out we'd collapse. Words had worn out, like old boot-laces, old leather soles: useless; no longer serviceable. The broom leaned in a corner, the dustpan beside it.

Monsieur Fauchon coughed and we both woke from our reveries. He fingered his naked chin: it's to go with the photo on the new papers. He covered his face with his long fingers. Brown skin calloused from work. I waited. He knew I was waiting, that he'd have to speak, he'd have to agree. I was resolved not to speak before he did. Finally he murmured: I'd rather consult your mother first.

My mother's face: pale, big-eyed, dark hair swept back. Hovering in front of me like a photograph. When someone got taken away, if you were lucky, you still had a photograph of them. If you didn't, for how long would you remember what they looked like? Already, I couldn't remember really what Madame Fauchon looked like, nor the two elder children. I couldn't remember the sound of her voice. But of course her husband remembered her. The tiny moments that made up his life with her; her portrait. She stood at the window and put out food for the birds. At night, in the dark, she pulled the sheet up over their heads and whispered her secrets. When she was angry she stamped in a killing dance. Was that true? I didn't know. Would he find her again and if not what would he do? Perhaps he'd hammer nails into himself; a kind of shoe. Nail down his tongue so he couldn't cry out.

I remembered what Monsieur Jacquotet looked like. With the eyes of my soul. He'd burned into me, like pokerwork on wood. The touch of his fingers, which helped shape me, which helped give me shape.

I said: we've got to hurry.

How much had Maurice charged? How much had the whole operation cost them? Their life savings, my mother had said. Their life savings to save their lives.

Monsieur Fauchon said: all right. Take the children today. I've got to wait another couple of days, for the papers, and for my guest to be strong enough to travel.

We shook hands. I said: give your guest my kind regards.

I went out. The sunlight jumped at me like a dog. The light licked me, bit me, forced itself against me. I could see nothing. I didn't know what time it was. I forgot. I was emptiness in sunlight.

Afterwards I tried and failed to draw it. A picture book for children. Brightly coloured images in comics. See it as the younger Fauchon child seemed to. Seven years old, he didn't yet live in the grown-up world. Tintin darts by with Snowy. Jagged balloons contain exclamations. Wham! Bam! Monsters! The older child, nine or so, small for his age, clenched himself, solemn and silent. He allowed me to hold his hand. His little brother jumped up and down.

Explosions of noise like gunfire break up the white spaces on the page into black stars. On their coats the children wear yellow stars. German words fly shaped like sprays of bullets. A voice shouts commands in capital letters. The younger Fauchon child claps his hands and laughs. An enormous revolving grey-green broom, a carpet-sweeper, bursts out of a side street, bristles towards us through the place. A broom robot. Rigid arms swing back and forth. Boots flash. Metal helmet shapes a metal skull. Grey-green cleaning machine sweeps the square clear of all rubbish wham bam.

The children gaze, astonished. Child artists compose an adventure story, observe wind-up clockwork gadgets, a busy little army of grey-green sweeper toys. Model soldiers with knifing legs, marching to do their duty. They won't bother us.

Next image in the comic strip: on the far side of the *place*, a man in a white shirt and dark trousers, hatless, a dark coat over his arm, opening the door of Monsieur Jacquotet's house from inside. He comes out on to the step, glances idly across the *place* in our direction. I close my eyes. Open them. I'm a child too: I turn away my head so that I haven't seen Maurice and therefore he hasn't seen me. Nor the two children. Their yellow stars blaze. Maurice goes back inside and closes the door.

Now: the convent parlour. Sister Dolly, who opened the door to us, has gone off with a hiss of dismay, flapping her penguin wings. The two Fauchon children grip my hands, blink in bewilderment at the half-naked figure, nails piercing his hands and his feet, dripping blood, which hangs on the huge crucifix suspended between the windows. It's not real. We're inside an illustration in a cookery book: how to butcher meat. The children don't want to learn to cook. Butchers in our town hang up joints on huge silvery hooks. You don't nail up live animals. The little Fauchons' eyes swivel over the brown walls, the stiff brown chairs, the brown oil paintings of holy scenes. You must be hungry, I say: we'll get you some tea in just a minute.

The two children blink once more as a second penguin waddles in and clucks at them. Mother Lucie's beak pecks the air: we'll keep them here in the convent. We'll put them in the old lumber room upstairs. Then if anyone comes looking we'll be able to say truthfully we haven't any Jewish children in the orphanage or the school. I want to scream at her to be quiet. She kneads her rosary, rattle and click, and the children fold up their faces against her.

I wanted to draw a comforting picture in soft pastels near the end of the story book, an image of rescued children safe in the convent lumber room, fed bread and milk for supper then tucked up in bed, told a tale of hide and seek. They gaze at me with their big solemn eyes, nod. I put their little coats into one dust-coated cupboard, their wooden-soled boots into another, run to the clothing store, find them felt slippers, overalls, night-gowns, bring these back up to where they wait, clutching each other's hands.

I've rubbed them out of the picture. I've turned them into orphans. I've made them disappear. I kneel in front of them, doing up their overalls, buttons and belts. I say: I'll try to come and visit you very soon. But I've got to go now.

I close the door behind me.

I began the walk back to Ste-Madeleine. Wishing I'd thought to borrow Émile's bicycle, avoided asking Maurice for a lift. Stupid girl. Too late now. Weariness turned the light to spots in front of my eyes. The sun struck down; repeated blows. I plod-ded along. Little shade from the tall spindly trees in the hedgerows: I started sweating. Flies buzzed round my head. My feet swelled, rubbed on my shoes. I cursed myself for wearing high heels. You couldn't stride in them. Mincing over the dry ruts of mud underfoot, I kept turning my ankle. Soon I began to hobble. My heels burned as blisters began to form.

Rattle and roar of an engine. Don't look round. A gleaming black nose pushed alongside me. A German officer stopped his staff car. He wound down the window. I had to look at his pink face, small eyes. He lifted a hand in polite greeting. Fräulein Johanna, isn't it? Do let me offer you a lift, my dear.

Impossible to refuse. I didn't recognise him, couldn't call him by his name. Pig number one pig number two pig number three. I put on a calm and relaxed expression. Like smoothing on make-up. Just one of the piggy-pink clients. Be nice. The uniform-encased driver stared ahead, expressionless. The officer pushed the door open. I got into the back of the car beside him, sat well back on the leather seat, turned my face towards him, managed the movement of muscles called a smile. His cap perched between us like a chaperone. The car smelled soapy, as though it had just been washed. The officer smelled of sharp-sweet eau de Cologne. He smiled hesitantly. Nice white teeth.

I chopped him up like a sausage. His fat fingers fell off. His round cheeks. I sliced his ears on to his grey-green shoulders. He mentioned a concert in the town hall next week. Are you fond of Schubert? I am, very. His small blue eyes gleamed in his fleshy face. His blond hair was crimped into crisp waves. His lopped pink hands had well-manicured fingernails. Despite being dead he could still speak, so I minced him into pink and grey-green stuffing while he droned about classical music. He stopped, sensing my inattention, and gave me another shy look. Obviously he liked girls; he meant me no harm. He loved his mother. She taught him to clean his fingernails, clean inside his ears, not to pick his nose in public, to change his underwear every day. Naked in bed he'd be a darling pink piglet with a little curled tail. He was still alive, snorting and grunting. Intolerable. My mouth locked in its rictus grimace. To kill pigs the farmers hoisted them up by their back legs above a wooden tub, slit their throats. The blood poured down in a red stream and the farmers' wives collected it for use in cooking. That stopped pigs smiling.

In Ste-Madeleine he got the driver to park the car outside the bar. Come in and have a drink. He wanted a French girl to sit with, to display. Any French girl would do. He was just a German officer offering me camouflage. Any German officer would do. I owed him for the lift and so I followed him in. The *patronne* gave me a swift disdainful glance. The German took my arm, shouldered through the café to the far end of the bar.

We sat at a table in full view of everybody. My arms and legs seemed bent the wrong way. I stared at my blue crêpe knees. I looked up as the door scraped open, the bell pinged as feet crossed the mat. Through the haze of cigarette smoke I saw Marie-Angèle and Maurice enter. I turned my head away. So did Marie-Angèle.

Our business concluded, Maurice and I avoided each other. His attention moved to the new women who had arrived in the house. Cheeks, fat or sunken, coated in beige paint. Eyes tinted black and blue like bruises. Semi-destitute and desperate for work. Invisible labels round their necks: willing to do anything. Just like me.

My mother had insisted I did not go back to visit her again. Stay where you are, don't run any more risks, I'll be all right. If necessary, I'll call on Madame Baudry. She's a decent woman when all's said and done. It's not her fault her prospective son-in-law has to work under the Germans.

Inside me: a dark space of loss, bitter and empty. Dark writing on a dark page. A list of names. A dark book inside me, listing the names of the lost. Once, in the night, they called to me from a snow-heavy pine forest. I noted the book's existence, then shut it, pushed it deep down under snow and ice.

I obeyed my mother. Stayed put in Ste-Madeleine. Kept my head down. Hung on in the *patronne*'s house. Watched tides of grey-green uniforms washing through. All through the following year we continued with our lives. Pretended we believed in the future. After the war, Émile and I would say to one another: after the war. After the war we'd go on a walking holiday together. We'd sleep under hedges, build fires on river banks, grill fish and drink beer, roam freely wherever we wanted, with no rolls of barbed wire barring the way.

When Émile disappeared, I didn't cry. What was the use? I summoned a night council in the kitchen. Hortensia and Violetta listed methods. Scalding hot baths jumping off the kitchen table drinking meths poking myself with a knitting needle. Pivoine said: who round here does any knitting, you idiots?

I said: OK, forget it, let's have a drink. We waited until the *patronne* had gone to bed then collected wine dregs from upstairs, tipped them into a pan, heated it, added stolen cooking brandy and sugar-beet. Our version of punch. That'll get rid of it if anything can, Desirée said. At the bottom of a tin Hortensia found a handful of large biscuit crumbs. She said: midnight feast!

I went to bed, waiting for the cramps to begin. Hoping they would, hoping they wouldn't. I lay facing the wall, which ran with damp. I put out a hand and touched its wet clamminess. I threw up, but the baby hung on.

Maurice's first-born was a son. He named him Hubert. After the christening he brought the *patronne* six bottles of Taittinger and a handful of lace-edged paper cones, decorated with blue rosettes, brimming with pale blue sugared almonds. The girls crunched these pebbly sweets while he popped corks but I hid from the party, stayed in the kitchen. In the morning, I poked around between bottles and glasses, trails of ribbon, fragments of icing and nuts. I picked up the empty paper cones, flattened them out into half-circles. Late at night, after work, I drew on one of them with my last stub of charcoal. I put it away with my other drawings, in the portfolio I made from an old cardboard box, tied up with black ribbon I filched from one of Madame's cupboards. After the war I'd decide which ones to keep.

I climbed into bed. After the war I'd return to Ste-Marie, take proper care of my mother. After the war I'd find Émile again. After the war we'd live together with our child. After the war I'd try to find out what had happened to those lost ones, whose names I could not speak.

After the war. One day. If they felt able to. People might tell each other what had happened. In confidence at first, not in public. Whispering tête-à-tête, as you did in the confessional. As I'd once done. As the nuns, presumably, still did. How would someone like Sister Dolly shape her version of these times? Did she have a confidante? Who could that possibly be? Falling asleep that night, I tried to imagine Dolly, later in her life, talking to a friend. I tried to imagine what she might say.

Dolly

That hard day began with the rising bell jerking me out of a bad dream. Kneeling by my bed to say my morning prayers I wasn't fit for God to see. That dream must have come from the devil and I'd let it in. A bunch of evil spirits flinging red darts at me and jeering.

The devil wouldn't let go of me. My clean coif was missing, and my underskirt. Something had come for me in the night and thrown my things about. At last I found my poor little slipper, hidden under the bed. I had to hurry, not to be late for the Office. In the cloister the devil tripped me up and I cannoned into Mother Lucie, plodding along like a cow off to pasture. That slowcoach. She was sent to try me. She never noticed anything, not my treading on her heel, not my exclaiming and saying sorry. In chapel she knelt in her stall, eyes shut, smiling, as though someone had given her a big present. She never seemed bothered by the cold, nor by how hard the kneelers were. She didn't need to. She had a soft life, just teaching in the school. She could afford to look so pious and pleased with herself.

The day got worse after lunch with the bang on the back door. Ill tempered and impatient it did sound. I opened up to my sister-in-law Adeline. What a mess she looked! Other women would have got tidied up to come into town but not Adeline. She wore her work clothes. A man's grey cap well pulled down, shading her eyes, a grey cotton shawl. Her shabby frock, a washed-out blue, flapped round her bony kneecaps. She was bare-legged, in an old pair of lace-up ankle boots, and she was carrying a cloth-covered basket that was much too small. Small as a pumpkin in a bad year.

She pecked my cheeks. I said: I was expecting you an hour ago. What happened?

She pushed past me, into the kitchen. I said: manners!

Her voice leaked out sour as old milk. A gendarme came round with an inspector. Making trouble. Counting our sacks of grain. They nearly caught us.

On the one hand, you should tell the truth. On the other hand, not declaring everything was a way to fight back against the Boches. I didn't know which was right, so I kept my mouth shut. Adeline scrabbled in her basket, held out half a savoy cabbage, a shrivelled onion, a black-spotted cauliflower: can't do any better than this. The *patron* says we can't go on giving away food for free. We haven't got enough for ourselves as it is.

I felt very upset. My own family was turning against me. I said: but your duty of charity! Adeline stared at the floor. Come off it. He can't give you what he hasn't got. I said: you mean he's found people who'll pay for it.

My insides were squeezing together. That my brother should send me such a message! Family was family, even if we didn't always see eye to eye.

I said: how can you do this? Times are so hard for us.

She knew perfectly well I'd never want to fall out with my

brother. He was falling out with me first. It was his fault. I was almost in tears.

Adeline practically spat at me. Times are hard for us too. The *patron* said to tell you he's sorry, but there it is.

I could hardly get my voice out. He's turned very mean. And I know who's behind it!

As kids, my brother and I had been thick as thieves. We ran about together all day long. When we played priests, we took turns saying Mass and handing out Holy Communion. For hosts we'd use daisies or dandelions. We were the two mischiefs. Always getting into trouble. So when one got beaten, the other did too. He and I, as the two eldest, had to keep an eye on the younger ones, and so we looked after each other as well. At night we slept next to each other in the big bed full of children.

My poor mother had so much work to do. She needed us to keep out of her way. If we got under her feet she'd bawl at us. My brother answered her back, then ducked. He was so bold! He wouldn't take anyone bossing him. He couldn't stand the nun who taught us our catechism. Why? Because she was dried-up and ugly. Walking home from church one day he said to me: I'd like to get hold of one of her saggy old tits, pull it right out then let it go – ping! I pretended not to hear and ran ahead shrieking we'd be late, we wouldn't half catch it.

Later on, when I entered, my brother said: good riddance! *Les bonnes soeurs*, he used to say with a nasty smile, spitting on the ground: there's many outside the convent just as good as that lot inside.

I didn't like nuns much, either, when I was a girl. They weren't like us. Sharp-eyed, always on the lookout. Going on about holy poverty but always asking for money for this or that, not realising we had none to give. Behind their backs my parents would roll their eyes. That didn't stop me from being bundled off to the convent as soon as I was old enough. One less to feed. Twelve children. Too many girls: get rid of one of them. They chose me. I heard their night whispers: best to let her go, she's so plain, no chance of her catching a husband, poor thing. My brother said: you fool! I answered: no choice, have I?

He wouldn't say goodbye, he was out mending a fence when I left, and that was a right blow to the heart. I offered it up for the holy souls but I still missed him.

In fact the life wasn't too bad. Enough to eat, a cubicle to sleep in all to myself, curtains you could draw right round your bed. Cold and narrow it felt at first, lonely, but the nuns explained: it meant being respected. The Good Lord gave me a helping hand when I needed it. I had no trouble with kitchen work, none with keeping the children in order. You just had to be very firm, let them know who was boss.

Best were our feast days. In May we made lily-of-the-valley posies for the Virgin, dressed her in garlands of white lilac, and took her round the garden on a bier. We sang Ave Maria and then the prettiest child crowned her. For Corpus Christi we made little altars at the edge of the lawn, with lace cloths and red roses. Throwing rose petals and singing, we went before the priest carrying the Monstrance. Gold rays flaming like the sun. We knelt down at each altar as he raised the Monstrance for us to adore. Afterwards we'd have almond cakes and wine at supper.

Mother Lucie made the cakes. Just once or twice in the year, on those special occasions, she deigned to come into the kitchen. So proud of herself, coming from a baker's family. Anyone can cook up treats if they're not on a tight budget. Still, she didn't know any better and she meant well. She'd get all flushed from the heat of the oven, pull out the tray, cry: they've risen! She didn't know how foolish she looked, her coif slipped sideways and flour smeared across her cheeks. I'd go over to her, stroke the flour off her face, pull her veil straight, generally brush her down. Once she laughed and said: you're grooming me! And she shut her eyes and purred.

Another good thing about the convent: we had no mirrors, and so I could forget about what I looked like. It just didn't matter.

My brother did sometimes come to visit me. He talked about the fields and the animals, the harvest, and I listened. He was still my brother, and I was godmother to his first child. A girl. Big brown eyes, soft pale skin, thick brown curls. Just like her mother. My brother doted on that child. He brought her in on his visits to the convent, to show her off. When she whimpered and jumped from his lap he'd get up and throw her in the air and let her ride piggy-back on his shoulders. Round and round the parlour, while Adeline smiled. I cautioned him: you'll spoil her! He said: shut up!

I said to Adeline: you want to come in?

She said: if you like.

We stood in silence, side by side, near the range. Adeline smelled of sweat after her walk from the farm. She threw down her cap. She sighed and chewed her bottom lip. Her short hair, curling like a sheep's fleece, was going grey, but her thick eyebrows were still black. Her hands were raw and scrubbed but her fingernails were crusted with earth. She saw me looking. Hastily I asked her: so what's the news?

She could only tell me new things. She didn't know the old things. Those were pictures from childhood, before she arrived on the scene. She was from Ste-Madeleine, not Ste-Marie, so as a child I hadn't known her. In any case, like my brother, she didn't talk about the past. The two of them got on with each day as it came. But I remembered the goats it had been my job to feed, the calves I'd been allowed to name, the way the small stone house and barns grew straight up out of the green land. No flowerbeds or high walls like the convent. Just a thin fence, and the orchard to one side.

Adeline said: what d'you think? Trying to manage, aren't we. Watching our backsides day in day out in case someone informs on us.

I said: what's he up to, my brother? Adeline shrugged. She put down her basket on the table, next to her cap, looked around. Trying to catch me out somehow but she couldn't. The place was all in order. Sparkling clean. Finally she said: the *patron*'s started supplying someone here in town. Seems an OK sort. Understands the way things are. Not like some.

She was trying to hurt me. Words like a smack to the belly. I felt winded. That she should show me such contempt! But I wouldn't let her see I minded. I shoved my hands into my sleeves and just waited for what she'd come out with next. She put her palms flat against the oven door. Wriggled her fingers up and down. He comes with his girlfriend. Good sturdy lass. She helps him carry the stuff into the car.

I said: I could starve for all my brother cares. My hands jumped out of my sleeves, rummaged in my pocket for safety pins. I fastened back my wide cuffs. I fetched out my mop from the broom cupboard. I said: I must get on. I've work to do.

Adeline said: you've always had such a temper! That's what the *patron* says and he's right. Why are you in such a huff?

She picked up her cap, her basket. She paused. She was obviously trying to think of something nice to say before she left. Then she'd be the good one not the nasty one. But her words squeezed out like rabbit droppings. You don't know how well off you are. A roof over your head, no responsibilities, no decisions to make. You might as well still be a child!

We kissed each other goodbye. I said: I'll pray for you.

I knew that would annoy her and it did. She stomped out. But I kept my word. Once the door had clacked shut behind her I said a Hail Mary, nice and slow, then picked up that good-for-nothing cauliflower from the table top and balanced it in my open hand. Hey there, I said: you old misery. The cauliflower stared back and said nothing. Before the war, I'd have made *choufleur au gratin*, with a couple of capers to give it a kick, cream and cheese sauce crusted golden on top. Now we were in 1942 and vegetables had to work harder all by themselves. A bath in boiling water for you, chum, I said: and perhaps a hat of toasted breadcrumbs if we're lucky. The cauliflower looked at me with its little black eyes.

Annoying as children, that cauliflower, that cabbage. What are you going to do with us, eh?

I spent my days working out how to make our rations stretch to feed us all. I had no time left over from all this scrimping and scraping by, yet Mother Lucie refused to see that those two Jewish kids gave me extra work. I was running up and down the stairs after them all day long. We should have kept them in amongst the orphans, hidden them that way, in the most obvious place. In this case, right under the Germans' noses, with the Jew-man gone from next door and his house made over to some sort of barracks. The children would have been perfectly safe with us in the school. On the farm, you kept the animals together. You took the cows out in the morning, after the milking, herded them into the pasture, brought them back at evening for the second milking. A cow on her own, that meant she was ill, or about to give birth. Sometimes you left cows in labour alone for a bit, to let them get on with it in peace. They didn't always want you there.

I admit, I didn't always want those two children there. They didn't need special treatment. They weren't ill. They could have just been part of all the others. Yes, all right, always supposing no one was looking. Always supposing no one was going to tip the wink. But they wouldn't, would they? People in town respected us. They didn't enquire into our doings. They didn't gossip about us. But Mother Lucie had got it into her head that the Jewish children must be kept separate at night, in case someone came in and counted the others. Who was going to do that? Some gendarme was going to storm into the dormitory with a list and tick off the little ones' names? Why would they bother? Mother Lucie said: please, dear, just do as I say. So on top of coping with two extra mouths to feed I had to climb all that way upstairs to tuck them up at night, keep an ear cocked for their crying.

I was at my wits' end over their naughtiness. Smacking them only made them cry harder. So I'd say: if you don't stop crying, your daddy won't come and fetch you. That usually did the trick. That hushed them up all right.

Mother Lucie got it all wrong. If only she had listened to me. But she didn't.

That stupid Jeanne. Of course she was seen. What did she think she was up to, bringing the children over to us in broad daylight?

Jeanne in her fancy get-up, her tart's clothes. We all knew how she was earning a living. I had it from Madame Baudry, on one of her visits, who'd had it from someone else. She could hardly speak for being so upset. Jeanne's mother had been her protégée, after all. That poor woman, what must she be feeling? Madame Baudry said: this will break her heart. Oh, she doesn't deserve this.

What a cheek Jeanne had to show herself at our door! People were going through so much, suffering so much, and there was Jeanne making mock of good French wives and fiancées. I couldn't stay in the same room with her. I dashed out and called for Mother Lucie. We'd tried so hard with Jeanne, we'd done our best, but blood will out, you couldn't expect anything better, not with her background. Of course Mother Lucie took the children in, such a soft heart, but I told her: you mark my words, Jeanne brings nothing but trouble!

It wasn't my fault, what happened afterwards. I couldn't stop them. Nobody could.

I was sweeping the entrance hall, in the middle of the afternoon. I was still feeling very hurt about my brother's behaviour, and there was nobody I could tell. I wasn't due for confession until Friday. Reverend Mother would have said that I shouldn't get so upset about my brother, that I lived in the Holy Family now. Mother Lucie might have been too nice and so made me feel even worse. I thought I'd never speak to my brother again, not even if he sent Adeline over to say sorry.

They hammered on the front door. Two gendarmes. Blank-faced boys in uniform: I didn't know them. Sorry, I said: what? I let them in, took them to Reverend Mother's office, then went away to say a prayer. I knelt in the shrine opposite the office, in the red passage, in front of the Blessed Virgin. At one point they raised their voices and so I heard some of what they said. This way there'll be no fuss, no disturbance. We don't want any of you good sisters making a scene. Later, when Reverend Mother spoke to me, she said some of it over again. She sighed. She said: I always meant to get that entrance closed off but I never got round to it. It never seemed to matter.

Her face set white, like a blancmange, then wobbled. She said: I know I can rely on you to do what you're told.

When I'd entered, my mother had packed me a bag with what the nuns said I'd need. A change of stockings, a night-gown, and suchlike. She added in her own rosary beads, which she'd been given for her First Communion. That was a mistake, it turned out, because they got taken away as soon as I entered and given to someone else. My nightdress and underwear vanished too. So much for all that careful laundry-marking I'd spent hours on. I lost my stockings as well. They danced away on to someone else's legs. In this new life you got stockings just as they came from the wash. Ownerless. Often mixed up. You couldn't be sure everything came in the right pair any more.

I found two spare pairs of children's long winter socks, and rolled them carefully into balls, so that they wouldn't get sepa-rated. In the kitchen I gave the little Jews their soup, then tugged them down the corridor and along the red passage, through the big black door, into the convent entrance hall. I took them upstairs to their makeshift bedroom on the second floor as usual. I put them to bed fully dressed, so that I could stuff their coats, extra socks, scarves and nightclothes into a pillowcase for them to take with them. I left their slippers on them, and set out their boots at the ready. I put in two apples, a piece of bread.

I didn't want them to get upset. We didn't want a lot of crying, and Mother Lucie waking up and getting into a terrible state. So I put my finger to my lips and told them: you mustn't make a sound. Your daddy's coming to fetch you tonight, because you've been so good, but it's a big secret. It's a game, like hide-and-seek. So no crying. Your daddy'll be here soon.

Good little chaps they were indeed. Quiet as mice. Just sat there watching me, the blankets pulled up round their chins. After a bit they lay back, sucking their thumbs, then their heads lolled and they fell asleep. I did as I'd been told and stayed with them, perched on the edge of one of the beds. I pulled out my beads and said my rosary. When the children stirred I sang to them gently, to lull them. *C'est le clocher du vieux manoir, du vieux manoir, qui sonne le retour du soir, le retour du soir. Ding! Ding! Ding!*

Soon as it was nearly proper dark, I heard a thump upstairs. The gendarmes, entering from the neighbouring house. I heard them open the door in the attic cupboard that let them in through the wall. They clumped across the floor over our heads, down the stairs, opened our door, came in.

I don't properly remember the order of what happened. All so quick. I jumped up. Their beam of light leaped about. I waved my hand: sssh! I stuffed my beads into my pocket. The children were fast asleep. I started humming, so that if they woke they wouldn't feel scared. I pulled back the bedclothes and the gendarmes lifted up one child each. I said: switch off that torch! You'll wake them! They laid the children over their shoulders like little sacks of grain. I followed them, carrying the boots, the pillowcase.

We went out into the little hallway, climbed the stairs up to the attic, went through the cupboard door in the wall, arrived in the house next door. We'd stepped into some kind of lumber room. Very bare. It smelled of fresh paint. Out of it we went, down the stairs, several flights in the half-dark. The children were so good! As good as gold. They didn't make a sound. I kept murmuring to them, so they'd know I was close by. Nearly there. Nearly there.

Out of the house we went, by the front door, into the *place*. The convent, when I turned to look, was completely dark. Everybody asleep. The truck was parked just in front. A tarpaulin covered its back, its lower part left unlaced. A hand pulled the tarpaulin aside. A white face glimmered. I whispered to the gendarmes: gently! Gently!

One gendarme handed up the children, very carefully, to those outstretched hands. Then the little pillowcase-sack. The other gendarme pushed the boots back at me: they won't need these. The truck revved its engine, rattled off.

Next day, Reverend Mother got Monsieur Baudry to come in and seal up the opening in the attic cupboard. He built a wall of bricks at the back. I left the boots there, I don't know why.

Soon afterwards, Monsieur Blanchard bought that house, it didn't suit the Germans as a barracks after all, and he did the place up. Renovated it, re-painted. A couple of the other lay sisters went over to give Madame Blanchard a hand with the cleaning, but not me. I stuck fast in the kitchen, with my pots. I kept my head down. I waited for the war to end.

Jeanne

Towards the end of the war I began seeing the days of the week as coloured squares. Andrée was born on a Wednesday, which was green. The Tuesday she went on to solids: dark red. The Saturday morning when I agreed to get a job in England: pale blue. Marie-Angèle delivering me a passport, a few franc notes: a brown Thursday. Leaving France: a yellow Friday. I collected up the squares of colour, arranged them in patterns. Controlled them. They couldn't stretch arms to me and wail. The colours could clash all they liked. They hurt each other not me.

Yellow Friday: the curé himself escorted me to the boat, I suppose to make sure I did actually leave. Marie-Angèle sent her brother over with the message. Marc Baudry was only a boy still, but he acted as though he ruled the roost. He just shouted in through our door: you'll be called for at eight tomorrow.

I packed my black papier mâché suitcase, a postulant's cast-off donated by the convent, with my art things, a change of clothes, and Maman's cookery book, which she gave me as a parting present. Its lavender cardboard covers were crumbled away at the edges. Over the cracked spine she'd pasted a strip of brown paper. Her face snapped shut like a volume someone smartly closes.

The curé and I took the bus to Ste-Madeleine. He glanced at me slyly when he thought I wasn't looking. What did he see? A thin, red-eyed young woman, wearing a grey woollen hat, a cheap navy-blue jacket and skirt. He and I didn't bother speaking to each other. Not on the train to Paris and not on the train from there to Le Havre.

What had the port looked like before the war? Jagged edges looming in the shadowy dusk, it hardly seemed a town at all. Bombs had reduced it to rubble, poking up in raw heaps, which made you feel broken inside. We picked our way between hills of debris that must have once been streets. Outside a mound of collapsed masonry we boarded a bus to the docks.

Beyond a low wall, the backs of dark huts, screaming gulls skimmed a black flatness. Coldness came off it. I realised it must be the sea. It wanted to tilt into me, drown me, so I held myself very upright, lips closed.

The sign for departures pointed us to a bleak pre-fab shed. Inside, the waiting area locked in a crowd of people muffled up in coats and scarves. The curé repeated his instructions. On the boat there'll be some kind of lounge where you can sit. One of the London nuns will be on the quayside to meet you at the other end.

He paused. You be a good girl, Jeanne, do as you're told, and you'll be all right. He lifted his hand and made the sign of the cross over me. I stared at his black toecaps.

His raincoated back retreated. A bell clanged. I joined the queue of foot passengers straggling towards a pair of metal doors. Out on to the black quay under the black sky we went, filed up the narrow, ridged gangplank. Black water depth I stumbled across. At the top, sailors reached out and pulled us on to the deck. They glanced at our tickets, waved us forward. We stood in a huddle in the noisy darkness. People pushed and pulled on every side. Children squealed and whimpered.

If I looked frightened, someone might dart up and hit me. I clasped the cold iron of the handrail, trying to look as though I were admiring the lights of the town strung out in the black night. My fellow passengers chattered to each other, shouted down to the dark silhouettes of people standing on the quayside come to see them off. More people, clutching luggage, straggled on board: families, couples, a young man in naval uniform, peaked cap under one arm, leather grip in one hand. Above me invisible seagulls called and cried. I smelled rust, and salt water. I began to shiver, and to wonder if I dared to find the passenger lounge. Did you need a special ticket to go in? Would it be full of people? What would I say if someone talked to me? I crossed my arms over my thin jacket to try and trap warmth inside me. Perhaps I wouldn't venture into a lounge. I could lie down on one of the benches lining the inner side of the deck, or under a tarpaulin in one of the lifeboats. No: much too cold. I'd freeze, be found in the morning rigid as a sheet hung out in winter, a panel of white ice.

I was beginning to feel plated with cold, glassed-in, stiffening up as the night air scraped closer to me. A howl unwound itself in my stomach. I pressed my lips together. My jacket flapped open. The cold formed a layer on top of my skimpy clothes. The wind knifed up my skirt. I clenched my knees together.

Can I help you? Need a hand with anything, *mademoiselle*?

A male voice, speaking French with a foreign accent. I looked round. I hadn't noticed him drift up and stand next to me. A gentle presence; almost apologetic. The young officer I'd seen come on board. My height, young, with an open face, a high forehead. Brown hair already beginning to recede. He wore a dark uniform with gilt buttons and yellow stripes on his cuffs and carried a peaked cap under one arm.

I'm the ship's purser, he said: Bernie Mathers. At your service, *mademoiselle*.

I said: you're English? He said: certainly.

The shouts of men down below on the quay, undoing the hawsers, mixed with the blare of the ship's hooter behind us. I glanced back: clouds of black smoke belched from the funnel into the black sky. The unfastened ropes were flung up on to the deck, caught by the sailors. A dark gap appeared between us and the edge of the stone quay. It widened. The sailors rapidly coiled the thick hairy ropes, which poured like water from their hands, into neat heaps. You need somewhere to sleep? Come with me, *mademoiselle*.

Bernie Mathers picked up my suitcase and took me below, clattering down metal companionways in front of me, turning round from time to time to check I was following him. The cream-painted passageways were busy with travellers, with porters hefting cases and trunks. Nobody took any notice of us. We walked deep into the ship, past the noisy engine room, then went back up two short companionways to deck level. Bernie Mathers escorted me to a cabin he assured me I wouldn't have to pay for. No one except him would know I was using it. The stewardess wouldn't be along, because these were the crew's quarters. He made me a little mock bow, smiling.

I said: you speak good French. He said in his odd accent: I've got to go and do my duty, but I'll be back soon and then we can have a drink. What d'you say?

214

I said: what's your duty? He explained. As the ship's purser, he sat in his office below decks, behind a little window, and checked the passengers' passports. He did this twice: when they got on and before they got off. That was the rule. They just had to stand patiently in a queue and wait for him to check and stamp their documents. He also opened his office at a certain moment during the voyage in order to change people's money, from French banknotes into English ones or vice versa. He was kept busy: he snatched just a few hours' sleep during the crossing.

He said: you don't need to queue up outside my office. You're OK. Stay here and get some rest. He pulled down the bunk, sheets and blankets tightly tucked in, from the cabin wall. Lavs are along there. He waved his hand in the direction of the corridor. The door shut behind him.

An open leather grip stood on the metal chair. It must be Bernie's. The one I'd seen him carry on board. This was obviously his cabin. Too late to do anything about it now. The floor of the cabin rose and fell, rose and fell: we had left harbour and were putting out to sea. When I pulled aside the little grey curtain, the round grey metal porthole showed blackness tumbling past. A round grey-lipped mouth wanting to spew black bile.

I forbade myself to feel seasick. I removed my woollen hat and threw it into the wastebin, took off my jacket, kicked off my shoes, lay down on the bunk under the orange blanket. I shivered, then grew warm. The waters rocked the ship and the ship rocked me, up and down, up and down. At least no one could find me here and scream at me. I was crossing over, between two lands, two parts of my life. Tearing myself in two like a piece of coloured paper. Bits of paper dropped into the sea. Disintegrating. Sinking. The sea received me, closed over my head. I sank, spiralled down into green depths green seaweed green-bearded mussels all of us green water.

A click. Strip of brightness, then wedge of yellow light as the cabin door opened and the stewardess peeped in. She wore a white veil over her wavy brown hair. Her dark eyes gazed at me. No, she was the Blessed Virgin, doing her rounds for the night. No, she was my mother, tying on her lace mantilla before going out dancing. Dance with me, Jeannette, come and dance. She nodded at me then twirled off to find Monsieur Jacquotet.

The boat rocked on, over undersea continents, all the people I'd lost, coral-clad, fish-bejewelled, waving with feathery green. My mother, a compact island, rose up, surrounded by white breakers. I rowed to her, docked in her little bay. The salt water of her words met me; her sharp spray. Seagulls nested in her wild hair. I stumbled up the wet grey sand of the beach. Debris marked the shoreline: pieces of broken green glass rubbed to emerald, seashells, grey-blue pebbles glinting with quartz, bladderwrack, starfish, tiny bits of white bone, fingernails, teeth. A child's cry startled up. My daughter lay, struggling, in the shade of a rock, waving her fists in the air. All mouth. Wailing and wailing.

It was that woollen hat, Bernie said: any girl wearing that hat had to be a real personality. Jeanne. That's Joan, isn't it. Named after Joan of Arc were you? Proper Joan of Arc hairdo you've got there.

Tiny squares of coloured paper whirled in the air. Confetti. Military flags. Red white and blue bunting. I shut my eyes but a blade forced them open. Sun-reddened faces. A blister of heat. All round me people gabbled and shrieked. Turkeycocks with wobbly red throats, pimpled and ribbed, opening their beaks to cackle and screech. Banging of drums, shrill trumpets, clashing cymbals, a roar like fire sweeping up. Tears stuck, scraped like grit in my throat. I wanted to throw up. I hiccupped and the fire and the banging drums faded. I tilted more whisky into my mouth.

Bernie had come back into the cabin once his duties were done for the night, snapping on the light and waking me up. Now we reclined at opposite ends of the bunk, propped up on one pillow each, my legs tucked next to his under the blanket. He wore blue pyjamas and I wore a sheet wound round me. We passed his silver hip flask of whisky back and forth between us. He said: it was my dad's. Just about the only thing of his I've got.

Harsh taste of smoke. At first I just took sips, then swallowed more. It warmed me inside, an amber flame scorching my stomach. Bernie called it a nightcap.

He'd brought in a couple of sandwiches and offered me one: thought you might be hungry. A Friday sandwich: thick yellow slice of cheese, yellowish bread. I reached out, took the sandwich, bit into it, devoured it. Bernie said: how about a kiss to say thank you?

The squares of coloured paper drifted down, along the pavement. I shook my head. Bernie held out the second sandwich: go on, then, have this one as well. I polished it off.

My eyes kept closing. He said: babes in the wood, you. He switched off the light. Sweet dreams, mademoiselle Joanie. We fell asleep, clutching each other's feet so that we wouldn't fall out of the narrow bunk that tilted back and forth like a seesaw.

We docked at Southampton in the early morning. Bernie

departed to check passports. I went up on deck, case in hand, wanting to see England.

Mist blurred the edges of the harbour. Grey, rainy sky. Seagulls swooped overhead, mewing. The quay teemed chock-a-block with porters, officials, clumps of overcoated people under umbrellas. To one side of them stood a tall nun with a calm triangular face, thin body encased in a long black raincoat, a transparent plastic hood tied over her black veil. Her black-gloved hands clutched a black handbag. Her gaze swept the deck. Was I supposed to carry a sign so that she'd recognise me? What would it say? I painted out those words, in a rush of dawn tints. Colours jumped up, intense in the wet greyness: red printing on notices, the blue paint on the window frames of sheds, a yellow sou'wester. The red words translated themselves to me no no no and I decided to obey them. Do not cry do not let them see you mind do not give up do not fall down.

Go where you can. Enter where they let you in. Around me on deck everyone was talking a foreign language. French had been put away into their suitcases. The crowd collected itself, pressed forwards, taking me with it. We flocked towards the gangway. What should I do? Let the nun claim me? Hang back? I crossed the deck like anyone else and nobody looked at me more than once. All too eager to get on to land. Here came Bernie hurrying up, changed into civvies, leather grip in hand. Hey, Joanie, wait for me! He picked up my case, swung it under one arm. Fingers steering my elbow, head bent towards me, attentive and smiling, he escorted me off the boat as though we were a married couple coming home from holiday and we sailed past the raincoated nun hovering at the foot of the gangplank and she didn't even glance at us.

218

The railway terminus opened off the far side of the Customs shed. Just two sets of tracks: hardly a station at all. Black lines stretched away into not-France. Bernie left me hopping from foot to foot on the wind-scoured platform and went off to get us tickets. In his severe, hard-edged blue uniform he'd looked like a boy pretending to be a man. Now he seemed even more boyish; but more real. He hurried back, waving. He opened the carriage door: after you, *mademoiselle*.

I said: thanks for buying my ticket. I'll pay you back as soon as I can. Bernie said: that's OK. Later on is fine.

He pulled shut the carriage door. Clunk. The seat received me and defined me. Back upright, knees together. I leaned my head on my arm on the elbow rest. The rackety clatter of the train, very regular, gave me an excuse to look as though I slept. I half-dozed all the way to London. As we slowed, entering the grey and yellow brick suburbs of the city, I sat up and said: but aren't you supposed to be back at work? Shouldn't you be on the ship? Bernie lit a cigarette and flicked the match out of the window: I've got a few days' leave.

Tumbling out of the carriage at Waterloo, jostling through the crowd past the uniformed ticket collectors at the ticket barrier and across the concourse, under the arched roof, I felt tiny, adrift in a stormy babble of foreign voices, accents, indistinguishable words. Above me: a sculpture on a plinth of an enormous striding man in a flapping coat, knee-breeches, a rakish hat. I'd entered a cathedral and this must be its patron saint. That's Johnny Walker, Bernie said: that's what we were drinking last night.

Outside the station we had a late breakfast in a café smelling of hot grease. More like lunch: fried eggs and chips and toast.

Brown sauce, out of a bottle, tasting of vinegar. Thick, sweet coffee, also out of a bottle. My eyes smarted with not enough sleep. The café's colours banged me: the silver steel of the hissing hot water urn, the orange lace curtains looped back with yellow ribbons, the red-topped tables, the blue and pink flowered wallpaper peeling where it met the windows. Behind his counter the *patron* darted to and fro in a cloud of steam, shaking his pan of sizzling bacon. He turned a tap on the urn and a jet of water drove down into a big brown enamel pot.

Bernie lit a cigarette and smoked. I stared at the congealing rind of egg yolk on my plate, the lacy flap of egg white with crisp golden-edged holes. I pushed grains of fallen salt back and forth on the table top. Music blared on the radio. I said: it's kind of you to help me when you don't know anything about me. Bernie stubbed out his cigarette and lit another. You can tell me in your own good time. First things first. I'm going to take you to meet my mother. She'll put you up for a bit. She takes in lodgers to make ends meet, so she's used to people just turning up. She'll fit you in somewhere.

I said: but she's never met me. Bernie said: any friend of mine is a friend of hers. Then we'll see about getting you a job.

We boarded a tall red bus like a little moving house, stairs twisting up to the top deck. We sat at the front, so that I'd get a good view. The clippie whirled the handle of her little silver machine: punched pale mauve tickets shot out. She twanged the cord above our heads: ping ping! Off we rumbled. Bernie leaned back and lit up. We trundled across a bridge slung above grey water. See that? That's the Houses of Parliament and Big Ben.

The city flared open around me. As though the bus were a knife, tearing into flesh. A wounded city, pitted with craters, like Le Havre. The city had fallen into the gaps made by the bombs. Houses teetered, their fronts cut off, their side walls missing. A brown-tiled fireplace dangled from an edge three storeys up. Other houses had tumbled to heaps of bricks, tufted with green weeds. Roadworks everywhere, protected by low wooden barricades. Men digging in pits half-roofed with corrugated iron.

I wanted to buckle the bus on to me like red armour. A red corset. Shiny red bus would fly away like a ladybird, fly me away with it. I stopped looking out of the window and listened to Bernie talking, telling me about his father who'd died in the war.

We pitched out of the bus in a district Bernie called Camden Town. Shabby grey shops held each other up behind broken pavements. We halted in front of a small house in a side street. Bernie explained: Mother lets the ground floor and the upstairs rooms. She lives in the basement.

We opened a gate in a row of black iron spears and dropped down a flight of steep steps. We ducked under some wreathing greenery and found Florence sitting at her kitchen table, smoking and reading a newspaper. A rounded, hazel-eyed woman, with a mass of curly, greying fair hair falling out of its combs. She wore a grey skirt, a faded pink blouse and cardigan, and fur-edged short suede boots. She gave me a steady look. She poured cups of a mahogany-coloured liquid she called tea. *Thé?* No. Tea. She brought out a blue-spotted plate of biscuits she called digestives. I said to Bernie: in France that's a drink! He said: not *digestifs*. Digestives. She says she's been saving these for a special occasion.

Green and white striped spider plants in pots jostled begonias and cacti on the window sill. A budgerigar in an orange wire cage swung to and fro and chirruped. A radio stood on a small red side table, a scarlet armchair next to it. Bernie and his mother chattered in their language I could not understand. He translated. Mother says you can stay here for a while.

That night, Florence unfolded a bed for me in the kitchen and set it up. Narrow strip of cream canvas held tight by wooden poles threaded along the side seams. She and Bernie wrestled shorter poles along the top and bottom edges, yanked them to meet and fit into the longer ones. She went off to find blankets and sheets. Dad's camp bed, Bernie explained: Mum likes having his army things. In the loft she's got his bivouack case, his service medals, all his stuff.

I slept wedged in next to the cooker. I dreamed I was a ship with multi-coloured satin slips for sails, rocking up the river Thames. A tidal wave broke over my head and I woke up, my heart bumping. Wind shook the house, rattled the window sash. A cat yowled outside. Something scratched in the wainscot, trying to get in. I wrapped the sheet round me, pulled it over my face.

Next day I got up feeling wobbling, light-headed. Florence put me into her red armchair, brought me cups of her brown tea. She didn't try to talk. Just let me be. I pretended to doze, so that I wasn't there. I wasn't anywhere. Gone away.

In the late afternoon Bernie declared he needed some fresh air, took me out for a walk. My legs kept bending. The world had enlarged itself: England, London town and London suburbs. Too many opportunities, which might have sharp points; might pierce me. The streets in Camden Town wavered and swayed, as though the bombs were still falling. The pavements rose up at me like stone hands. Break my knees. The walls shoved me along. Swaying. I leaned against a metal rubbish bin: hold me up. My skin felt rattling and loose; uncoupled like a train carriage. I might spill out. I might crash. I needed to hang on to someone or something.

I said to Bernie: shall we have a drink?

The pub embraced us, drew us in. Glittering and dark as a chapel. Warmth smelling of beer and tobacco. Glass-glinting bar, shelves threaded with strings of lights, the bottles posing calmly as saints. Drifts of blue smoke like incense, big engraved mirrors with bevelled edges.

Bernie bought beer, a pint for him and half a pint for me. I mopped my eyes. He patted my hand: everything's going to be all right. I tipped down my rich, sweet glassful and asked for another. Warm froth swilled round me, blurred the edges of the world beyond the pub table. Brown polish brown as the beer. Bernie propped his chin on his hand and gazed at me: you Frenchwomen are so emotional. You're adorable. His words scooped into my insides, a spoon seeking sweet love. He looked so defenceless, beaming at me with such affection. I wanted to shout: take care I don't hurt you!

Golden glow of alcohol soothed my jumping insides. Bernie dipped his forefinger into a puddle of beer and drew squiggles. He said: I don't want to go on living with Mother for ever. If I were married I could get on to the waiting list for a council flat.

Night-time, and again I couldn't sleep. Piece of paper thrown into the sea. Almost disintegrated but not quite. The tide had washed me up here in Camden Town. I'd fetched up on a stranger's folding bed in a stranger's kitchen. Yellow light from the streetlamp outside reached through the thin cotton curtain drawn across the window above the sink, gleamed on the cream enamel edge of the gas cooker, the metal handle of the oven door. Sizzled-fatty-meat smell of the lamb chops we'd had for lunch. Bernie, eyeing the bloodstained paper-wrapped package Florence took out of her shopping basket, had said: Mother must like you. That's her meat ration for the week. Florence displayed three tiny scraps of grey meat. Grilled, they had been gristly and tough. Bernie said to me: there are French restaurants in Soho. We'll go to them together. Just you wait and see.

Over the meal they called high tea, bread and margarine and a hard-boiled egg divided in three, Florence and I had taught each other some words: fried, roasted, baked. Bernie had said: she says she'll teach you to cook English dishes and you can teach her to cook French ones.

I lapsed back into silence. Not understanding English: a good excuse for not speaking. What could I have said? People who don't know who they are can't speak. Florence eyed me, tilted the white spout above my cup. I dropped in two sugar lumps, stirred the brown liquid. I couldn't speak, but I could act. I seized the bread knife, picked up the loaf then cut the bread in the way I'd seen Florence do the evening before, curving my arm around the loaf to hold it close, spreading it with margarine then shaving off a paper-thin slice. Florence smiled, and said something. Bernie translated again. She says she can tell you're the resourceful type. He passed me my crescent of egg: you'll make a go of it here, Joanie, I know you will.

Did I want to? With him? He'd captured me, somehow. My life was finishing here. In front of a blank wall. Yet he said I'd captured him.

224

I could leave before they woke up in the morning. Hardly anything to pack: I could be away from here in five minutes. Who was the person who'd flee? Who was I? I didn't know. Squares of paper lost in the sea. Would I ever start existing again and who would I be if I did? If I thought about it too much I might go mad. I'd disintegrate completely. But Bernie was saying I might become a wife and Florence was saying I might become some kind of friend.

I could turn into someone English. Learn the language, put on the clothes. Mrs Mathers. In a grey felt hat. Then I'd be a person, belong somewhere. Know people. Be accepted by them. Good morning, Mrs Mathers. I could pull all that round me and hide inside it. Keep safe keep warm. Layers and layers of soft, thick clothes so people's fingers couldn't jab at me.

And then.

Baby crying. Calling for me.

I was biting my thumb, ripping at a piece of skin with my teeth. Don't think any further ahead than that. Don't. Or you really will fall apart.

Shivering, I got up and switched on the light. I put on my jacket over my nightdress, dragged out my suitcase from under the camp bed and opened it. I laid out my possessions on my pillow.

Maman's cookery book. If Florence wanted French recipes, here they were.

I Want To Cook, by Brigitte Marisot. I held the volume in both hands, its spine braced by brown paper, let it fall open. Brittle pages yellow at the edges. Recipe titles in bold. On the flyleaf my mother had written my name under my father's inscription. Josef. Liliane. Jeanne. There we were, the three of us.

I turned the pages. Not just any old cookery book. Her

cookery book. The one my father had given her, the one I used to flick through.

Why hadn't I noticed before? The book's copyright date was 1920. Not just the year my mother got engaged but the year she had converted. She had told me often enough. She used jokingly to call the book her Bible. Now I wondered: had she decided to learn specifically French dishes at the moment of converting? Was this a version of the catechism for good French wives?

The book certainly handed on a precise French tradition. I could hear Madame Marisot declaiming: this is exactly how you do it! An allegorical figure of Cookery, with the brass scales for flour and butter in her hand.

Turning over the crisp, friable pages, I noticed something else I must have seen before but had not bothered to think about. My mother had adapted her adopted tradition, scribbling little marginal notes, altering proportions of ingredients, adding comments and question marks. The cookery book had given her instructions and she'd talked back to it. She'd entered into discussion with her Bible. She'd insisted that she and the Word of God were equals. No, if I were cooking for a dinner party, I'd prefer a little raw onion, rather than cooked, chopped on to the cream topping celeriac fritters. No, for babas I think you'd need two tablespoonsful of rum not one. No, I don't think lamb's liver will do, I'll insist on calf's. When had we eaten these dishes? Never, in my memory. Perhaps she'd cooked them for Papa, before we became so hard up.

The recipes she knew by heart had come from her mother's family background in eastern Europe. She hadn't had a Polish cookery book, as far as I knew. Nor a Jewish one: did they even exist?

The cookery book was a memory box. You lifted the lid and days of your past flew up and out. White pages. White oblongs striped with black type. The recipe for *Délicieuses*, snowy beaten egg whites folded with grated gruyère and quickly deep-fried to become fat puffs, which we'd had on my thirteenth birthday. Salt and hot oil on my lips, the billowy cushion of egg white melting to wateriness on my tongue. The recipe for Nuns' Farts, the little sweet choux buns, very delicate and light and airy, which Maman made just once, on the day I left the nuns' school. Laughing fit to bust.

From between the flyleaf and the title page a loose piece of paper shook itself free. No bigger than a playing card. I pulled it out.

The recipe for Liqueur 44.

A square of cream-coloured paper cut from a school exercise book, pale brown lines criss-crossing it; ruled in red down the left-hand side. My mother's handwriting, shrunk down to fit into the small space. Fine point of her nib. Dark brown ink. Cramped lines of curly words, with scrolling flourishes over the capitals. She had written me a letter. A recipe that began: my dear Jeannette.

A recipe that was a love letter. From my mother to me and no one standing in between to stop her words darting across the sea. No one to catch her words, intercept them. Her message reached me. Do you remember how you didn't like this liqueur the first time you tried it? I've still got a drop or two left in the bottle. It'll have to last until our reunion. You can only make it with proper coffee beans. Rationing will be over at some point and oranges will come back into the shops. Use the best quality ones you can afford. Stab them forty-four times. Don't forget, once you've made your liqueur, you leave it for forty-four days. Remember you tap the bottle forty-four times with a knife before you open it and take your first sip. Papa's favourite aperitif, did I tell you that?

My mother had written a recipe like a poem, a song. Each word, each ingredient, in its right place; chosen and measured. Cooking, speaking, writing meant selecting. This not that. But also: this and that. Judge well, mix well. Don't waste food. Don't waste your words. The art of using leftovers: out of waste scraps make something beautiful and new.

I traced Maman's handwritten words with my forefinger. Traces of herself. She was invisible, she was absent, but she was present too, curls of writing like brown lace, like the frilled edges of pancakes, the brown crust at the neck of a bottle of liqueur, I pressed her to me, paper and ink to my lips, paper was flesh, I smelled her lily-of-the-valley skin.

Hot skin. Smell of fresh sweat. Long ripples of green. A field of grass blowing in summer sun. Hands reached down and hauled me along through the thicket of tall green stems tickling my bare legs. My bare feet sticky inside my sandals. Grass twitching with heat, jostling very close; fizzing with insects. Swaying folds of a yellow skirt on one side. Blue trouser-legs scissor along on the other. Over my head their butterfly voices dizzy back and forth. They press into the green meadow-forest, they push it back on either side, dividing it, they cut a path through and pull me with them. Birds spiral up at my elbow, flash into the sky, ribbons of singing. Blueness swings over me. I lose my balance and stumble, nearly fall over. Hands lift me, scoop me into the air. Suddenly I'm high up riding above the green field on Papa's shoulders he clasps my ankles grips my feet against his chest and Maman is laughing we're making towards the river we'll always be going on here together we're rocking through the green field this is now this is for ever it will never end.

Wetness fell on to the pages of the cookery book, soaked in. I put out a finger to wipe my staining tears. Behind the thin curtain the basement railings drew strict black vertical lines. Fleur-de-lis tops like splayed pen nibs. Iron bars that melted. Streams of ink flowing down.

Crying broke me open, gouged my guts. All the people I'd loved were gone, they were all lost, I was on my own. Embracing a bundle of barbed wire. Nobody could take that pain away from me and nobody would. It was mine.

After a while I made myself stop crying. I began yawning. Tiredness fidgeted under my eyelids, scratched me to stay awake. I put down the cookery book, replaced it with my other things in the suitcase, pushed it under the camp bed again. Shivering, still wearing my jacket, I got back beneath the blankets, pulled them up round my ears.

If I stayed, I'd take sticks of charcoal, gouge paper with them, stroke paper with them. I'd take sticks of oil and chalk pastels, make coloured marks, rub them, soften them. But if I stayed, how much of the truth would I tell Florence and Bernie?

Find a language. Not their English foreign language. The language of food. The art of composing a menu. Compose a menu. Menus exist in the future tense: I want to sit with them at the kitchen table, tell them this really matters, ask Bernie to translate, wait, dare to look at their faces.

Her crumpled face when she was born, her shut eyes, her red crinkly legs bent up like a tiny frog's. She is my truth. Write a recipe for truth.

How far back to begin? Eggs inside eggs inside eggs. Take one mother and one daughter, crack them, separate them, don't let them touch, beat them in their separate bowls, whip them well. Take also one young man and one young woman, add one future mother-in-law, mix well, stir well, season with bitterness and despair, when the mixture curdles add the milk of human kindness, the yeast of doggedness, leave it to rise for as long as necessary, punch it back down, take the resulting story with a good pinch of salt.

Take as many Jews as you like, crack them whip them beat them put into the oven turn on the gas wait till they're well crisped throw into the rubbish pit take another batch start again.

In the cold dark kitchen.

The words tottered like a baby trying to walk.

The father's name was Émile. I lost touch with him at the end of the war. I gave my baby up, I left her behind in France. Everyone except my mother said it was for the best. What did my mother say? She coughed and covered her face with her handkerchief. What happened when we said goodbye? Greyness.

I spoke to myself as a nun might, taking a child into the orphanage. It's all right it's all right calm down. Well-worn phrases. Nothing wrong with those. Meant to offer soothing. Possibly true. I needed to settle, recover a bit. Here, people offered a haven. Don't make a fuss. Crawl inside. Let them shelter you.

Not good enough. Need ripped me open. If ever I saw my daughter again, if ever it were possible, I'd try to explain. If she wanted me to. I'd try to find her again, I'd try to talk to her.

I'd ask her to forgive me for abandoning her. I'd try to tell her what happened. Bring the memories into language. Put the words together. Give them a shape, out in the world. Tell her the true story.

One day I'd try to discover what happened to those dear others. Those lost ones. I whispered their names. I'd try to find out. Uncover the true facts. I'd write to my mother, ask her to help me.

The story stirred in me, wanted to jump out and fill the room. Fragments of the past, like dying cinders in a mound of grey ash, made a faint glow. Ghosts shuffled in, formed a crowd of shapes standing round me.

Black paper cut-outs. Burnt paper shrivelling to black fragments. Black shadows with the light behind them. Ghosts were dead people who hadn't had time to tell their stories. They'd come, in their black mourning clothes, to listen to one another, to speak. To tell the story of what had happened. They invited me to become their witness.

Shivering. Blanket round my shoulders in the cold kitchen. Would I be able to hear them out? I hoped so. I didn't know.

Acknowledgements

Many authors' books helped my research. Among these are:

Carmen Calil, *Bad Faith: A Forgotten History of Family and Fatherland*
Laurent Douzou, *La Résistance française: une histoire périlleuse*
Adam Nossiter, *The Algeria Hotel: France, Memory and the Second World War*
Richard Vinen, *The Unfree French: Life Under the Occupation*

Thanks to Ayesha Karim and all at Aitken Alexander Associates. Thanks to Alexandra Pringle, Erica Jarnes and all at Bloomsbury, and to editor Gillian Stern and copy-editor Audrey Cotterell. Thanks also to Patricia Duncker, Sarah LeFanu, Hermione Lee, Jenny Newman, Bill and Hilary Startin, and Richard Wainwright.

A NOTE ON THE AUTHOR

Michèle Roberts is the author of twelve highly acclaimed novels, including *The Looking Glass* and *Daughters of the House*, which won the WHSmith Literary Award and was shortlisted for the Booker Prize. Her memoir *Paper Houses* was a BBC Radio 4 Book of the Week. She has also published poetry and short stories, most recently collected in *Mud: Stories of Sex and Love*. Half-English and half-French, Michèle Roberts lives in London. She is Emeritus Professor of Creative Writing at the University of East Anglia, a Fellow of the Royal Society of Literature, and a Chevalier de l'Ordre des Arts et des Lettres.

A NOTE ON THE TYPE

The text of this book is set in Bembo. This type was first used in 1495 by the Venetian printer Aldus Manutius for Cardinal Bembo's *De Aetna*, and was cut for Manutius by Francesco Griffo. It was one of the types used by Claude Garamond (1480–1561) as a model for his Romain de L'Université, and so it was the forerunner of what became standard European type for the following two centuries. Its modern form follows the original types and was designed for Monotype in 1929.